PLANNING BLISS

A BLISS SERIES NOVEL

MICHELLE JO QUINN

Cover design: Alyson Hale
Cover image: DepositPhotos

ISBN: 978-0-9951506-0-7
Print ISBN: 978-1-7750256-1-0

To Ethan and Violet,

*I hope you never tire of fairy tales
and happily ever afters.*

ACKNOWLEDGMENTS

I'm grateful for everyone who's been a part of this book,
from its early life years ago as a short story, to the
expansion on Wattpad, and now...
here, like this, a book with the prettiest cover.
To Joe, who knows what would happen
if I didn't have your support and understanding,
and knowing when to buy me cake and coffee?
To Ethan and Violet,
thanks for being awesome children!
Thanks to my parents for showing me that there's such a
thing as true love, even after being married to that same
person after almost forty years!
Thanks to my sister who constantly gives me
encouragements and who gets my humor,
and to my brother who's brave enough
to live his own adventures.
A huge thanks to my entire family
for cheering me on.
Thanks to friends who like me, quirks and all—Cathy,
Aline, Jenna, Brenda, and others.

Thanks to author friends who never let me feel alone even though the process of writing itself can be lonesome. Thanks to Trinity Hanrahan, Amie Stuart, JE Warren, Liz Durano, Roderick, Amanda Cheairs, and many, many more for the chats and words of wisdom throughout this journey.
To Samatha Harris for giving this a thorough read and offering ideas to make it better,
you are wonderful, and I'm lucky
to have you as a Beta reader.
To the founders and staff of Wattpad for creating a platform where a writer like me can share thoughts and dreams to millions worldwide, thank you!
To thousands of readers and followers I have there, I'm always grateful for the support.
Thanks for swooning with me along the way!
A huge thanks to Lucy Rhodes of Render Compose for my previous gorgeous covers, and to Alyson Hale for my new beautiful ones.
Many thanks to editors, Noel Varner, Dayna Hart and Elizabeth Roderick for helping me polish this book until it shines as brightly as the sun.
I can't thank bloggers and promoters enough for spreading the word about me and my books.
And to you, readers, thank you for choosing my book out of millions of others.
You have no idea how much it means to me.

❧

Don't miss news or updates!
Subscribe to Michelle Jo Quinn's newsletter and receive

an exclusive bonus chapter:
http://madmimi.com/signups/220738/join

THE GROOM

I was surrounded by perfection. Anyone else would wallow in it, but the minute flaws screamed at me. It was a hazard of my job. That, coupled with the nervous anxiety bubbling in me, I was a wreck.

My hand itched to reach over the table and adjust the crystal wine glass opposite me. It needed to move a half-centimeter to the left to meet the standard 45-degree angle. Don't get me started with how the napkins were folded; I'd already dealt with those as soon as I sat down, and before I moved both plates closer to the edges of the table. I was proud of myself. I didn't even take out my trusty measuring tape. As an event planner, I'd set thousands of table arrangements like these; I could do it blindfolded. After sipping on sparkling water, I placed the glass back on the table, and at the last second, fixed Jake's wine glass to meet industry standards. There. I should be good for a few seconds before I could find something else amiss.

Above me, ornate gold and crystal chandeliers cast a glow in the atrium, bouncing off the towering pillars with gilded crowns. I'd never been here when the fog cleared and sun shone through the glass dome, but I could imagine how beautiful it would be. Closing my eyes, I thought of this scenery at night when the lights were dimmed to add romance to the air. A few feet away, a seasoned pianist played a light classical piece. A mixture of aromas permeated the air. It was a scene right out of a fairy tale. I breathed a heavy sigh as I opened my eyes.

I glanced at my watch. Jake was ten minutes late. There was nothing unusual there. Even on the first night we'd met, he'd been late to an event. In the coming weeks after, I'd realized that it was typical of him never to arrive on time. It was a hazard of *his* job, I supposed. Surgeons were often called away on emergencies and worked endless hours. The waiter came by to refill my water just as a whoosh of warm, fragrant air passed me by. Jake. God, he smelled so clean.

"Sorry I'm late." He leaned over and kissed my cheek. "Nica, you look amazing. Is that a new scarf?"

The scarf was a present from Jake. His last present to me, in fact. Why did I think he'd remember?

I fiddled with the soft silk. "No. It's not new." What was the point in telling him that it had come from him? I swallowed the lump in my throat. "So, what's up?"

Jake and I hadn't seen each other since we broke up. When he'd called me last week to invite me for lunch, I'd been too focused on how my heart exploded in my chest to ask him why.

He pressed a hand over his tie before settling across me. "Mom says hi. I told her I was going to see you today." Interesting.

If it hadn't been for his mother, Jake and I wouldn't have met. She'd hired me at the last minute when her event planner blew up on her three weeks before the charity event she was planning. We'd worked a few more events together since, but that was mostly because I was dating her son. Now that Jake and I weren't together, I'd had to keep my distance, which also meant that my business suffered.

"I'll make sure to send her an email today." Our waiter asked for his drink order, and Jake requested a bottle of champagne. *For lunch for two people on a Tuesday?* Something was up. "Are we celebrating?" My chest tightened. I kept my trembling hands under the table and plastered a sweet but nervous smile on my face.

Jake pinned me with his blue gaze. Gosh, I missed him. Drawn to the brightness in his eyes, I crossed my hands on the table and leaned forward, mesmerized by his dreamy look of adoration.

"Sandrine and I are getting married, and we'd like you to plan our wedding." He reached across the table for my hand and gave it a light squeeze. "Nica, will you please say yes?"

In the midst of the opulent dining room, serenaded by romantic classical music, I heard the desperation in those words. I saw pleading blue eyes—eyes that I stared at and got lost in—eyes I'd woken up to, kissed, adored. He pouted with his full lips. A crease appeared between his brows. His hand fought to warm the chill that had spread on my fingers. Jake—*my Jake*—had pleaded. I was so focused on that, on him, that I ignored the cracking of my already fragile heart. With both trepidation and thrill, my heart beat a mile a minute, my gaze swept over our interlaced fingers, and I nodded.

Jake jumped up with what I could only describe as pure elation, lunged on one knee and hugged me. "Thank you. Thank you, Nica."

And for that moment, in that tight hold, wrapped in

warmth and heavenly scent I craved so much, my head swam in ecstasy and into a different future. The future where I was Mrs. Veronica Benjamin, loving wife of Dr. Jacob Benjamin, like I had imagined many times before.

I was dreaming of a simple church ceremony, vintage French laces, pink peonies and white *lisianthus* bouquets, and uttering the words 'I do' to the man of my dreams in front of our families and closest friends.

But I was ripped back into reality when he breathed out, "Sandrine will be so happy."

Jake released me, whipped out his cell phone, and dialed his fiancée's number.

Thoughts of my dream wedding collapsed. I clasped my hands on my chest, trying to prevent my pounding heart from breaking out of my ribcage. If I listened carefully, I would be able to hear the tearing of my heart muscles.

Jake broke my heart once again, and I just sat there and let him.

I remained silent when he spoke on the phone with his fiancée, a woman I'd never met. My fortitude cracked each time he told her he loved her.

"Madam." The waiter returned with the chilled bottle Jake had requested and two champagne flutes. I gave him a polite smile, but underneath, I was drowning in tears.

"Champagne's here. Yes, my dear, I will see you soon." Jake rang off and pocketed his phone in his gray suit jacket. "She's so happy." *Someone had to be.* The waiter popped the cork and poured each of us bubblies. Jake picked up his glass, but before he could say anything, I chugged mine.

"Thirsty?" he asked, entertained.

"Yeah," I replied, slamming the glass back down on the table. "You know…" Twisting around, I reached for my purse and stood. "I just remembered…I have to meet new clients for an event. A birthday or baptism or something," I rambled.

"Oh, but we didn't have lunch. Do you want to..."

"No!" I cut him off, raising a hand in front of me. My insides churned. I hadn't been able to eat properly since I'd thought of this meeting. My wild imagination had got the best of me. No, we were not here to reconcile. He'd asked me here to plan his wedding. *His wedding!* Pain stabbed through my chest. If I didn't leave now, I wouldn't be able to stop the tears from flowing. I grabbed Jake's hand and shook it, a little too aggressively. "We'll talk soon," I promised, and left.

❧

To CLEAR MY HEAD, I took a couple detours after leaving the restaurant. I wanted to feel a different kind of pain—other than the one wrenching my heart—a pain that made me hold my breath, and caused numbness in my fingers and toes. After swerving a little too closely to a car beside me, I knew I had to stop somewhere. Parking the car on a sketchy street, memories of how Jake and I met invaded my mind.

We were inseparable for six wonderful months. I loved him, and he loved me. The night we met, Jake rescued me from an aging playboy aristocrat at a gallery event, which I'd planned and organized. Of course, I was used to advances from wealthy, ogling, men old enough to be my grandfather whenever we threw parties for the rich and famous. Most of them probably thought that being the event planner meant that I was also available for a quick romp in the coatroom. I wasn't, at least for them...but I thought about it the instant I met Jake.

A man three times my age had me trapped between a

table and the nearest exit sign. From across the room, I caught Jake's blue gaze as he entered the grand space. I might have sent out a desperate SOS with my eyes, because after speaking momentarily with Levi—a person I avoided like the plague and whom I learned, later on, was Jake's best friend—he'd walked straight to me.

"I'm so sorry I'm late, dear, traffic was horrendous," he'd said in front of the aged ogler and butt-squeezer. Sparks flew all over the room when he grazed my cheek with his soft lips.

"No worries, babe. Glad you're here now." I hung my arms around his neck, giving him an admiring look.

We were convincing, and it worked. The geriatric Casanova waltzed off, no doubt looking for his next young wife.

Jake and I spent most of the night chatting whenever I could—I had to be professional and keep in mind that I was still working. At the end of the night, we were lip-locked in a cab heading to whomever's apartment was closer.

He was such a beautiful man, inside and out. Following in his mother's footsteps, Jake was a philanthropist, having been born into a wealthy family. He gave money unselfishly to each and every charity thrown at him. He was also the best lover I'd ever had—never selfish, always willing to give and give and give. Double sigh.

We spent every non-working moment together. Every time I woke up beside him, I stared at his beautiful face and wondered why he was with me, out of all the girls in San Francisco, why had he chosen me...up until three months ago...when he met Sandrine in a gala in Paris, the city of love. How could anyone compete with Paris and their exotic women?

When he'd returned from France, he was upbeat and upset at the same time. I had never seen him so happy and so distraught. He had confessed that he'd met someone else, and although I was an extremely beautiful and caring and intelligent (his words, not mine) woman, Sandrine was out of this world (my words, not his). Although he cared deeply for me, he hadn't fallen madly in love with me. But in one night, in a single moment, he had fallen for Sandrine.

Being the gentleman that he was, he didn't pursue their relationship further than a chit-chat the evening they'd met. He flew back the day after to talk to me and tell me about this woman who had swept him off his feet.

Knowing Jake, he'd told her about me and what I did for a living, and I was sure he had exaggerated my talents. She, probably as smart and glamorous as she was in my head, thought it would be fantastic to have me plan their very large and very expensive wedding. I, being the idiot that I was, had accepted, because, in the deep recesses of my mind, I hoped that Jake would see his mistake and find his way back to me.

The word 'no' glared desperately in my mind, but foolhardiness to have him back in my life had won out, even if it was on borrowed time.

As soon as I entered the kitschy office of Bliss Events, the business idea which started at one drunken night in college, Chase was on me.

"So, are you guys back together?" There was a little glimmer of hope in her eyes. Her hands were clasped, her breath held. She was a closet romantic, reserving the truth to the only person she was close to—me.

Chase had been an amazon fighter at one point in her life. She was tall, curvy, rough, and sexy at the same time.

She stood six inches taller than me, and on teetering heels, almost double that. She also had a semi-permanent scowl on her face that scared off anybody who came near —men, women and children. We were college best friends.

And in two seconds, she would probably want to bitch slap me into oblivion.

I shook my head as I walked to my desk, dropping my purse on it, and slouched on my chair.

"What! What do you mean?" Chase stood in front of my desk, smacking both her hands on it.

"He asked... He's..." I couldn't even form the words properly. "He asked me to plan his wedding to Sandrine."

Chase let out a guffaw, which had Jewel and Mateo, the two people who comprised our small staff, turning their heads toward my small office. Once she managed to suppress yet another laugh, she said, wiping off tears from her eyes, "You're kidding. This is your idea of a joke."

I whispered, "No."

She clammed up, realizing that I wasn't kidding. "Ah, shit." Chase slumped in the chair in front of me. I nodded in agreement. "So, what are you gonna do? Wait, you said no, right? C'mon, he's your ex, and she's the wildebeest who stole him from you. I mean, they haven't gone out for more than four months."

"Three." I corrected her, holding up my fingers.

"Three? Are you sure? Isn't that too short? That's gotta be too short. Three months?"

I sighed. "But that's Jake, when he's sure of something, he'll just go for it."

She scrunched up her face and straightened. "Well, I thought he was sure with you." She wasn't Jake's biggest fan, but she accepted that he made me happy. When he left, she picked up the pieces.

"Yeah." I sighed again, pressing my face onto my upturned hand. "I thought so too."

"What are you going to tell him? He would understand if you declined."

"Chase." I looked her straight in the eyes. "When have I ever said no to Jake?"

"Ah, shit," she muttered again.

Those six months that Jake and I were together, I had never said no to him, not even when he asked me to let him go the night he broke my heart.

Chase shook her head and mumbled something incoherent. When she looked back at me, she waved her hand in the air. "Get up."

"What?"

"Get up!"

"Chase, not now."

"Nica, please get the eff up." I rolled my eyes but obeyed. "Turn around."

"Chase—"

"Please, Nica." She didn't sound bossy, which was highly unusual for her, so I gave in. I turned on my heels. With the palms of her hands, she patted me from the nape of my neck to my lower back.

"What are you doing?" I asked, glancing over my shoulder.

Chase sucked her lower lip between her teeth, then let it out with a pop. "Checking for your backbone."

I stepped away from her, pouting.

With her arms crossed, she cocked her head to one side and pinned me with a serious look. "I know you're still in love with Jake. Otherwise, you wouldn't have said yes to his ridiculous request. That's gotta be the only explanation since you clearly still have a backbone."

"It's not that easy, Chase."

"Yes, it is. Say it with me...no." She squeezed my lips together, making them form a small 'o'. "No."

I slapped her hand away. "Stop. It's complicated."

Chase seethed, and we had a stare down. I guessed she saw all sorts of emotions cross my face since she threw her hands up in the air in surrender. "Fine. But after this, you better grow that spine back." She firmly grabbed my arms and shook me lightly. "You're too nice for your own good sometimes. Next time you meet with that ass, make sure I'm around."

I nodded, but my fingers were crossed. This was just the beginning, and I wouldn't put it past Jake to come up with something else that would surprise me or his future wife.

THE BRIDE

For the next four days, I had more conversations with Sandrine over the phone than with my own mother. And that was saying a lot since my mother called me up every hour to tell me about the most mundane things in her life. I might seem like a pushover, taking over Jake's wedding plans, but in my head, I was not—I was simply being professional.

I had a business to run. The commission I'd receive from this wedding could keep us afloat for a while. When Jake and I broke up, that effectively severed my connection with San Francisco's elite community. While my heart wailed as I planned his wedding, I focused on the advantages this would bring to our small business. Yes, this sounded less insane than the fact that I would let Jake do just about anything he wanted with me.

Chase had been supportive in her way, but every time the phone rang, and it was Sandrine calling, she huffed and stomped out of the room. Apart from that, she was my personal cheerleader.

Jake would often visit me at the office, mostly to talk

about Sandrine and their future. However, one day just dropped by to bring me tea and pastries from the bakery across the street. Okay fine, he got called in to work before we started talking about his wedding, but still...

Finally, on the fifth day, I had the chance to meet Sandrine...but not before Chase pulled me back into my office, locked my door, sat me down on the loveseat, and told me her own plan. Her new, brilliant plan. I wasn't quick enough to take note that she was too happy, which usually translated into she wasn't up to anything good.

"You're going to steal him back." She held both my hands, her azure eyes squinting at me—a sign of ruthless determination.

"Steal who back?" I knew whom she meant, but it was an audacious thought, not unusual for Chase, but completely out of left field for me.

I was always the good girl, and she was the devil dressed in a designer black, form-fitting dress paired with sky-high stilettoes.

Her head sagged, and she said, huffing in exasperation, "Jake. You have to steal him back." She trained her eyes back on me.

I blinked at her. "Why would I do that?"

"Because you're meant to be together. I know you still have feelings for him. And think about it...he asked *you* to plan his wedding. There are hundreds of wedding planners in the city, but He. Asked. You." She punctuated those three last words by pointing her finger at me. "Maybe he was self-sabotaging. How does he know that you won't mess this up? Or, maybe he *does* want you to screw things up, so he can get away from this engagement. Maybe he got her knocked up and he doesn't want the kid. What if it's not even his?"

I groaned, frustrated that I had to defend my ex-boyfriend's honor to my best friend. "He asked me because he likes what I do. He's seen what I can do to the most ordinary events. And, it wasn't entirely his idea, it was Sandrine who told him to ask me." I blinked furiously, as though it would exaggerate my point, ignoring the last bit of Chase's theory that Jake might have gotten Sandrine pregnant. My heart could only take one heartbreak at a time.

Chase was such a great person to have on my side, and her mind was an excellent tool for the business. She had been my anchor when I was floundering on the ocean of self-doubt, and when my heart tore into pieces, she helped me glue it all together by keeping my mind busy with new projects (and loads of tequila shots).

When Jake broke up with me to be with Sandrine, Chase stepped in and offered to hold my hair when I needed to throw up (after said tequila shots). She nursed me through the heartbreak, but she couldn't quite cleanse me of what I felt for Jake, though not for lack of trying. She had pushed man after man my way, hoping one of them would snag my attention. None of them was ever good enough. Not one of them ever came close to Jake's perfection.

I might sound picky, but I was convinced that once I met the perfect guy, I just couldn't look elsewhere. I craved him like he was part of my soul, like my every breath depended on his presence, like every heartbeat only responded to his voice, his touch, his kiss.

Through months the late-night sobbing and ice-cream bingeing, I cursed the heart that was too quick to love a man, a trait I had inherited from my often love-sick mother.

Chase adamantly shook her head. It was her way of telling me that I was being stubborn. If I continued the conversation, she would lay out a plan for me, which she most likely had been working on since I told her about Jake's engagement.

I stood up in defiance; arms crossed over my chest. "I won't do it, Chase. You know why." She opened her mouth ready for a rebuttal. I held my hand up in front of me. "Stop. I don't want to hear it. I'm meeting with Sandrine in ten minutes. I just want your support. If not as my friend, then as the co-owner of this establishment."

Grabbing my bag, I left, leaving her sulking in my office.

❧

OF COURSE, on my way to the restaurant to meet Sandrine, I kept hoping that she had a massive overbite, her teeth yellow from chain-smoking—as a true Frenchwoman, I'd imagine, would—and her hips and butt would be massive from eating calorie-filled French pastries, full-bodied wine and stinky cheese. But, when a statuesque goddess with perfect olive skin and a thick, wavy, healthy *coif* introduced herself to me and kissed both my cheeks, I berated myself for ever thinking those thoughts, and that a woman any different from the one seated before me would have attracted Jake in the first place.

Picture an even more sexed-up Marion Cotillard with higher cheekbones, bigger, more expressive eyes with impossibly full lashes, thick eyebrows that only looked good on Europeans, pouty lips that any model would kill for, and throw in long, soft, graciously moving limbs on a body that didn't seem to have any fat on it whatsoever. She was perfect!

Chase would hate her.

"I'm so 'appy to meet you, Veronique." Her French accent was so distinct, sexy, and sultry that I couldn't even courageously correct her from saying my name wrong because it sounded right coming from her lips.

"When Jacob told me that you were the best planner in the city, I knew I must 'ave you. And, like I said on the phone, money is no worry." She said his name like a caress. I groaned inwardly.

She had mentioned many times over the phone that perfection was what she desired, and it didn't matter what the expense was. I had also learned that she was the only daughter of one of the richest couples in France. Not that she needed their money at all, since she was a doctor, and was doing very well, according to Jake.

"Yes, I'm glad we finally get to meet. This wedding may be the biggest I've had to plan." My high-wattage smile was plastered on my face. Chase called it 'the joker smile', but it was the one I wore for every uncomfortable situation.

Our waiter showed up and told us the specials. His attention was more focused on Sandrine than on me, even when it was my turn to tell him what I wanted to drink. I would have bristled, but he wouldn't have noticed.

"'Ow many weddings 'ave you done?" she asked when our waiter left.

I counted in my head. Weddings were my favorite type of event we planned, but I hadn't done nearly as many as I wanted.

"I'd say about fifty."

"Ah, *c'est bon!*" Sandrine pressed two dainty fingers on her full lips. "So, you are an expert then."

"Expert?" I chuckled. "Not at all. Well...maybe a little."

"*Mais*, it is not important. Jacob thinks you are the best, and I believe 'im." Her smile flashed before me, and I was nearly incapacitated by the supremely white rows of pearls. So, no crooked, yellow teeth then. Darn!

Once our waiter brought us our drinks and took our food orders (and stopped mentally undressing Sandrine), I pulled out my iPad from my bag to show her what ideas I had so far. She had no real inclinations toward a specific location or theme, except that it had to be larger-than-life, a real show-stopper. I couldn't help but wonder how Jake felt about it. When our relationship had become serious, I had imagined a beautiful wedding, but nothing grandiose. He wasn't that type of man. He wasn't a show-off...unless being with Sandrine had changed his ideals.

One important factor did matter, so I asked. "Before I forget, have you decided on a date?"

"*Oui!*" She perked up, clasping her hands together. I was momentarily blinded by the 5-karat emerald-cut engagement ring on her dainty finger. My knees weakened, my jaw dropped, and I almost spat out my drink. "The twenty-fourth of August," she announced with extra flourish, flicking her hand in the air.

I gaped at her. "That's a month from now." I scrambled to get into my calendar on the iPad, barely noticing the waiter returning with a bread basket.

For some reason, that was the only Saturday that I had no events to organize. I had plenty before and after, but not on that day. The wedding gods must be smiling down on this woman. But still... "That's in a month!" I said again.

"Oh? Is it too far away? Shall I move it closer, you think?" Her head cocked to one side, eyes as wide as Bambi's caught in headlights. She had no idea.

Pinching the bridge of my nose, I composed myself before I pulled her into the reality that I lived in. That everybody else lived in.

"Sandrine..." I started, just as the waiter came with our meals. I had to shoo him away before he could say anything else, an action that gained me an evil look. "Sandrine, a month is too short to plan what you have in mind. We are talking four hundred guests, at the very least. Even if you have the money, it is nearly impossible to..."

"But I..." She stopped me with a hand raised. Then she brought that hand to her heart. "You 'ave only to tell me what it is you want, and I am sure that between Jacob, and you, and me, we can all do it. We can make it 'appen." She fluttered her thick lashes. I waited for the trumpet sounds after her spiel. Nothing came.

Going through the mental list of what was needed for a wedding as grand as hers made my head throb. I massaged my temples. Why the rush? Unless she was...I glanced at her fingers and checked for any sign of swelling around her sparkly engagement ring. No, Jake was too careful for that. He couldn't have gotten her pregnant, could he?

"Veronique?" Her voice pulled me back from my musings.

I swiped my fingers on the iPad. "One of the locations..." I tapped on the screen and displayed my wedding ideas to show her again. "The country club just outside the city. Jake's country club..." I paused, remembering how he had once taken me to the exclusive Goldengate Club for lunch with his family, along with a round of golf, which I found out I was quite good at, and which, thankfully, bought me approval from his father. "His family have been members for years, and they might have enough influence for the club to allow you to have your wedding there with short notice. Provided nothing's booked that day."

Morphing yet another gorgeous smile on her face, Sandrine stated, "Say no more." She reached out for my hand at the same time she speed-dialed someone on her phone.

"*Mon amour*." Her words were silkier and sultrier than

before that there was no mistaking she was talking to Jake. "Veronique said the country club would be perfect, but that the time is so short... *Oui...Oui...ah, fantastique!* I shall tell her. *Je t'aime, Jacob.*" As she hung up the phone, she flashed me a sweet, confident grin.

Trying to act clueless (or hopeful that she had another boyfriend), I couldn't help but ask, "I gather that was Jake?" I took a bite of the salad in front of me to avoid gnawing at my own lips.

Nodding her head, she said, "*Oui.* Yes. He said it is done."

"What's done?" My fork, speared with a cherry tomato, stopped midway to my mouth.

"It is done," she repeated, making a gesture with her hand. "Jacob said that if the club is what we wanted, then it is what we shall get. 'e will call me as soon as he confirms it." She picked up some salad on her fork and appealingly ate it, like there wasn't a wedding looming and she had all the time in the world to enjoy her meal

Being in the event planning business, I'd experienced some miracles. Some so off-handedly impossible that I still couldn't believe that Chase and I had pulled them off. More often than not, mentioning a certain name with certain standing in the community paved the way to our goals, but it was not without hard work and persistence. And a promise of something in return.

Sandrine's phone rang just two minutes after talking to Jake. He called back to tell her that he'd booked the club for their chosen wedding date. No questions asked. Though I had spent only a bit of time with Sandrine, with all her beauty and grace, I only felt pure jealousy when I realized that Jake would give her the moon if she had asked.

I wondered if he would ever have done the same for me.

THE BEST MAN

*T*here were only a handful of people whom I couldn't stand the very second I met them. I was friends to many, and friendly to all, but when I met Levi my skin crawled.

I recalled seeing him a few times before, during galas and charity balls and whatever posh events, always with a model *du jour* on his arm. I made darn sure we never crossed paths otherwise since the first time I met him. So, when Jake introduced him to me as his best friend, I almost lost my lunch.

Sure, Levi was wickedly handsome, rich and a quasi-celebrity, but he was as slithery and slimy as the old geezers who would grope and proposition me. Whenever Jake and I attended or met at an event, I steered clear of Levi, even if it meant letting go of Jake's arm. The several times I couldn't quite escape, Levi's actions and words left me seething, and sometimes wishing that I had Chase's guts and quick wit to parry with.

He would ogle every woman who passed us, even when he was with someone. Most of his dates couldn't offer a word of intelligence during conversations, often saying "like" at least five times in one drawn out sentence.

Jake and I had agreed to meet at a café near my office. I just couldn't let myself be alone with him, not when I was planning his wedding, and especially not after meeting Sandrine

"Levi's going to be here soon," Jake told me. I'd just sat down, but I stood up the second after his announcement. His hand pressed onto mine.

Oh, how I missed his touch.

"Wait, Nica. I know you can't stand him, but he's still my best friend and..." He tugged on the collar of his shirt. Uh-oh... "And my best man. With Sandrine away for most of the planning, I do need him to be here with me, with us." His ocean blue eyes darted to mine. "He promised to behave." This was his final plea.

I thought about it for a moment, but to be honest, I was still enjoying his touch and his gaze on me. I sat back down with severity plastered on my face, which didn't mean much. Picture a docile Yorkie trying to act like an angered bull.

I opted for pouty instead. "Fine, but one smart-butt comment from him, Jake, and I'll..."

"He won't. I promise. And if he does, I'll remove him. I'll even kick him out of the bridal party if he tries to say or do anything stupid around you." Jake's hand remained, enveloping mine with warmth.

"Who's being stupid?" A baritone voice asked from behind me. Jake's hand flew away, leaving mine cold and bereft.

Levi pulled a chair up between Jake and me, angling it my direction, and sat with his legs spread wide. I inched away to avoid any physical contact with him.

"Veronica." He nodded my way, with a grin, wide and full of malice.

I gnashed my teeth together, and raising an eyebrow at him, I simply said, "Levi." Then puckered my lips like I'd tasted something sour.

Jake clapped his hands together once, trying to diffuse the tension. "Great. So, the team's here. Why don't we get some coffee and snacks," Jake happily suggested, motioning for a young server nearby. The kid with dreads came over and stood before us, ready with a pad and pen. "An espresso for me and a chocolate croissant."

"Make that two of the same," Levi interjected, raising the index and middle fingers of his left hand.

Jake continued, "And a chai nonfat latte and cranberry scone, please, for the lady." He smiled knowingly at me. He remembered. The kid nodded then left.

"What? You don't drink coffee? It's not good enough for you?" Levi asked me. He was languidly seated with an arm hanging off the back of the chair like he was Mr. Oh-So-Cool.

I glared at him, but before I could answer, Jake said, "Veronica doesn't drink coffee, except after drinking alcohol. Coffee makes her too bubbly."

I smiled at him, recalling the many times I'd tried drinking coffee on a regular day, only to end up sounding like a mumbling idiot who couldn't stop giggling. Jake thought it was cute, of course. I wondered if he'd still think that.

"Bubbly?" Levi's question pulled me out of my thoughts. "If you get any bubblier, you would be..."

Before Levi could give his opinion, Jake jabbed him in the ribs with his elbow and shot him a warning look. After Levi's quiet protest, Jake turned his attention back to me.

"I'm sorry again that you have to do this with me, with

us guys." Jake gestured between them. "I know next to nothing about weddings, apart from what you've already told me, but Sandrine insisted I meet with you while she's away. She just has a few things to take care of back in France." How convenient.

"No worries. I've been able to catch her on the phone a couple of times before she rescues the world from another disaster." I stopped, hoping that I didn't sound petty. Jake had a serene look on his face, which told me that he appreciated what Sandrine did. Levi, on the other hand, rolled his eyes and then focused on a girl sitting near us.

"Anyway, this is what I have so far." I pulled my iPad, and their wedding binder full of information—forms, ideas, costs, swatches, and samples—out of my bag.

"Wow, look at that!" Jake cleared his throat at the sight of the binder. "I've seen you work before, but I never thought I'd witness you planning my wedding."

Ouch! And the knife in my heart dug in deeper.

Levi chuckled. When I shot him a warning look, he clammed up and shrugged, but he was clearly still enjoying a little joke in his head. Thankfully, our orders came…a welcomed distraction.

I went into planner mode—or what Chase called OCD mode—presenting what I had done so far (and in such a short amount of time), and then suggested what we do for the rest. Jake was pleased with the progress. Even Levi offered a few thoughts and suggestions. His comments I readily ignored, but some of his suggestions were a bit…genius. He was clearly an intelligent man; I didn't understand why he had to act like an idiot most times. Correction: all the time.

We ordered two more rounds of drinks and pastries. With Levi behaving well, it was easy to be around him, listening to him, and even laughing at jokes he made. Jake became more agitated as I explained to him time and time again the difference between Casablanca lilies and calla lilies, French and Italian lace, bone and porcelain china, and, the most frustrating of all, the difference between white, cream, off-white and ivory.

At a certain point, Levi and I were the only ones talking about damask and brocade patterns. He was knowledgeable. He knew as much as Chase did, even telling me the history behind Coalport and Radnor bone china. He became bearable.

"Well, as much as I enjoyed being a girl..." He stretched out his long arms above his head, and his outstretched legs touched mine. "I'd rather be *inside* one than *be* one." Just like that, the Levi I often ignored was back.

He got to his feet before either Jake or I could say anything, picked up his remaining espresso and sauntered over to the table where the girl he had been eyeing earlier was seated. Only slightly appalled by his behavior, I shook my head as Jake chuckled.

"Boys will be boys, I guess." Jake shrugged. "Tell you what...I need to go to work. Everything looks good—no, better than good—everything's great. I knew I could count on you. We'll stop for now and touch base later."

As he stood up, he held onto the back of my seat, leaned down and planted a kiss on my cheek. His lips warmed me, and his scent brought back many fond memories. Memories of us in bed together on Sunday mornings. Of dancing to a song on the radio in my kitchen. Of impromptu picnics at the park and frolicking on the beach. We had the type of romance that people wrote about. What happened? He fell in love with someone else. It was as simple as that.

"Thanks for being such a sport. I'll call you tomorrow." Then he left.

I touched the side of my face that he'd kissed. The skin felt heated. My chest constricted. I let my mind wander into the wicked world of "what if?"

After several minutes of reorganizing the binders and inputting information into my iPad, my eyes wandered to where Levi was slowly seducing the girl. She looked to be a freshman at SFU, blond, innocent and cute. I should warn her, but she seemed quite taken by him.

Levi was always overflowing with charm and, any second now, he would have charmed the pants off her. I didn't want to be a witness to that impending disaster. I gathered my stuff and headed out of the café.

As I crossed the street, I heard Levi calling my name. I threw my bag in the back of the car and stood by it, waiting for him, wondering what else he could add. Gosh, I hoped he didn't think that we could be friends.

When he reached me, he hooked his arm around my shoulders, trapping me between his warm body and my cold car. "You didn't even say goodbye," He said in a low murmur.

Really? That's why he chased me down? I raised a brow and scoffed. "Sorry. You looked pretty busy back there."

"Oh yeah...her..." He smirked. "She was too young for me."

I didn't realize he actually *had* standards.

"I like my women with a bit of experience." Suddenly, his arm on my shoulder felt a little constricting, so I tried to move it with very little success.

I couldn't make myself comfortable. As I continued to shrug, he clasped my shoulders tighter. If I leaned against my car, his hips would press against me. I sagged in defeat and avoided direct contact with his eyes. This was worse than him thinking we could be friends.

"Since you're big, bad boss of this whole operation,

what's going on with the bachelor party?" The man wriggled his eyebrows at me when I looked up. It was such a laughable action.

Levi was the ultimate bachelor...and rebel. He kept his hair long, rarely shaved, and often dressed in button up shirts with the first three buttons undone and sleeves rolled up, showing off his constant tan. He exuded bad-to-the-bone. And he loved it.

No doubt he had particular ideas about what Jake's bachelor party should be like. I had more than enough of a fight to deal with, why would I add a few more in the way of silicon-filled strippers?

"What bachelor party? I'm not in charge of that. I've never planned one, and don't intend to start. It's your job as the best man to figure it out." I poked my finger at his chest. Hard, warm chest, with a steady fluttering from his heart.

"Is it?" He took my hand in his and flattened my palm on his chest, halting my protests. I stared at my fingertips touching his exposed skin. "Maybe you and I can get together soon, just us, and you can give me ideas." A number of salacious scenes flashed in my mind. I gulped, realizing my mistake, but the heat had ebbed up my neck and cheeks.

Drawing back my hand, I replied, "If you need help, you can call Chase." I spun around to the back of my car, reached in and took out a card from my purse, ignoring the blush on my cheeks and hoping he would, too. The hand that was squeezing my shoulder smoothed its way down to the small of my back when I faced him again. I tried not to focus on the sudden, pleasant warmth in my belly. This was Levi, Casanova of the Bay area...and beyond!

He took the proffered card. "She's the expert on all

things...naughty." Chase would kill me if she found out I gave him her number. "I have to go."

He removed his hand from my back and held my door open for me. As I settled in my seat, he stuck his head in my car and surprised me with a swift kiss on my cheek, rendering me speechless with how pleasant it felt. Levi had never been this close to me before. I'd never allowed it.

After shutting the door, he leaned his arms on the opened window and cocked his head to one side. Playfulness washed over his face. "Veronica, you may not like me, but whether you like it or not, I will be around whenever Jake asks me to be there. So you'll have to get used to us being together...a lot." It felt like he was trying to say more, but I simply nodded my head, and started the car, waiting for him to back away, before I sped off. I was flustered enough to accidentally run over the guy.

During the short drive back to my office, I managed to shake off whatever reaction I had from Levi's touch and chalked it all up to a combination of exhaustion and excitement of being around Jake. After parking my car, I flipped the visor down, checking to see if my cheeks had returned to their normal hue, only to realize that for the first time in my life, I'd been kissed by two different men, and reacted to them in quite the same way.

What was I saying? No, they weren't the same. Levi wasn't Jake. Jake was sweet and a real gentleman. Levi would jump any woman that batted her lashes his way. Lucky for me, I wasn't the type of woman who batted lashes at someone like *him*.

No way.

I went to work without another thought to this ridiculous idea.

After waking up bitterly hungover the morning after agreeing to do Jake's wedding, Chase had decided that I needed a fresh new me, one with a stronger backbone. I'd been dragged out of my fuzzy slippers and pink pajamas to join a prestigious gym and enlist in a boot camp called *Torture*. It hadn't been a misnomer. Every single morning at the unholy hour of five o'clock, Chase shook me out of my bed, poured me into exercise clothes and trainers, shoved pre-workout smoothies into my mouth, and dragged me to (be) *Torture*(d).

The only cherry-on-top factor was our trainer, a sexy man named Diego, whose gluteal muscles were possibly firmer than marble, and whose skin looked as smooth as silk and the color of milk chocolate. And he always smelled like coconuts.

Since missing this morning's class due to an impromptu meeting with the chairman of a non-profit organization, Chase and I had to attend the evening class. I was bone-tired but with the afternoon I'd had, I couldn't help but hope a little bit of Torture would excise all the unwelcomed thoughts in my mind.

After the last cycle of pushups, squats, inclined crunches and lunges, I dragged myself to shower off the smell of a hundred liters of sweat. I took longer than usual and didn't rush drying my hair.

When I came out of the locker room, I found Chase sipping her post-workout smoothie and eyeing Delicious Diego, who was standing on the other side of the room, talking to a gaggle of his groupies.

Chase offered me an identical drink. "Thanks. I'm starving." As if to prove a point, my stomach grumbled.

"Ladies." That deep baritone resonated in my core, which still ached from the workout.

Chase and I turned to the source—Delicious Diego

(DD) was sauntering toward us. Without glancing her way, I knew Chase was unabashedly licking her lips.

"Great job today." DD's smile nearly blinded me. "Chase, your range is excellent..." He turned to me (I bet he didn't have the same praise), and continued, "and Nica, you've managed to keep up with the class. You're constantly improving every day. I admire that about you." Hot dang, he was a smooth talker.

DD stepped closer to me— I swam in the masculine cologne he wore—and produced a card. I mechanically took it as I drowned in the depths of his chocolate brown eyes. "I'd like you to consider some private lessons with me."

Chase made a choking noise at my side, forcing me to take my eyes off DD. I patted her back. "Sorry, went down the wrong pipe," was her excuse. The smile that broke on her face was suggestive, giving the Joker a run for his money. "I'm gonna wait outside." She traipsed toward the entrance after waggling her eyebrows at me.

The corners of Diego's lips lifted, producing an achingly drool-worthy smile, paired with a set of dimples on his face. "Or maybe we can have dinner sometime." He didn't pose it as a question. DD had the right to be confident, but it never came off as arrogant.

"Dinner? Ahm...I...uh...." Was I ready to date another man? I glanced to where Chase was watching with unveiled interest. She gave me a thumb's up. She'd been suggesting I needed to get out there if I wasn't going to steal Jake back. "Yeah, dinner. Sure."Flipping the card in my hand, I nodded and gulped the lump that formed in my throat, but kept my eyes trained on the embossed letters on his card.

"Wonderful. Have a look at your very busy schedule, and give me a call." As I raised my head, he winked at me, and I could swear my uterus jumped.

I strode away, adding a little bit more sway into my walk, just in case he was still watching.

Chase and I contained ourselves until we reached the car. We didn't stop talking about how hot our trainer was and all the dirty things she would do to him, which made me double over from laughter until we got back to my apartment.

THE MAID OF HORROR

The next day, Jake's sister barged into my office and stopped in front of my desk, hands on hips, Louboutin heel tapping on my office floor.

"Isobel! What are you doing here?" I gnashed my teeth.

"I need to talk to you." She turned on her heels and slumped on the loveseat in my office with a heavy exhale.

I rolled my eyes. Isobel could be such a spoiled brat when people let her, and people often did. It was always easier to give her what she wanted than deal with her moods.

I spoke to her in my most sarcastic tone. "Sure, it's not like I'm busy." Sweeping my hands over the piles of paperwork I had in front of me.

"Oh good," she said, oblivious to both my sarcasm and the work on my desk. I had a feeling that she didn't come for a social call, so I stood up and closed my office door.

"I'm the maid of honor," she spat out, tilted her head onto the back of the loveseat, and covered her face with her thin hands, as though the weight of the world was on her shoulders.

This was news to me, and being the wedding planner, I needed to know important details like this, but I kept quiet. There was no need for Isobel to run back to Jake and Sandrine telling them that I'd been slacking off, even if it was their omission.

"I'm glad it's you," I said, with a saccharine smile.

She grinned at me as I sat beside her, and then she leaned her head on my shoulder. Isobel could be an affectionate person, whether people thought it was fake or not. It was one of her redeeming qualities. Although, often, her affection was followed with a request that was hard to turn down, even when I should.

"I don't like her." She pouted. *Uh-oh*. "I don't like her, and I don't want to be her stupid maid of honor. She's so pathetic! She doesn't have friends." She was on a roll. "And you should see the designs for the dresses! They're atrocious. Made my skin jump." Isobel grimaced, stuck a finger in her mouth, and made a gagging noise. "She has no style. She's...she's...she's so French!" she finished, throwing her hands up as a sign of exasperation and then crossing them over her chest.

I honestly couldn't agree with her. Sandrine definitely had style. She had that elegant French style, and it worked to her advantage. I didn't know about her lack of friends, and since it had come from Isobel, it could be tainted idealism, a rumor at best.

Rubbing my temples, I tried to muster the energy to oppose Isobel. "You might not like her, but she's still marrying your brother. We don't have a choice on Jake's preference of a wife."

Ever the dramatic, Isobel straightened and gasped. "How can you say that?" She glared at me for a moment, then her features smoothened. She pouted. "He should be marrying *you*." This was *not* going to be good, coming from

Isobel. My heart did twitch at the tiny hope, but Jake was a one-woman kind of man. She continued, "You guys were perfect for each other. That French twit stole Jake from you."

I tutted at her choice of word for Sandrine and worried that it hadn't been too long since I'd heard the same conversation from Chase. Neither one had said anything like that to me when Jake and I broke up. Chase had tried to set me up on dates immediately, and Isobel had been out of the country. I was out of her sight and out of her mind. Until today.

"Again," I touched her arm to soothe her. "There isn't anything we can do about that. Sandrine is his choice."

"But there is something we can do. Something you can do!" This was not going anywhere good. I could almost see the horns growing out of her salon-styled hair. "You can sabotage their wedding! It's perfect, and they won't even find out until it's too late! Come on, Nica." She kept bouncing on the couch, her little butt making squishy sounds against the fabric. "We can do it together. I'll help you. They have so much trust in you. Really, they expect you to handle everything for them. She's not even in the country for most of the planning!" she said, rolling her eyes.

"Stop, Isobel!" I held her wrists in my hands. She pouted again. Time for damage control.

"Isobel, Jake and I are over. He picked Sandrine and like you said, they have entrusted everything to me. This is my job, my career. This company is all I have. When...if they found out, and they would, that I was trying to sabotage their wedding, it would destroy me. You know that it would. It won't be good for you or me, or Chase, or my company, and all the staff I have employed." I pinched the bridge of my nose, trying to get my mind steady. "You have to understand this, Isobel. My hands are tied. As much as I would like to be with Jake again, I...it's not going to happen."

It hurt to say it out loud, even to Isobel, but I was not the steal-your-man-behind-your-back type of girl. If Jake did want to come back, I wanted him to do it because he wanted me, because he loved me, and because he couldn't live his life without me. I should remember to say the same to Chase.

Isobel was quiet for a while, and I hoped she was trying to understand. Then she opened her plump pink mouth.

"Don't worry, Nica. I got your back. You and Jake will be back together again. I will make it happen." Her lips curled into a devious smile.

I realized that she only heard the last part of my remarks. Before I could say more, she gave me a kiss, a hug, and sashayed her way to the door.

"Isobel," I began, but her black Louboutins were already out of my office.

Leaning my head against the back of the couch, I wondered whose bright idea it was to make her the maid of honor, and why I wasn't told. After a few cleansing breaths, I got up to call Jake, while sending Sandrine an email.

Jake answered on the first ring.

Bypassing the pleasantries, I spat on the phone, "You guys forgot to mention that Isobel is the maid of honor."

"Hi to you too, Nica." He knew I was upset, and he was waiting for me to greet him back, but I had no energy for games.

When it was clear that I wasn't in the mood, he told me, "Sandrine and I just decided this morning when she flew in. We had breakfast with the family, and she asked Isobel then." He paused and softened his voice. "I was just about to call you to see if you could hang out with us tonight. You know, dinner and maybe dancing?"

I had to look at my cell phone in disbelief. Did he really think it was going to be that easy for me? What could be better than a date with my new *favorite* couple?

This was his way of making amends. Honestly. Jake was a peacemaker. I hoped that the reasons I'd given everyone as to why he'd picked me to plan his wedding were the truth, but only he knew. He wouldn't take advantage of my feelings for him, would he?

"Fine," I answered before I could convince myself otherwise. "Dinner would be great, but I'm not sure about the dancing. We have plenty of things to discuss, now that I finally can get the two of you together."

"Great. We'll send a car at eight. See you soon, Nica."

I sighed a goodbye.

I organized my thoughts, finished sending my email to Sandrine—just for safe measures—and went back to the bar mitzvah planning.

It didn't take long before the day was over, and the sun began to set. Chase popped in for a bit, asking me about everything else but Jake and Sandrine's nuptials, to my surprise (and suspicions). Then she asked if Diego had called me yet.

"No." I tried not to sound too sad about that. I still wasn't too sure if I was ready to start a relationship. Not that Diego was thinking of that. Probably not. Maybe. He just asked me for dinner, just dinner. That was all.

She pursed her lips. "You should call him."

"No! Not yet. I'm not ready."

"How would you know if you don't give it a try? You deserve to be happy too, Nica." Before she could say more, I informed her that I was heading out to meet clients for dinner and that I would be late if I didn't leave right away.

It was a total cop out. Thankfully, she didn't ask with whom.

We said our goodbyes and our 'see you tomorrows', and off we went in separate directions.

§

SECONDS AFTER PARKING my car in front of a restaurant, my phone buzzed. I fished it out of my purse. Looking at the caller ID and not recognizing the number, I hesitated to answer it, but it could be a possible new client. "You've reached Veronica."

"I have, haven't I?" Diego's chuckle was even deeper than his voice and much sexier. Closing my eyes, I imagined hearing that chuckle in person, and it gave me goosebumps. "I know I asked you to give me a call, but I don't want to risk not getting a chance." There was a pause on the other end. I gripped my phone tightly, eager to hear more. "Would you have dinner with me tomorrow?" he asked.

I couldn't imagine any hot-blooded woman turning this man down. But I had baggage. After my break up with Jake, I found it difficult to connect with other people, new people, men. With the swirling confused feelings I was harboring, I wasn't sure if I was ready for this.

"Veronica, are you still there?"

"Yes, I am! Sorry. This is quite a surprise." Chase's last sage advice entered my mind. I deserved to be happy. This could be my second chance at happiness. "I would love to have dinner with you tomorrow." I didn't even bother checking my schedule for fear that I would find an excuse to change my mind. I would have to worry about the rest tomorrow. Chase would agree to anything I asked her if I told her the reason was Delicious Diego.

"Wonderful, then. I shall pick you up at eight." By the way Diego answered, I sensed his smile. He was adorable.

"How about seven?"

Diego chuckled again over the phone, and my stomach clenched. Did this man know his effect on women? "I'll pick you up at seven. Text me your address. I will see you tomorrow night. Good night, Nica."

I looked at the restaurant and wondered what kind of night I would have. "You too, Diego." I ended the call and hugged the phone to my chest.

When I entered the restaurant, I was shocked to see the group that was waiting for me. I was expecting Jake and Sandrine, naturally, but Isobel and Levi were also there. The more the merrier, but also, too many cooks....I plastered a smile on my face. I'd only brought my iPad, thankfully, and not the bulky binder.

"There she is!" Isobel said as I neared the table. She jumped up to give me a tight hug. "Remember, I've got your back," she whispered before letting me go. My breath faltered a bit, but the smile remained on my face.

I received the European two-cheek kiss from Sandrine and surprisingly, also from Jake—which caused a twist in my gut. It was quick, and his lips barely touched my skin, but it still kicked up a sense of nostalgia within me. Not to make my building anxiety obvious, I nodded at the rest of the group. I got an easy salute from Levi before I sat down as far away from him as I possibly could. He was starting to feel like dangerous waters. Dangerous waters in a white button-down shirt and dark jeans, looking all mysterious and deep, with aviators on. I mentally rolled my eyes at him. Seriously, who wore sunglasses indoors at night?

"The whole party is here," I muttered between clenched teeth. Yeah, me and the impending doom of having to deal with the four of them with the rest of the planning!

"Oh, not quite yet. Landon and Trent are on their way," Jake said, more to everyone than directly to me. They were Jake's cousins. Also heartbreakingly good-looking guys, but with more respect toward women than Levi showed. "Groomsmen," Jake added as an explanation to me.

Good. More information. I pulled the iPad from my purse and started typing. "And who are the bridesmaids?" I asked, but when I looked up, three of them had confusion written on their faces. I couldn't tell what Levi was gawking at behind those sunglasses. "What?"

Sandrine spoke up. "Veronique, we did not ask you to come so you can work. We wanted you to come so you can take a break from all of that." She pointed at my iPad.

"Oh," I said glancing down, protectively clutching my iPad against my chest.

Sandrine reached out for my hand. "You've been working so 'ard and everything 'as been flowing very well." Yeah, because I've been working my butt off these past days, no thanks to either one of them. "And the rest are minor details now that we 'ave the date and location figured out, *n'est pas*? Correct?"

What did she know about wedding planning? What did any of them? I suppressed a 'but' and sighed.

"Yeah, Nica, chill out. Everything will work itself out," Isobel added with a wink.

Jake poured me a glass of wine. "Just relax for tonight, Nica. Put that thing away before I hide it from you." He nodded toward my iPad.

I hugged it tighter to my chest, protecting all the important dates and details in it. Before anyone else could threaten it again, I slipped it back in my purse. How I wished Jake had been clearer that this was a social visit. I could have made time to change from my work suit to a nicer dress. Honestly, I could have made time for it. The shoes I was wearing were not meant for dancing if that was the plan.

"Well, I'll just go to the little girl's room to...loosen up." I had no better way to describe it. It did garner a few laughs from the table, even though I wasn't trying to be funny. Levi just appeared amused with that smirk plastered on his face.

After untying my hair and unsuccessfully using the hand drier to make it voluminous, I re-applied lipstick and a thicker coat of mascara and liner. With my suit jacket off, I didn't look half bad. The satin blouse I wore had ruffles along the neckline, and jewel buttons, which shone when they caught the light. When I returned to the table, Landon and Trent had arrived with, I assumed, their girlfriends, two waif-thin models with perky boobs and professionally done hair and makeup.

I was suddenly thankful for Isobel's presence. It would have looked like a group date if she wasn't there. Or, maybe right now, I looked like the spare tire, *sans* partner, underdressed and frumpy, despite my earlier attempts in the bathroom. Compared to all the other women at the table, I looked dowdy and unsophisticated. I made a note to keep a pair of high-heeled pumps and better accessories in my purse for emergencies.

To drown my sorrows, I started drinking wine...then champagne...then wine again. I think I even took a bite of whatever the waiter served me. Levi started handing me colorful drinks once we all walked into a nearby club, except for a pouting Isobel, who was sent home after the restaurant. Being twenty had its disadvantages at times, even if you had the perfect, youthful skin. My skin had suffered from staying at late night events, not for fun, but for work.

When somebody suggested shots, we were all in.

They wanted me to loosen up, and I was doing it expertly. How else could I relax in the presence of my ex and his future wife, his Adonis of a best friend—who was also a slithering playboy—his two gorgeous cousins and their equally gorgeous partners?

We were all seated in the VIP lounge. The music boomed, colorful lights flickered in all directions, and hordes of people were starting to fill the place up.

Jake and Sandrine sat across from me, separated by a low oval marble-top table. "Let's go dancing, *mon cher!*" Sandrine smoothly suggested. I noticed how the men reacted to her—act first, question later. Nod first, then follow through. I never had that kind of power over men.

She didn't look drunk at all. I followed the line of her fingers caressing Jake's arms and shoulders. My heart took a beating at the sight of Jake exploring her curves with his hands in return. There were full champagne flutes sitting on the table, and I guzzled each down without thinking, and I chased them with more sweet drinks in chilled martini glasses. They kept coming, and I kept drinking.

My increasingly hazy focus was too much on the happy couple for me to notice whose strong pair of hands led me to the dance floor, where I tried my hardest to move in sync with the music. The operative word being 'tried'. The flow of alcohol rushed through my veins, filling my head with unfettered thoughts. A hand grabbed and squeezed my behind. Dancers bumped me with their butts and jabbed me with their elbows. My contacts had dried up and irritated my half-shut eyes. I couldn't see who was grinding against me. Or, was I grinding against them? I was clearly not in any shape or form to dance, but the alcohol had made everything woozy.

Was that even a word? Woooooozy...

The overhead light show created colorful waves on

gyrating bodies on the dance floor. I'd lost track of where everyone in my group had gone. At some point, I stopped caring about anything else and danced freely in the rhythm and beat of the blaring music. With my hands wrapped around the person undulating his hips behind me, I turned. Clear blue eyes settled on me. My body moved of its own accord. My fingers played with the ends of his hair, absently noting that it was longer and softer than any man should have, and then my hands moved to stroke the stubble on a chiseled chin, up to a pouty bottom lip. I grazed that lip with two fingers, and the end of his tongue poked out and licked my skin. Electricity flowed from the tips of my fingers down to the soles of my feet.

The room spun around me, and the bass pounded in my brain. I stopped swaying, stood on my toes and tugged at his collar, which brought his head down to me. I breathed his scent in—a delicious mixture of man and sweet champagne—before I pressed my lips to his. He growled into my mouth before we separated. I panted, dizzy from man, music and champagne.

My hands gripped his shirt when I pulled him in, playfully bit the outline of his ear and whispered, "Take me home." I wasn't sure if he heard me until he intertwined his fingers with mine, and we made our way to the exit.

We slipped inside a waiting limo parked just outside the club. More champagne flowed. Although I was raised in a part Scottish, part Irish and part Filipino family, and supposedly should have been able to handle my booze, there were still such things as too much alcohol. After all, I stood at five-foot-four and weighed an average amount, according to my doctor.

With two bites during dinner, one bowl of cereal for breakfast and a skipped lunch, the alcohol surged through me. I could remember flashing lights, bumping and grinding, lots of kissing and groping, and more booze.

In my twenty-five-year history, an abundance of alcohol in quick succession only equated to an extreme level of danger. And I didn't know how much danger until the next day.

THE BLUSHING BRIDESMAID

he pounding in my head wouldn't stop.

Whenever I got super drunk, I could never remember to close the blinds. So when the bright sun was up, it would hit me like a battering ram right when I tried to open my eyes. It was punishment. Oh, Universe you are so cruel to me!

The pounding continued, followed by a wheezing sound. Where was that coming from? I didn't want to open my eyes, knowing full well that leaving my contact lenses on would cause me major issues. But what was up with the wheezing? Maybe I had a nosebleed again. It happened sometimes when I had a bit too much to drink, and I'd certainly had more than enough last night.

I was about to stuff my head under my pillows when a grunt and a groan, which came from my side, stopped me.

It also made me open my eyes, which was a huge mistake. Sunlight assaulted my brain. I shut my eyes tight. Bright spots danced under my lids. I tried it again—slowly, the second time around.

Blurs started to form into shapes, shapes into objects—

familiar objects like my dresser, my lamp, my shirt on the floor, my bra hanging over my sleigh bed, and a hand. That last one wasn't so familiar. It was a large hand resting on the blanket on my right hip.

A man's hand.

Oh. My. Goodness.

I assessed my state under the blanket and flinched when I saw nothing but skin. I was naked in my bed with a man! But which man? Panic set in.

What had happened last night wasn't at all clear. I pinkie-promised myself that I would never touch any type of liquor again. A voice in my head, sounding a little too similar to Chase's, screamed in protest.

I tested my vertigo as I sat up. Then turned toward this...stranger in my bed. He wasn't facing me; his head was hidden under a pillow. One arm was stretched toward me, keeping a connection between our bodies.

His back—a sexy, toned back, I noticed—faced me, and the rest was thankfully under the blanket. I hoped that maybe he wasn't naked underneath there. That would be beyond bad. But, I knew better. I stared at what was in front of me, trying to find a familiar marker—a freckle, a scar, a tattoo—that would indicate who this man was.

I'd never come home drunk with a stranger before. I had a system. I was too organized for spontaneity. Last night, I was ambushed, lured with the possibility that I would be able to continue working with Jake and Sandrine on their wedding plans.

That's it! I was with Jake and Sandrine. I fought through the haze in my head. We went to a club after dinner. Had I picked up a man from the club? Chase would have been proud! I groaned at the possibility. Moreover, I wondered if Jake had seen me leave with this man.

Oh, the horror!

Tugging the blanket up to my neck, I poked him a couple times on his shoulder. He moved his arm that was on my hip, with the fingers precariously placed over the front of my right hip once I sat up, a little too close to my nether regions. But he didn't rouse.

I gave him another poke, this time with two fingers instead of just one. And again. I heard another groan, so I continued jabbing my fingers with their grapefruit-pink polished nails on said stranger.

He turned his whole body away from me, the blanket falling off his back and revealing the top of his naked, tanned butt. My mouth dried up. I held tightly to my blanket, reached out, and poked him again.

He grunted. "Please don't tell me you're a morning person." The pillow muffled the sound of his voice, but it was clear enough for my addled brain to place it.

That voice, rich, low and gruff. There was no mistaking it.

"Levi?" I jumped off my bed, tried to take the covers with me, but he tugged them and won. So I grabbed whatever clothing off the floor and used it as armor. "What the hell are you doing in my bed?" I soon as I yelled, I regretted it, fearful that my head was close to exploding. I squeezed my eyes shut to ensure it wouldn't, then opened them.

Levi sat up, the blanket sliding down his torso and scandalously revealing more naked parts. And it was morning. It was evident that Levi was like any other man, judging by the tenting of the blanket. I gulped and trained my eyes to look elsewhere.

"Veronica, please don't yell. Oh...my head." He brought his hands up and covered his eyes and half his face then dropped them on his lap. He squinted, taking in the room.

My room. My bedroom. "Why is it so bright in here? Don't you believe in curtains?"

I ignored his question. "Just tell me why you're in my bed," I demanded, stomping a foot on my bedroom floor.

He leered at me with tired eyes. Then his amused smile popped up. This moment was going from not-so-good to catastrophic. "You don't remember?"

"Would I ask if I did?" I snapped at him.

He looked me over, so I held onto the fabric armor tighter. Why didn't I run to the bathroom to grab my robe? My common sense had abandoned me.

"Veronica, I'm assuming you're naked by how tightly you're grasping that, and I'm..." he peeked under the blanket. I turned my head away. "Well, I'm also very naked. What do you think happened?" he said, finding amusement in the situation.

Oh, crap!

"I... I don't remember," I said sheepishly. "But please get dressed." I snuck a glance back through my curtain of hair.

"Funny," he started as he maneuvered his legs slowly over the bed, picking up pants off the floor then putting them on, sans underwear. "I don't seem to remember a lot either. It's a shame really."

When he turned around, his pants were zipped, but he wore the wickedest grin. "Maybe..." He sauntered toward me, rounding my queen-size bed. I moved further away from him, still clutching the clothing over my nakedness. "Maybe you should remind me." Levi waggled his eyebrows and bit down on his lower lip.

"What?" I asked, astonished.

He pulled away whatever fabric I was holding onto like it was my lifeline, revealing my naked bits. My hands flew to cover my dignity. He chuckled, the SOB. Turned out, the article of clothing I had used to cover myself up was his white shirt. I noticed this as he put his arms through the sleeves. He kept his bedroom eyes on me, so I pivoted to grab a shirt out of my dresser.

Just as I was able to pull it over my body, he grabbed my arm, spun me around, and planted his lips on mine. It was a hard kiss, hungry and fervent, yet he had the softest lips. It was the type of kiss that made me forget who I was kissing. All that mattered was the warm sensation flooding my core and the shivers spreading along my spine. He gave the term "French Kiss" another meaning. My intention was to fight him off, but something deeper stirred in me—a desire brewing, a longing—so I closed my eyes, and I let him kiss me. My fingers hovered over the smattering of dark hair on his toned chest. I moaned against his mouth, which caused him to deepen our kiss.

When his roving hands started to move down, and the cool air hit my naked bum, I broke our connection and pushed him away. I should have slapped him, but that was overly dramatic. He chuckled again, sticking his tongue out and licking his own lips, and muttered, "Sweet."

I exaggerated the way I wiped my lips on my sleeve.

"What happened?" I demanded. I tried to look mad, not shaken and affected by his kiss. My legs trembled a tad. My thighs pressed together. Under my long shirt, I was very much aware of my nudity.

He shrugged, buttoning his shirt up. "Lots of drinking. You were doing this incredibly sexy dance in the club..." I sadly knew what he meant. Chase called it my 'mating dance,' only performed while fully intoxicated. "It was kinda cute too. Then you asked me to take you home, we kissed, got naked...and then...you know." Levi winked, puckered his lips and made kissing noises.

Oh, Holy of all holy. I did know. Or, I could speculate. What else could it be? I went back under my covers to hide my shame. I could not have had sex with the snakiest of playboys in this city, my ex's best friend, and his best man. What was I thinking? I was mentally chiding myself when I felt my bed sag by my feet.

"Veronica..." His voice was laced with sweetness. "There's nothing to be ashamed of. You were such a good..."

I groaned and lifted a finger above the blanket. "Please don't say it. Will you just please go away? Just leave, okay?" I sank deeper into my bed.

In all of my twenty-five years, I had never been so...irresponsible, and never with someone like Levi. The men I dated (count three) were dignified, responsible, and *not* man-whores.

He remained quiet for a beat or two and then sighed heavily as he stood, my mattress springing back up. I couldn't see what he was doing, but I heard shuffling about, followed by his footsteps leaving my bedroom. A few moments later, the door of my apartment slammed shut.

THERE WEREN'T a lot of reasons that would keep me away from work. An earthquake was one unless I was already at work, and then I'd hide under the desk until Chase gave me the 'all clear'.

Heartbreak was another until Chase could convince me that she would run the place down to the ground if left to her own devices. But a drinking binge, and a possible wild night with Mr. Casanova himself weren't good enough reasons.

After reminding myself that I was human and allowed to make mistakes, I dusted myself off, showered, dressed, ignored the possibility that I might have had unprotected sex with Levi, and went straight to meet with Sandrine for lunch. The effervescent woman seemed quite refreshed after last night—no saggy bags under her eyes, no blotches on her face, and she was even a tad cheerier. The kind of cheer that only a woman who got a little something-something last night, and possibly this morning, could have. Life was so unfair!

"I was so grateful that you came out with us last night! Did you 'ave fun?" she asked as I ordered a cup of the strongest black coffee.

Since nodding still hurt my head, I answered her, keeping my voice low, "Yup, for the most part."

"Ah, you mean the alco'ol? Ah, *oui*. It is the devil. But you kept up with the boys. I was impressed. And you danced so well. Did you take lessons when you were little?"

"Yeah, my old man was part Irish, and my mother was a dancer, so I may have gotten my impressive skills from them." My mother would have been appalled. Well, what she didn't know wouldn't kill her. "What time did you get home?" I needed some more insight of the previous night. Maybe I could recall the rest with her.

"I wasn't so sure. I drank so much champagne, *non*?" Apparently, not as much as I did.

When my coffee arrived, she let me sip a few sips. I refused any food, as even a tiny smell could turn my stomach.

"I 'ave something to say." Her hand was over mine.

Uh oh. This was the time she'd tell me that I was fired because I slept with her best man. Not to mention the feelings I still had for her fiancé. "Go on." I kept the coffee cup close to my mouth, running excuses through my aching head to counter her with.

"Veronique, I 'ave two friends. Shalom and Natalie. They are both *docteurs* like me, but they're... 'ow do you say..." She made gestures with her hands. "Quarantined."

I nodded, encouraging her to continue. Maybe she would ask me to postpone the wedding until they came back. Maybe this time, the Universe *was* on my side.

"And my other friends, they don't talk to me anymore." She pouted her rouge lips. "Jacob said they chose sides. I had to ask Isobel to be my maid of *honeur* since she's Jacob's little sister." So, it wasn't her idea after all. "And I was wondering..."

"Uh huh?" I said over the coffee, my brows knitted.

"Since you 'ave every knowledge of the wedding and you are our friend—" I raised a brow "—will you be my bridesmaid?" Hope gleamed in her eyes.

My hand shook, spilling some coffee on the table. I piled napkins over it, but the waiter was so attentive he had it cleaned up in seconds. I checked to make sure that Sandrine was fine, and she was. I, on the other hand, had a blot of black coffee over the crotch of my new white linen suit.

As I tried to dab at the spot, I remembered what Sandrine asked of me. "You want me to be your bridesmaid? Sandrine, I'm already your wedding planner. I can't be your bridesmaid too."

It was like chiding an orphaned child. I didn't know how she did it. She looked crushed, and it made me feel horrible.

"Oh, I know, and I 'ate to ask you, but I felt I 'ad no other choice. You've been so good to me, to us, and 'ave been so involved, but I didn't want to ask Landon and Trent's girlfriends from last night. They were so uncouth and lacked class," she explained. Everything was clear to her. No wonder she was so freaking cheerful.

"And I did?" I snapped at her, briefly recalling the earlier mention of my dancing skills, which was clearly a way to butter me up. Mating dance equaled zero class.

"You 'ad more than those two girls combined. I will double your fees. All you need to do is stand during the ceremony for a little while. Then you're free to do whatever wedding planners do." Her back was straight. Her chin was held high. She believed that her idea was divine.

I shook my head until it felt it was going to come off. "I cannot be in two places at once. What if something happens during the ceremony? Who will attend to that if I'm standing next to you?"

"Well, maybe you can ask your partner to be there too? I will pay 'er as well. I will cover your whole staff's fees. Jacob wants his cousins as his groomsmen, and 'e said I needed a bridesmaid. I do anything, Veronique. Just please, please be my bridesmaid?" Her dainty surgeon fingers clasped under her chin. She'd give cute puppies a run for their money.

Fudge my life.

That day I realized that not only could I not say no to Jake, somewhere along the way I had also lost that ability with Sandrine. She clapped her hands with glee and hugged me tight when I gave in and nodded. "Perfect! We will fly to Paris in three days for dress fittings."

"Whoa! What?" Did she just say Paris?

"*Oui*, my mother's friend is a designer, and 'e insisted 'e makes all the dresses for the wedding party. We will only spend a few days there, don't you worry. It will be *fantastique!*"

I stayed silent after that, letting her tell me about Paris and the French designer, and his plans for her *haute couture* wedding gown. My spotted crotch forgotten, my unplanned romp with the best man became secondary.

Every girl has a dream.

I was lost in my own when she mentioned Paris.

THE BOUQUET

$\mathcal{I}$ was a walking zombie when I returned to the office. Chase was ready to hear my stories as soon as she saw the puffiness under my eyes. When her gaze drifted down to the coffee stain on my white pants, I held up a hand. "Don't ask." And headed straight to the tiny office kitchen to rummage for liquid soap and vinegar.

"I spilled coffee this morning," I explained anyway as I removed my pants and ran it under cold water. The stain had set in.

"Do you also know that you smell like you bathed in alcohol?" she asked, sniffing my hair.

Shocked, my eyes widened at what she'd just said. "What?" I grabbed a chunk of my hair and inhaled. Twice. She was right. I sagged in defeat and returned to washing my pants in the sink. "This is great. I had breakfast at a posh restaurant with a posh French woman, and I smell like a drunk skunk. On top of that, I don't think I have enough time to go home before my date tonight. Maybe I'll cancel."

"I beg your freaking pardon...date?" Chase shut off the

faucet and made me face her. "Did the girl too busy planning other people's happily ever after say she has a date? Tonight?"

Crap. I completely forgot to mention it to her. Avoiding eye contact, I replied, "Yeah, I hope it's okay. It was a little sudden. Just happened last night. Diego called me before…"

"Did you just say, Diego? As in the most delicious human being on earth?" she interrupted, her eyes and grin widening.

"Yes. Him." I turned the faucet back on and returned my attention to my pants.

"Yes? Him?" she said, incredulous. "Nica, Diego is not just 'him.' Diego is perfection wrapped up in muscular goodness. What time is your date?"

"He's picking me up at seven. Oh, shoot. I have to text him our address."

"He's picking you up here?" she shouted, like I'd done something so heinous.

"Well, I have work to do and…"

"No. I won't allow this." Chase shook her head, pushing her fingers through her thick hair and tugging in frustration.

"What? Chase, I have stuff to do and this trip to Paris will require a lot of preparation."

"What trip to Paris?"

Right. I forgot that one too. I paused scrubbing and slowly pivoted. "I'm going to Paris in three days on Sandrine's dime for a dress fitting." Before she could explode, I continued, "I'm now her bridesmaid, and she's taking me to Paris to get measured by one of the best couturiers in France. It's only a few days, and I know we have quite a bit to do this weekend, but she's practically tripling our fees and…it's Paris." Hopeful, I bit my bottom lip and shrugged. She knew it had always been on my Bucket List. "I'll make calls today to make sure you're covered while I'm gone."

"Woman, please. I know how to do my job." I raised a brow at her. "Oh, shut up. I do. The only reason I don't do much is I don't want to get in the way of your perfectionism and OCD tendencies." She waved her hand in a circle in front of me. "But this is huge. Diego and plans to Paris in less than twenty-four hours. Anything else I should know?"

Yes. "Nope. That's all." I focused my attention back on my pants and ignored the need to tell her about waking up next to Levi. I wasn't sure if I was ready to admit *that* to myself yet.

Once my pants were dried, thanks to Chase's hair dryer, I settled back into work, ignoring the hazy throb in my head. I kept hydrated and by lunchtime, my stomach didn't feel like it was turning itself inside out. Every now and then, something would cause me to pause, close my eyes and try to remember what happened last night, but nothing solid would come. Once I opened my eyes, I ignored Chase's curious looks.

Jewel, one of our semi-permanent staff, walked into my office with a bouquet of flowers that she could barely carry half an hour after sending Diego my home address. "Delivery," She announced.

Chase hopped up from the couch and grabbed the card stuck in the arrangement, which Jewel placed daintily on my desk. "To Sweet Veronica."

My head jerked up. "For me?" My cheeks warmed.

Chase waved the little card in the air. "Yup. Somebody lurves you."

I scooted forward, examining the beautiful, massive

arrangement of every flower that ever existed (or close to it). "Who sent it?" I held my hand out for the card.

Instead of giving it to me, Chase flipped it in her hand. "Doesn't say. You have a secret admirer." The way she waggled her brows reminded me of someone...someone who didn't have the right to invade my thoughts. It didn't matter how sexy he'd looked in my bed. *No, Nica! Stop it!* I couldn't let myself think of Levi. Or his naked behind. Or that toe-curling kiss.

Looking at the bouquet, I named all the flowers I knew in my head, from garden variety round bulbs of pink peonies and white ranunculus to the more exotic yellow and purple lady slipper orchids to keep my thoughts away from the man who'd woken up in the nude next to me.

"Who would send me flowers?" I asked under my breath.

"Maybe it's from DD!" Chase's grin spread from ear-to-ear.

I smiled at the thought. I tried to recall the last time Jake had sent me flowers and couldn't remember it. An ache replaced my giddiness. Maybe this whole dating thing was a good idea after all.

AT EXACTLY 6:55PM, Diego knocked on my door. I opened it to greet the debonair man in a collared shirt, light blue V-neck sweater and dark jeans. He completed the look with a navy blue blazer, a white handkerchief folded neatly in the breast pocket. I was truly attracted to this man, physically, but when he greeted me with a kiss on the cheek, with the slight quiver in my belly came a surprising stab of guilt.

I blinked, thinking it would be enough to erase that last unwelcome feeling. It wasn't. "Hi," I welcomed him in.

"You look…" He swept his eyes over me. "Wow."

I blushed, most likely the same color as the tight dress I was wearing (that Chase insisted on, but I must admit I rocked it). "And you don't look half-bad."

"I know it's a bit of a change from my usual trainers and gym clothes." Which he never looked bad in, either. "Shall we?"

"I just need to grab my purse. Why don't you come in?" I let Diego close the door behind him.

It was awkward having a man standing by my door. I didn't date much. Jake and I hadn't gone out much due to time constraints and our never-ending responsibilities. Even the few blind dates that Chase had arranged for me would meet with me at an agreed-upon location.

After grabbing my clutch from my dresser, I went through my scarf drawer (yes, I had one, so should everybody) to pick something that would both compliment my dress and keep my neck warm. My breathing faltered when I immediately spotted the scarf that Jake had given me. Like a ticking time bomb, I went around it carefully and chose a black silk-cashmere blend instead. I breathed a sigh as I wrapped the scarf around my neck and walked out of my bedroom to meet my hot date. One who wasn't engaged to be married. One whose wedding I wasn't planning.

Diego was such a gentleman. That wasn't much of a surprise. He helped me shrug into a light coat, opened and closed the car door for me, held out his hand when I stepped out of it and slipped my arm around the crook of his elbow while we walked. Whoever said chivalry was dead had not met Diego. He smelled incredible too. He didn't have his usual coconut scent but a more appealing, more masculine allure.

"So, where are we going?" I asked as we turned on Noe Street in Castro.

"Do you like French food?"

If I had been drinking something, I would have sputtered and spat all over my date. Or, if we had been walking faster, I would have fallen on my ass. French? Was he kidding me? I looked at his polite smile.

He was serious. Of course he was, because he wouldn't have known about the one French person I knew—Levi. Admittedly, I hadn't been able to get him out of my head, no matter how hard I tried. As soon as I stepped into my bedroom again after coming home from work, he had invaded my mind. I blamed it on the fact that I couldn't remember anything that happened last night, but...the kiss we shared was hard to ignore.

"Yeah. Sounds great."

We arrived shortly at *La Mer*. Diego greeted every staff member who came our way. The restaurant was busy, but everyone, including the chef, made an appearance at our table. Diego, once again, ever the gentleman, introduced me to every single one of them. They all seemed ecstatic about my presence.

"Do you work here?" I asked Diego when Chef Jean-Luc left.

He laughed that delightful, hearty laugh. "I don't. Not anymore. I used to be a sous-chef when I first moved here." So, he cooked too! He really was the perfect man.

"You're not from San Francisco?"

Diego took a sip of water. "'Fraid not. I was born in Atlanta, and I moved around a lot with my family when I was younger. Military brat." He pointed at himself. "I lived in Georgia again before moving here."

"Oh, nice. What brought you here?"

Luciano, our server, returned and brought us a bottle

that Chef Jean-Luc recommended. Diego did the wine thing (checking the label, swirling, tasting, making faces) before nodding at Luciano.

"I didn't know you were a wine connoisseur," I observed.

"I'm not." He leaned forward and lowered his voice. "I pretended I knew what I was doing to try to impress you. Can you keep a secret?" I nodded, then he glanced around. "I cheated on my sommelier test."

My eyes bugged out of my head. "I promise not to tell." Hot, sexy, can cook, and funny? This date had promise. I'd be stupid not to enjoy it.

Satisfied, Diego sat back. "Love."

What? "Pardon me?"

"You asked me what brought me here. It was love. Love brought me to this city."

Wasn't he the most adorable man that ever existed? "What happened?"

Diego sucked on his bottom lip before answering, and pulled on his left ear.

"Life happened, I suppose."

What could I say? First dates could be awful with awkward chit-chat. This wasn't exactly first date conversation, but I asked a question, and he answered, truthfully. Time to change direction. "Thanks for the flowers, by the way."

Immediately, from the confused look on his face, I knew they hadn't come from him. "Flowers?" he asked, with one corner of his lips tilted.

"I received a bouquet of flowers this afternoon at work." Why didn't I stick to that first awkward topic? Did Jake actually send me flowers? He might have done that once before, but why now? What did it mean?

Diego shook his head, still smiling. "I wish I had thought of that. I'm a little rusty at dating."

I picked up my wine glass and swirled the clear liquid in it. "You? Rusty? That's hardly believable." His eyebrow shot up. "Have you seen yourself lately? Don't act all humble. You think all the girls in Torture go there for fun? And don't include Chase. She *does* do it for fun."

He probably had a good comeback for me, but Luciano brought an *amuse-bouche*, a lobster-topped *choux* pastry—creamy, flaky and so yum!

"So, who is it?"

"Who?" I asked, taking a sip of wine.

"Who sent the flowers?"

Whatever wine I had left in my mouth sputtered out a bit. Se-xy. "What makes you think I know?"

Diego chuckled, pouring a bit more wine into my glass. "When I told you I didn't send them, your eyes got all...squinty."

"Squinty?" A giggle burst out of me.

Diego played with his napkin on the table. The confidence I'd seen on him time after time was waning. "I'm going to level with you, Nica." He stared me right in the eyes, folding his hands on top of his napkin. "I think you're great. You're smart, accomplished, talented, and you're beautiful."

"I don't know about that," I said, looking down on my fingers.

He reached over and tilted my chin up, forcing me to meet his gaze. "You. Are. Beautiful." Diego threaded his fingers together, cleared his throat and continued, "As I said before, I came to San Francisco for love. My fiancée, ex-fiancée, found a job here, and I followed her. I was never a believer of long distance relationships, you see." He paused, laughing at something I didn't quite catch. "I know

I'm breaking a lot of rules here—talking about past relationships during a first date."

I straightened on my chair and fiddled with my own napkin. "So, you've been briefed by Chase too?" We both chuckled at that.

Luciano reappeared to serve us a fresh baguette and our appetizers of rillette of rabbit and salmon terrine. I was starving, and the smell of food set my stomach grumbling. I waited for Diego to start, but he urged me with an offer of bread. It was a great compliment to the wine.

"Marissa, my ex, had a great job at a marketing company. She was doing well. And I wasn't." Diego raised his shoulders in a half shrug. "I also didn't look like this back then. I loved food too much. Way too much. I didn't exercise, I smoked, and I drank a lot, too. I was working here when Marissa left me for another man."

I cleared my throat for fear that I would choke on rabbit and bread. "I...don't know what to say."

Diego smiled, but it didn't nearly reach his eyes. "Marissa thought I wasn't going anywhere, that I wouldn't amount to anything. She said that if I couldn't even take care of myself, how could I ever take care of her?" No matter how long ago that had been, he was still hurt by it; it was apparent in his voice.

My mouth went dry. A confident, handsome-as-sin man was pouring his heart out to me. All I had to offer back was, "Is that why you look like this now?"

Thankfully, he thought I was being funny. "That would be a no. I did this for myself. That's what I was getting at." Chocolate brown eyes mesmerized me. "I didn't change for her. I didn't change for what she said. I woke up one day and asked myself what I had done to me. I changed for me." The confident man returned. He reached for my hand and squeezed. "This guy who brought you flowers, was he the reason why you came to my class?"

Jake? Was he the reason for all the physical torture I put myself through each morning?

"I didn't?"

"You're not sure? You didn't do it for yourself."

I shrugged and screwed my lips into a grimace. "Not exactly. Chase threatened to drag me if I didn't go, physically drag me."

His laughter boomed in the otherwise quiet restaurant. "But someone did break your heart. Is he worth it? The change? The process? The pain?" I nodded, shook my head, and nodded again. "You change only for you if you want to. You don't change for any man. But I'm curious about him. Tell me."

And as *faux pas* as it was, I babbled about not just one man but that man's best friend during a first date with a viable partner, over our lovely prepared dinner and wine, and minus the gritty details (the whole world didn't need to know my foibles). Over our shared dessert of *creme brûlée* and cups of tea, we went back to discussing who had sent the flowers.

"He's an old school romantic." I laughed at Diego's comment. "When I said your eyes became squinty, I knew that look. You obviously think about him enough. My friends used to tell me that too when I thought of Marissa. For him, the flowers said a lot. He knows you're smart. He knows you'll figure out they're from him. Ball's in your court now, girl."

I chuckled mirthlessly, wrapping a hand around my teacup while I scooped another bite of the dessert. "It's not really Jake's thing to send me flowers. He was more of a 'let's go out for dinner since we're too exhausted' kind of guy or 'let's cuddle on the couch and watch a movie'." But maybe being engaged to a French woman had changed Jake.

"Nica, Nica, Nica." He shook his head and rubbed his palms together.

I nibbled on the tip of my teaspoon. "What?" I huffed out a heavy sigh when all he did was cock his head to the side and continued to look adorable. Damn. "I'm sorry about this date."

"I'm not. I got to spend a wonderful dinner with a wonderful girl. It just so happens her heart already belongs to someone else."

Double damn. Why couldn't my heart beat erratically for him?

The chef came out again and thanked us for coming. I kept his card for future references. I'd never know when I would need a great French chef.

I excused myself to head to the bathrooms, and while I was reapplying my lipstick in front of gilded mirrors, my cell phone vibrated in my purse. Thinking that it was Chase checking on me and my date, I fished it out and was surprised by the picture that appeared on my screen. There he was, hair mussed, eyes lit up and lips slightly puckered. From the familiar floral print surrounding him, Levi had taken a selfie on my bed with my phone and took the liberty to program his number on it. This was bordering on creepy. *And cute.* I mentally rolled my eyes at myself.

Bypassing pleasantries, I snapped, "How did you figure out my password?"

Levi's chuckle caused a tickle in my belly that I didn't expect. "Veronica, one, two, three, four wasn't a genius password. You should change it."

"I never thought I needed a reason to. What do you want?"

"What happened to the Sweet Veronica I woke up to this morning?"

There it was. All the proof I needed that Levi had sent me the flowers. Sweet Veronica. And here I was thinking that a trip to Paris had changed Jake to what Diego called "old school romantic," sending me a large bouquet of flowers, and making my heart skip a beat. I couldn't help but feel slightly disappointed.

"Veronica? Are you still there?"

"Yeah...no..." I stammered. "Could you please let me know what you want? I have to go back to my date."

If I wasn't mistaken, there was a loud gasp on the other line, right before he asked, "A date? What date? With whom?"

"None of your business, Levi."

"It is my business."

"Why?" I propped a hand on my hip, leaning against the vanity.

"Because..." I waited for a few beats for the rest of his reply. "Of Jake. And Sandrine. You're their wedding planner."

"What's your point?"

"Shouldn't you be concentrating on their wedding instead of going out on dates?"

"Are you freaking kidding me? Levi, can you hear yourself? This conversation is ridiculous. I'm hanging up."

"Wait! No. Veronica..." The way he said my name did something weird to my chest. I held my breath, anticipating to hear what he would say next. "What time are you done your date?"

"I don't know. Maybe it won't end tonight. Maybe it will continue tomorrow morning."

There was no mistaking it. Levi sighed heavily on the phone. I felt bad. I was implying I'd do something that I didn't usually do on first dates, not counting Jake...or him. Not that what Levi and I had last night resembled a date.

I was about to apologize when he spoke. "If it ends soon, can you give me a call and we can finish what we started this morning? I'd like a repeat of last night."

I gasped, and my cheeks reddened. "Jerk! You don't deserve another chance with me. You shouldn't have had that chance at all. I was drunk, and you took advantage. I don't sleep with guys like you, Levi."

"What kind of guy am I?"

"A man-whore." As soon as I said it out loud, I regretted it, but I couldn't take it back.

"Well, you're wrong. You came on to me, Veronica. Apparently, you like man-whores."

"I hate you." I hung up and threw my phone back into my purse. When I returned to the table, I was still shaking, and Diego noted it right away.

"What happened?"

"It's the flower guy. You're wrong." Short of stomping my feet, I slumped in my chair and crossed my arms over my chest. Yeah, I pouted too.

"Wrong about what? Jake didn't send them."

"No, Levi did. He wasn't a romantic. He's a big butthole."

Diego laughed, and it was so contagious that I had to laugh too, even if it was at my expense. At times like these, all we could do was laugh. If not, I'd be on my knees crying at how bizarre my "love" life had turned into.

After saying goodbye to the staff, Diego and I walked out of *La Mer* the same way we came in, with my arm wrapped around his.

There was a chill in the air, and it smelled like rain. I snuggled closer to Diego, and he kept me warm. It felt like

I'd found a new friend. A new hot and sexy friend. If only I were the type of girl who kept friends with benefits.

"Thank you for the lovely night," I told him when we stood in front of my apartment door.

"I had a great time too." He squeezed my hand and raised it to his lips. "It's just my luck that I met you at the wrong time."

I could say I was sorry, that I wished I met him at a better time. But I thought this was a good time. Diego was perfect. Too perfect to be a rebound. With all the confusion surrounding me, it was unfair for a wonderful man like him to be involved with someone like me.

THE CAKE

*N*ormally, an appointment with the baker would have taken place at least six months before the wedding day, especially if said baker was the cream of the crop. We had a few weeks.

Lucky for Jake and Sandrine—who wanted only the best —I was connected to the best. Eddie was the renaissance man of cakes and pastries, and he made wedding cakes like no other.

In college, I had taken summer and night jobs to help out with my fees and basic life needs. Eddie had hired me on the spot; once I had proved that I was Queen of OCD, to sort out his disorganized mess. I had worked with him tirelessly until I had graduated. He had been a great employer, but what was more important was that he had become my family, and he treated me like the daughter he never had.

These days, Eddie's bakery was consistently busy, and his wife of three years, Nancy, was the one who kept him together. His reputation had flourished, and he only took four wedding cake orders every year. Jake and Sandrine's was the exceptional fifth.

"Hi, Eddie," I greeted the larger-than-life man behind the display counter as I entered the bright, clean and kitschy shop.

Eddie's eyes popped. "Baby girl!" He rounded the case and wrapped me in a teddy bear hug. "How's my darling girl doing?"

"Eddie, I spoke to you on the phone yesterday." I rolled my eyes as he pouted. "But I'm fine. Surviving this heat."

"Fine? That's not what I heard. Heard you're dating again." Eddie's arms straightened as he held me away from him so that he could train his eyes on me.

I scoffed. "Where'd you hear that?" I twirled the end of my ponytail with my fingers, avoiding his gaze.

Eddie's eyebrows knitted together.

"The Amazonian. And she also ordered me to give you as many goodies as I possibly can. She said you lost weight, and it sure looks like it." His eyes scanned me up and down. He knew that I'd never been one to be too concerned about my weight.

I dislodged myself from him and huffed. "Everyone needs to calm down. My weight should not be something to gossip about. I'm fine. I'm healthy. I'm exercising."

"Ah." Eddie chuckled. "But you are dating again. Who's the lucky guy?"

My mouth fell to the floor. Damn Chase and her big mouth! My phone buzzed in my purse, and I took it as a chance to escape what could turn into twenty questions. I fished it out and answered hurriedly, "You've reached Veronica."

"Nica! Oh good. Are you at Eddie's?" Jake rushed the words out.

"Yeah, I am."

"Sandrine's very ill. She's been throwing up all night, and I just got called in at the hospital. "

"Oh, well, don't worry. I'm sure I can reschedule." I wasn't taking crap from them, as they had valid reasons.

"No!" he said quickly. "I've sent someone else so you won't have to do it alone."

I tried to protest, but he wouldn't let me. "I trust you implicitly. So does Sandrine. I'm sorry, Nica, but I have to go. Don't worry. He has a discerning palate." More voices filled the line, as people began directing Jake and giving him more information. I could imagine the chaos surrounding him.

Wait, he? Did he say 'he'?

"Jake? Jake, who'd you send?" But his phone had already disconnected.

The ring at the door signaled an entry into the bakery. I didn't need an answer from Jake once I turned toward the front, right in time to witness Levi sauntering in, with his hotter than hot sauce looks and a killer, Cheshire-cat grin.

But he didn't. Come. Alone.

With claws wrapped around Levi's left arm, a woman strutted beside him in six-inch fuchsia heels. She flipped a chunk of platinum blond hair over her left shoulder as they stopped in front of me.

The fast and furious hammering of my heart threatened to rip my chest apart. This was the first time I'd set my eyes on Levi since waking up next to him. And he had the gall to show up with a twinset of double Ds?

"Well, lookie what we got here," Eddie piped up behind me.

I immediately had plans to kill Jake the next time I saw him.

"I guess you're the replacement," I spoke to Levi, careful not to inflect my tone.

I wished he would take off his gosh-darned wayfarers so I could look him in the eyes. The hot bastard shrugged and wiped the grin off his face. He was lucky that a marble top, bar-height table separated us, or I would be tempted to shake him senseless.

I cleared my throat as I made introductions. "Levi," his name sounded foreign on my tongue, "this is Eddie Stone, owner, baker, artiste. Eddie, this is Levi, Jake's best man...and his guest." I waved my hand between them.

"Pleasure," was all Levi offered. I waited for him to tell us what his date's name was, but he never did.

I stared at the woman. Her hand made its way to Levi's chest, and she started circling a manicured finger over his blue Oxford shirt. Her boobs pressed against his arm. A hiss escaped my mouth. I gripped my phone as I thought of the best way to escape this situation.

As soon as Levi started a conversation with Eddie about the bakery, I stealthily tapped a text to Chase and tagged it 911. Several seconds later, my phone vibrated in my hand.

"Excuse me. I better get this." I didn't wait for their acknowledgments. I ran to the back of the bakery, through double-swing doors, and watched the horror through the one-way glass in front of me. I had a good view of the storefront. Of Levi and his date.

"Chase! I need your help!" I rapidly expressed, my voice shaking.

"Nica? Calm down, what's going on?"

"Chase, he's here."

"Who?"

I narrowed my eyes at the people behind the mirror. "Levi."

Chase went silent, then said, "So? He's the best man."

"Yeah but Jake and Sandrine couldn't come so they sent

Levi over. He's not alone," I stated, eyeing the boob-popping blond beside him.

"Why is this a problem? What does she look like?"

"Porn star. I can't even call what she's wearing a dress. It's tight, it's white, and I think Eddie can see her nipples through it."

Chase sucked in a breath. "Bastard."

"You have to get me outta here, Chase. This has bad written all over it. Bad."

"Nica, it's only Levi. Just ignore them. Stuff your face with cake and choose."

"Only Levi? Chase, you don't understand...I...it's more complicated than that." I gripped the phone harder.

"Is there something you're not telling me?"

"No!"

"Then why are you acting all weird? You've worked so hard to be able to stand up to other people. Levi is other people. Stand up to him."

"Oh my god!" D-cups slid her hand beneath Levi's shirt. "She's feeling him up! In front of Eddie! I think she's pinching his nipple. Oh, I'm gonna throw up." I didn't like what I was seeing, but I couldn't look away.

Chase hissed. "Stop! Go out there and face them. Square your shoulders. Stick out your tatas and sashay those hips."

"You have to help me, Chase. Please."

It took an entire minute before she replied, "I'll figure something out. Don't worry."

"Fine. But hurry. I think they're ready to start making a porn film on the counter!"

"I'll hurry." Chase rang off.

I held onto my phone and sucked in my panic. Exhaled. Inhaled. With the next exhale, I rolled my shoulders back, lengthened my neck, stuck my nose in the air, and made sure my B-cups fit properly in my new demi cup lace bra. For good measure, I undid the first two buttons of my peach blouse to show off a bit of cleavage, and fixed my white belt, cinched at my waist. My clothes weren't designer duds—the 1960's June Cleaver floral circle skirt I was wearing was a vintage find. I opted for cute and comfortable. Not tight and porn star chic.

I had worked my damned ass off in Torture. I told myself that I looked fabulous no matter what I wore. I looked fine. No, more than fine...I was hot! Scorching!

When I returned, I touched Eddie's arm to take his attention away from Levi and his *pal*. "We should get started."

Eddie mumbled something inaudible and walked to the back of the store, shaking his head.

I schooled my face into something more serene. "We have four cakes to try," I announced. "Please remember, this is for a seven-tier cake."

Levi's lady friend hummed, but I was sure it was due to something else other than the thought of cake. Her hand seemed to have found something interesting beneath Levi's shirt.

I narrowed my eyes marginally as Levi finally took off his sunglasses and placed them on the table. He wasn't smiling. But he didn't seem upset either. He was stoic. The unfeeling man.

And he unnerved me.

I looked away and paid attention to my phone, tapping a text to Chase to hurry up.

Thankfully, Eddie returned with a tray of empty dessert plates, which he left on top of the counter. He then took out four lovely, intricately-decorated round cakes from the display cabinet, and arranged them before us. "What we have here are..." Eddie began but was interrupted by a ring at the door. Eddie looked stunned, making the rest of us turn our heads.

I stifled a gasp as a six-foot-four hunk of a man in a plain white tee, dark jeans that hugged every sinful bit of his lower half, sauntered in. Diego prowled like a male model on a catwalk. He was just plain sexy all over.

"Sorry I'm late," he said, eyes on me, as he neared. He kissed the side of my cheek.

"What are you doing here?" I whispered, then smiled.

"I knew you were gonna see Eddie, so I thought I'd surprise you and stop by. I would have made it on time, but I got stuck in traffic." Diego glanced over my head and nodded. "Hey, Eddie."

"Hello?" Eddie was right to question Diego's presence. On top of that, he didn't even know him, but Diego acted as though he did.

I tapped a finger on my chin, trying to make sense of what was happening. When I received the text from Chase: *Is he there now?* I got it. Diego was Chase's solution to my dilemma.

"Hi!" Levi's date spoke up in a high-pitched tone. Diego and I turned to her, and I swallowed a guffaw. She stretched out the hand that had been in Levi's shirt moments before and offered it to Diego. "I'm Ophelia."

Her name rolled over her tongue, and it sounded as though she said 'I'll feel yah.' I bet she would too. I shuddered.

Diego, ever the good boy, took the proffered hand and shook it once. "Very nice to meet you." He had to pull away forcefully from Ophelia's grasp. Then he angled his body and stretched his own hand toward Levi. "Diego," he introduced himself.

Levi's eyes narrowed into tiny slits. He looked down at

Diego's large, callused hand, up to Diego's face, and then to me.

I had to take advantage of the situation. The new me needed it. Levi brought Ophelia to either piss me off, or make me jealous, or whatever. I touched one of Diego's bulging biceps and left my hand on it. "Diego dear, this is Levi. Remember the wedding I told you about last night? He's the best man." I made sure to enunciate the 'last night' and didn't miss the understanding in Levi's eyes. Yes, he knew that Diego was my date. He didn't have to know that we had parted as friends.

Diego slowly retracted his hand. My face burned like I'd eaten a five-alarm hot pepper.

Eddie cleared his throat, produced dessert spoons and forks, and placed them on a linen serviette on the table. "Shall we continue?" We all returned our focus on Eddie.

I nodded. "Please."

"Our first cake is an homage to our lovely country: apple and cinnamon cake with brown sugar frosting." Eddie sliced the first cake and placed a piece of it on a plate.

"Diego and I will just share one, Eddie." The words just came out. Out of the corner of my eye, I could see Levi's mouth gape.

"That'll be the same for us," Levi said. His voice did not waver.

I looked at Levi and Ophelia, who was still eyeing Diego and seductively licking a spoon.

Eddie stared at the two couples in front of him. He was as confused as ever. "Very well then." He proceeded to cut the next cake, a mocha-colored frosting over yellow cake. "Next, we have almond with mocha icing, chocolate drizzle, and pistachio crumbs."

The third cake was decorated more elaborately with

Corneille lace piping, something I had become proficient in when I had worked for Eddie. "This is our blackberry and currant chiffon with raspberry filling and limoncello icing. My dear Nica's favorite." Eddie glanced at me, and I sent him a smile. "And last, but not least, dark chocolate with a whipped peanut butter mousse filling, and dark chocolate ganache. Rich, robust, and I believe it is still the groom's favorite."

"You're so good, Eddie. I can't believe you remembered," I quipped, even though I had reminded him about it yesterday when I confirmed this appointment. He passed along the plates, and I placed them on the table. Four cakes for Diego and me, and four similar slices for Levi and Ophelia. I hoped he choked. Well, not really. Maybe just a little.

Eddie had also provided carafes of water and glasses. Perhaps he could read my thoughts. *"Bon appétit!"*

Diego and I took a spoon and fork each.

I watched as Ophelia scooped a piece of the first cake, and lifted it to Levi, who slowly, like we had all the time in the world to eat cakes, opened his mouth to take the dessert. So this was his game. I copied Ophelia's actions and fed Diego a piece of the cake.

"Hmmm, very good. This is definitely a winner," Diego offered his opinion. He used his fork to lift a tiny slice to my mouth. "Here you go, my sweet."

My throat dried up upon hearing Levi's term of endearment to me coming out of Diego's lips. In my peripheral vision, I could see Levi's jaw drop. I made sensual sounds with my mouth. The cake certainly tasted divine.

"Good, huh?" Diego's eyebrows shot up. I nodded as he continued to feast on the cake. "So good."

"Sandrine's allergic to nutmeg. And if I'm not wrong, I

detect a hint of it in the flavors," Levi told Eddie in a matter-of-fact way.

Damn, I dropped the ball on that one. I knew she was allergic to it. I had it in my notes somewhere. "Yes, that's correct. Thanks for reminding us." I sent a quick, shy look toward Levi. "Shall we try the next one?"

The same thing happened to the second cake. Ophelia fed Levi. Diego fed me, and I fed Diego. And every single time he did, Levi would move his head from side to side and rub the back of his neck.

Levi noted the complimentary flavors of the almond and the hint of coffee and chocolate of the second cake.

It was good, but it wasn't elegant enough.

When we got to the third cake, my favorite, I added extra oomph in my moan, closing my eyes as I let the flavors of fresh berries and the sweet-tart combination of the limoncello icing explode in my mouth. My hands were pressed against Diego's broad expanse of chest, and as I let the last bit of sweetness melt on my tongue, I fisted Diego's white shirt. I opened my eyes marginally in what I hoped was a seductive gaze and smirked at Diego.

"That good, huh?" Diego's face was plastered with a wide, knowing smile.

"It's a perfect cake for a summer wedding," I replied.

"It's a bit tart." From the other side of the table, Levi's words sounded petty.

With my hands still over Diego's shirt, I turned to Levi. "Tart?" I raised an eyebrow.

Levi crossed his arms over his chest, exposing the tanned, toned forearms under the sleeves of his light blue button down. He narrowed his eyes at me. I shot daggers at him.

"Why don't we have a sip of water before the last cake?" Eddie suggested. He poured us a glass each, even offered one to *Oh-feel-yah*.

After a couple of minutes, we continued. I'd had the pleasure of tasting this cake before with Jake when we were dating. Back then, he had always made me promise that I would buy this cake for his next birthday. I never had the chance. Not for his birthday, at least.

I was pretty confident that this was the cake he would want at his wedding. Eddie could add some elegance to it by using a different type of icing, rather than a ganache so that he could display his skills in cake decorating.

Levi grabbed a fork and spoon off the serviette, cut a small piece with his fork, and pushed with his spoon. He raised the piece to his own mouth, and I could tell that he loved it. He made a small moan of approval.

I gave Diego a piece, and his eyes rolled back in his head as he ate the cake. "Divine. Simply divine, Eddie. You've outdone yourself. Can we take this home? I can think of many ways I'd like to eat it." There wasn't just a subtle hint in Diego's eyes. He made sure that everyone in the bakery knew what he meant. My cheeks burned.

I swallowed the nervous anxiety in my belly, smiled at Diego, and took the smaller piece of cake on his fork. It was better than sex. Well, at least the sex that I'd had. The decadent bittersweet flavor of the moist cake paired with the sweet-saltiness of the peanut butter mousse and the rich ganache was to die for. I didn't close my eyes as I tasted. Instead, I trained them toward Levi.

He was raptly watching me. We held our gazes together. With the tip of my tongue, I licked ganache off the corner of my lips, then bit my bottom lip. I might have seen him tremble, but it was so slight that I wasn't sure if I'd imagined it.

He rubbed the back of his neck again and then lightly scratched the five o'clock shadow on his chin. A muscle in his jaw twitched. He took a big scoop of the cake and turned toward Ophelia. She had been surprisingly quiet throughout the whole exchange, and she hadn't tried a single piece of cake.

Ophelia sneered at the piece on Levi's fork. "I don't want that."

"Just try it," Levi said.

"I don't eat cake. You know that. I told you." Ophelia took a step back. Was she afraid that the cake would jump off of the fork and force itself into her mouth?

Levi sighed. "Oh, just try it. It's really good." He moved his hand closer to her.

"It's full of calories. I can't have any more calories for the day. I can only drink water."

No more calories for the day? It wasn't even noon yet. How could she survive?

"Just. Try. It." Levi looked like he was going to lose it.

"I can't. I have a shoot tomorrow!" Ah-ha! I knew she was in the industry.

Levi lowered his hand a bit, and huffed, "A shoot? I thought you said you only have an audition for a foot ad?"

Ophelia's mouth formed a large 'O'. "It could be my big break. What if they think my feet look fat from eating cake?"

A laugh escaped my mouth. I clapped a hand over it when Ophelia shot me a menacing look. Diego leaned forward to peek at her very skinny feet.

"Just try the damn cake!" Levi pushed his hand forward, getting the forkful of cake closer to Ophelia's face.

Diego, Eddie and I watched in horror as the dark chocolate cake slipped off the fork and splattered onto Ophelia's white dress. And it didn't stop there. The cake smeared down the short length of the dress and flopped on top of her fuchsia stilettos.

Ophelia shrieked. Her hands flew over her head, careful not to touch the mess on her. "This is a new dress! It's Versace! Do you know how much this cost?"

I never took interest in what Levi did for a living. He looked and acted rich. With the company he kept, it wouldn't surprise me that he did indeed come from a wealthy family. Ophelia didn't seem to know much about him either. Levi could probably afford another one of those. Heck, maybe even four!

"I told you I didn't want to come here. I told you I didn't want to have cake. Now look at me!" Ophelia pointed her sharp fingernails at Levi, who seemed both slightly entertained and shocked by what had happened. Ophelia huffed one more time, and tramped her way out of the shop, with bits of chocolate cake trailing behind her.

Levi looked at her retreating form, at Diego, and finally at me. He brushed his hair back, seemingly unsure of what to do next. He dropped the fork on the table and followed his date, muttering to himself.

"That wasn't awkward at all," Diego said when the door shut behind Levi.

"Sorry about that. How did you end up here?"

He replied, "Chase was at the gym when you called her. She told me you needed help. I didn't know what I signed up for until I got here."

I shook my head, embarrassed that Chase had to resort to asking Diego to get me out of what shouldn't have been a stressful situation. If only I'd been honest with her.

"I gather he's your flower guy?"

I rubbed my temple and was about to say more when people started to gather outside the shop.

Eddie and Diego hurried to watch through the storefront windows. I couldn't help but join them, curious to see what was happening.

Outside, Ophelia was alternately waving her arms around, and pointing her fingers at Levi. A couple of times, she also pointed toward the shop. Levi spoke to her with the same gusto. I wished we could hear what they were saying.

I felt horrible. If I hadn't been so petty, this wouldn't have happened. All I wanted was to give Levi a taste of his own medicine. "I should put a stop to this." As I said the words, I watched, bemused, as Ophelia stepped toward Levi, anchored one foot to the ground, and sharply brought her knee up into his groin.

"Oh!" The two men with me instinctively cupped their own crotches, as did a few men outside.

Levi collapsed to the ground and curled into a fetal position. He was clearly hurt.

"Levi! Oh, crap..." I stepped toward the door, ready to burst outside and help him.

Diego grabbed my arm to stop me. "You can't go out there, Nica."

"Why not? Look at him. He's hurt. And nobody's helping him." My eyes were welling up with tears. I had caused this.

"If you go out there, his family jewels won't be the only things hurting. You'll hurt his pride too," Diego explained. "I'll go."

He didn't give me a chance to argue. Diego pushed me carefully aside before going out of the bakery. Eddie wrapped an arm around me, as we watched the exchange between the two men.

Diego helped Levi to a seated position on the curb. They talked, nodded at each other, and then both looked behind them, seeing me. I backed away from the window.

Diego then got up and stretched out his hand. Levi grabbed it and slowly stood. He bent over for a bit, placing hands on his knees and tucking his head to his chest. A moment later, he straightened, said something to Diego, and shook his hand. Then he walked around the black, shiny convertible parked in front of the store, got in, and without looking back, drove off.

When he was clear out of range, Diego came back in, scratching his head.

"Is he going to be okay?" I was extremely concerned. My chest constricted, and I started wheezing.

Diego nodded. "He'll be fine. Nothing that a bit of ice and rest won't fix." I wrung my hands together. He stared at them. He wrapped his hands around mine and spoke, "Nica, that man is so into you."

"Into me?" I pointed a finger at myself. "Me? Him?" I tried to process this. That couldn't be true. Levi had no business being into me. Not when I had feelings for Jake. "No. You're silly."

"Yes."

"No," I said defiantly.

Then I laughed and said it again, although the second time, I wasn't entirely sure what to believe anymore.

THE BRIDAL PARTY

I might have been a little too excited to go to Paris, readily ignoring all the screaming questions in the back of my head. How could I have ended up in bed with Levi? How could I not have seen that he wanted to be with me? Did Jake know? How could I continue to plan this wedding if I still had some sort of feelings for the groom?

Well, I pled insanity. And Paris was my asylum.

After tying up some loose ends for events happening during the weekend I was away, I dragged myself home, packed for hours, since I couldn't decide what to bring for Paris, and dropped onto my bed to sleep. Three hours later, I was fully awake but extremely tired.

Unfortunately, it gave me more time to rethink my wardrobe choices, and I had to go through my luggage again. By the end of it, the driver sent to pick me up had to rush so I would not miss the plane. I argued with myself that I might have packed too much, or too little. Were five pairs of shoes enough? Should I have brought another Little Black Dress?

When I arrived at the airfield, where a sleek private plane waited, I saw the bags being loaded and confirmed that I, indeed, hadn't packed enough. Counting at least three suitcases for Isobel alone, I panicked. I was going to look like a tourist.

Almost everyone was present, including Levi. I groaned at the sight of him. It was my first time seeing him since that dreadful morning at the bakery. I'd tried not to dwell on it, and busied myself with work. Good thing he was too busy on the phone to notice my arrival.

Isobel hugged me like we hadn't seen each other in years instead of just a few days. She insisted that we sit together, and I was more than happy to oblige. She couldn't stand to be around Levi, and I didn't think he'd ever warmed up to her.

We were promptly handed champagne as we took our seats, although I refused to drink mine since my last drinking debacle (cue Levi passing us). I asked for some sparkling water instead. As our plane was preparing to take off, I noticed that we were short two people.

"Aren't we waiting for someone else?" I queried.

Isobel looked around us. "Who? Everyone's here. Sandrine left yesterday to prepare for our grand arrival." She winced when she said Sandrine's name and snorted when she finished.

"How about Olivier?"

She quirked her eyebrow. She seemed confused. "Olivier?"

"Yeah. Sandrine mentioned he was going to be here. Who is he anyway?"

Isobel laughed out loud, and I felt a blush color my face.

"But he's here. Olivier." Her fingers flicked in the air.

She pointed across the aisle where Jake was engrossed in a book, and Levi was animatedly talking in French to our striking flight attendant. I quickly averted my eyes before he noticed me looking. I turned back to Isobel with a look that said that I had no idea what she was saying. She laughed again, brushing a tear from her eye and slapping her hands to her thighs.

When she finally quieted down, she explained. "Veronica, Olivier is Levi." Pause for effect. "Olivier Laurent. He's like French old money." She flicked her fingers in the air again, lowered her voice as she continued. "Apparently, he's a descendant of Napoleon Bonaparte. He's almost royalty, but you wouldn't guess it by the way he acts around people, women in particular. This plane is his, or his family's. Can you believe it? I mean, I've been in private planes before, but nothing like this. This is beyond posh. He's that rich." A smug look appeared on her face.

"Oh. I didn't realize." Ever since meeting Levi, I had taken little interest in him. So my theory was correct. He was born with a silver spoon in his mouth. And a jerk. And he had a very sexy body. And he wanted me. I shook my head to clear my wayward thoughts. "When Sandrine told me that this Olivier was coming with us, I thought it was one of her cousins or something. Well, thanks for clearing it up. It would have been embarrassing had I said something out loud."

Her hand patted my arm in a soothing manner. "I told you. I got your back, sister." She winked.

Once we had the all clear to take off, I immersed myself in some work I brought with me. Just because I was headed to Paris didn't mean I could slack off. I still considered a big chunk of this trip to be work-related. The company wouldn't survive on its own, and neither would Chase, not without my supervision.

One of the things that always stopped me from working was a full bladder. After having too many glasses of sparkling water, I stretched and headed to the bathroom that Isobel pointed out. I walked by Landon and Trent, who were involved in a very serious game of chess. They waved at me as I passed.

I reached the polished bathroom door and didn't see any indication that it was occupied, but I was obviously wrong.

When I opened it, I was surprised (only a little) to see Levi with the French attendant, about to join the mile-high club. I suppressed my shock, closed the door immediately, and hurried back to my seat.

"That was fast," Isobel said.

"It was occupied." I busied myself by picking up a Paris guidebook out of my purse.

"There's another one at the front. It's smaller but functional."

"Thanks." I stood up right away and walked to the smaller bathroom. I did my business, cleaned up, took off my contacts (the cabin air was drying my eyes out) and put my glasses on. When I returned to the seats, Isobel joined her cousins, Levi was still absent, and so was the glamorous Sophie-the-flight-attendant. The slight pang of jealousy jarred me, but I managed to shake it off.

Jake waved at me to join him, looking up from his book and patting the unoccupied seat on his side. I grabbed my stuff off my seat and settled beside him.

"Are you okay? I know you don't like to fly." That wasn't completely true. I loved flying. I just hated the touchdown part. I was touched that he remembered. I wondered idly what else he remembered about us. About me.

"I'm fine, thanks. I'm just doing a bit of work. What are you doing?" I nodded at the book in his hand. It looked like a manual, and he confirmed it by saying "work".

I smiled at him, let him work, and continued mine. A few minutes later, I felt a strong presence across the aisle. Without looking, I knew right away that Levi was back from his little tryst. I angled away from him, but I could feel his eyes trained on me. I managed to ignore him long enough in the end.

Although, when Jake stood up to stretch his long legs, Levi took the chance to sit beside me. I straightened upon hearing him sigh.

"You look adorable in glasses. Like a sexy librarian," he whispered, the scent of champagne tickling my ear. Seriously? Could he be any more cliché?

"My eyes were dry. They're just glasses." I bit back, pushing the spectacles closer to my face.

They really were just glasses, non-designer, black, and nondescript. They were glasses my grandmother could pick up from the drugstore, but I paid tons for mine. "Aren't you supposed to be...somewhere else?"

"Somewhere else? Like where?" I had managed not to make eye contact with him since he sat down, but that didn't stop him from trying to get me to look his way.

He fiddled with the papers tucked between me and the armrest. He even felt the fabric of my shirt. He reminded me of a five-year-old boy with ADD. Maybe that was it. He had adult ADHD, which might explain the constant changing of girlfriends, or partners, including porn stars and flight attendants. I just couldn't believe that I was now part of that list. I sucked in a groan.

Although I still had trouble remembering the sex part, which surprised me a little bit since Levi was a self-proclaimed Sex God, I was also relieved that I couldn't remember that much. It was enough to pine for the groom. I didn't have to lust after the best man too.

He continued to touch my things, which brought me

back to my point. He needed to be somewhere else. "Maybe Sophie, our flight attendant, needs help filling up the drink cart," I added her title in case he never bothered to ask for her name.

I felt him stiffen beside me, then eased. "That was you who opened the door?" Now that got my attention. "Are you jealous?" His smirk irked me.

"You've gotta be kidding," I mocked him, looking over my glasses.

A couple of beats passed, then he snuggled closer to me, whispering in my ear. "You've already spent one night with me, sweetheart. You know how great that feels."

I wanted to smack him...hard...right on the kisser, but that would only make everyone curious. So I settled for a retort, something I didn't usually do, but Levi brought the bitch out of me.

I took off my glasses, shook my hair as seductively as I could a la shampoo commercials, and sucked on my bottom lip. The trick worked, attracting Levi's eyes to my reddened lip. "Maybe it was one night with me that made the difference. You're just itching for a repeat performance." I leaned in closer. "I was so great that you had to have me again."

Our faces were so close I could feel the warmth of his breath against my cheek. His pupils dilated. My breath faltered. Neither one of us was touching the other, but electricity zinged over my skin.

His face turned serious, and slowly his lips curled into a seductive smile. My stomach fluttered, and my lower abs contracted. I hated that he knew how good-looking he was and that he could see the effect he suddenly had on me. Time to change tactics. "How's Ophelia?" I gave him a rueful smile, happy to get my mind out of this heady cloud.

He was about to answer me when Jake blurted out,

"Nica, you're not staying with us?" I gulped and sat back in my seat, crossing my shaking legs. He sat across from us, leaning forward, arms resting on his legs. "Isobel said you're staying at a hotel. We have more than enough room for you."

Levi laughed, keeping me from answering Jake's question, but the prick answered for me. "You're wondering why your ex-girlfriend isn't staying with you and your current lover?"

I glared at Levi. He might have been telling the truth, but he didn't have to be rude to his best friend. I turned to Jake, who had turned pale, and smiled.

"I'm considering this as work-related travel, but I would also like to experience Paris like a real American tourist. I want to explore the city a bit when I'm not needed, and I didn't want you guys to fuss over me. Plus, I've already booked a room at a mixed Baroque and Contemporary hotel facing the Eiffel Tower."

"Ah, the Baroque period," Jake said, clearly remembering a conversation we had in the past. His face softened, and the smile on his lips brought back happier memories. "Baroque is Nica's favorite art period. She thinks it's the most romantic." He tilted his head as he regarded me with an endearing look on his face.

Jake stretched his leg out and nudged my foot with his. "Remember when I argued that Renaissance was more romantic? You chewed me out talking about Caravaggio and Tenebrosi, Rembrandt and the Dutch Golden Age, and how chiaroscuro in The Baroque period was all about deeper, livelier colors filled with passion in contrast to the secretive darkness of the backgrounds." Jake shook his head as we both laughed.

"I think you fell asleep when I started talking about Vermeer's *Girl with the Pearl Earring*." I was shaking from laughter but quieted down when I turned and saw the sadness and confusion in Levi's eyes.

I couldn't let him affect me. This was the most Jake and I had talked about our past since our breakup.

"Levi, did you know that Nica has a Masters in Fine Arts?" Jake asked him, clearly noticing Levi's mood.

Levi shook his head, slouching into his seat and touching his fingertips together under his chin.

"Maybe you should take her to the Louvre so she can give you an art history lesson like she gave me when we went to the Guggenheim," Jake suggested. I just about wet my pants.

Levi, clearly liking the suggestion, sprang back up. His blue eyes lit with excitement. "You want to? I may be able to get you a private tour."

"No, thanks," I said, turning away from him, although I believed he could get me that private tour. I'd be lying if I said I was tempted by it.

"Why not? I'd be a great tour guide," he proudly claimed.

I shut down my iPad and rearranged my papers. "I highly doubt it." I noticed that Jake had gone back to reading his book. Clearly, our trip back to memory lane was over.

Levi didn't relent.

"Give me five reasons why you would be." I splayed my fingers up at him.

"Just five?" he gloated.

What a prick.

He raised his left hand, counting off his reasons. "I speak the language better than anyone on this plane and possibly than most Parisians. I lived there for a number of years, so I know the city rather well. I have connections to most, if not all, the places you'd probably want to visit. I can give you a piggy back ride if your feet get tired. And....and I'm great to look at."

Unbelievable! "How is that even a reason?" I asked, wanting to laugh in his face.

"How is it not?"

I shot an inquisitive eyebrow.

He became contemplative, chewing on his bottom lip. I quivered a bit watching him do that. Levi rested his arm on the armrest, creating a mild sizzle on my skin when our hands touched. "Fine. How about...number five, I won't fall asleep if you start talking about things that are interesting to you." He studied my face, and I wondered what he was searching for. His eyes were brilliant blue, his red lips pouty, and his minty breath tickled my cheek.

I leaned back in my seat, smiling inside and appreciating that he believed in those reasons. "I'll think about it." I picked up another packet from my bag, the beginnings of a charity event Chase and I were planning, which was taking place after the wedding, and placed it on my lap. "Now, go away and let me work, or stay there, but be silent." I didn't glance back at him, but I could feel the mega-watt smile he had on.

Levi didn't get up right away. He shifted, groaned and moaned, sighed and yawned, and stretched and whistled. When he realized that I intended to work for the rest of the flight, he stood up to join Landon and Trent and challenged the winner. With a secret smile held, I squashed down the fear and confusion bubbling deep within.

THE WEDDING DRESS

*W*hen we arrived in Paris, I was chauffeured by a kind old man who didn't speak a lick of English. But he helped me with my luggage even when I insisted, in a horrible attempt of the French language, that I was fine on my own. Sandrine had given strict orders when she met us at the airfield, and he had to oblige.

Three cars waited for us. One was just for her and Jake. Levi had mockingly declined to join the already packed second car that seated Trent, Landon, Isobel, and her army of luggage. I was terrified that he would insist riding with me in the third car, but he told us that he had to meet with someone and would see us later for lunch. He stood back as we drove away. I couldn't help but wonder who he was meeting. Maybe Sophie did need help filling her 'drink cart'.

Checking in at the hotel was a better experience than I thought it would be. One of the bellhops was an American, so he translated for me and for the desk clerk. He also helped me get my stuff into the room. His name was

Charlie, but everyone—and he insisted that I should, too—called him Chaz.

The first thing I noticed in the room was the view of the Eiffel Tower. It felt too surreal.

Although my heart belonged to San Francisco, my mind often wandered to Paris.

My single mother had helped pay for my education. Even though she would have been proud to work extra hours to support me if I had decided to move to this city to study Fine Arts, I had declined profusely.

When I started making more money with event planning, I never had time to travel unless it was for clients, and most of them remained in the US. As my career flourished, my priorities shifted, and Paris became a pipe dream.

I was taking in the view beyond the open windows under the blue sky when my ringtone startled me. My mother was calling to see how my flight had gone.

I spoke briefly to her, saying that I needed to get ready for the dress fitting and lunch. I did exactly that but took a longer shower to prep for the fitting. No one would want to take measurements of a stinky bridesmaid.

Promptly, I made it to the design house where Sandrine and Isobel were already waiting. Isobel sat bored and sulking, fiddling with her phone, and Sandrine appeared put out. They both jumped out of their seats, almost pushing each other to give me a hug and shower me with kisses.

Sandrine introduced me to Crâyon, the fashion designer in skintight black trousers and a colorful paisley shirt, with cheeks so hollow I wanted to pick him up and carry him to the nearest hospital. I tried not to butcher his name but did anyway.

He sneered at me the entire time.

His assistant handed me champagne and produced the dresses for me and Isobel.

A sea-foam green, beaded chiffon overlaying sparkly silver silk, with cute circular patterns along the hem for Isobel (which she merrily referred to as the puke green dress, even though it looked fabulous, like nothing I had ever seen before, and the fit on her was perfect), and a blush pink, layered trumpet dress for me. I had minor adjustments on my dress—Sandrine confessed that she had forgotten to ask for my bra size.

Both Isobel and I changed back into our regular clothes, and while we waited for Sandrine to try on the dress Crâyon had created for her, we drank champagne and ate caviar. I loved every minute of it until Sandrine stepped out of the dressing room.

For a bit, I wasn't sure why I felt like I was going to pass out. Perhaps I should have eaten something more substantial before the fitting. Sandrine had a killer body. She posed and sashayed in front of us. The long train glided on the marble floor behind her.

"So? What do you think?" she asked Isobel and me.

Then, like a lightning bolt hitting me, I was all too aware of why I felt faint. It wasn't the lack of food. It wasn't even the woman in the dress.

It was the dress.

It was a sweetheart neckline, heavily beaded bodice, vintage lace trumpet dress with a long scallop-hem train. It screamed great taste, boasted of great talent, and was definitely expensive. It was perfect.

It was also the same wedding dress that had filled my dreams. A fat tear rolled down my cheek. My hand flew my mouth to suppress the angst and sadness and disbelief.

Sandrine took them as tears of joy and hugged me. Crâyon spoke to her in French, cooing at the beautiful bride with the dreamy dress. My dream dress. Sandrine turned around so he could place the vintage veil over her perfectly shaped head. Sandrine was beyond perfect. She looked perfect in my dress. And she would look perfect in my dress when she married my perfect ex-boyfriend.

I excused myself for a moment, stepping out of the place, breathing in the Parisian air. But the city had lost its magic.

The air smelled stale and pungent. The street looked desolate and dirty. The buildings showed off their crumbling, old façades. The radiance dimmed. I had the urge to call Chase and tell her I was going back home immediately and canceling the contract with Jake and Sandrine. I didn't care what the repercussions would be. I just needed out. Surely, she'd be supportive and understanding.

Our company would probably get sued. It seemed like something Sandrine or maybe her family would do. We'd probably lose more clients Jake and his family had connections with. We might have to fire all our staff. I might have to move back in with my mother in Fresno. Grief struck like an ax through my heart at the possible loss.

With no other choice and a heavy heart, I plastered on my best fake smile and headed back into Crâyon's design house.

༗

BACK IN MY HOTEL, I closed my eyes for a couple of seconds, sat up on my bed and stared out the window at the tower still standing proudly in front.

I remembered the time Jake had promised to take me to this city. It was two days before he left for Paris. A couple of days before he met Sandrine. I was busy preparing for a huge event and couldn't go with him.

What if I had been able to go? Would we still be together? Would he have met Sandrine? Would I be in some beautiful hotel room months later, alone and in constant tears?

I cried and cried for an hour until my head started to hurt. I showered again, trying to cleanse myself of the afternoon's events and unanswered questions.

Out of desperation and sheer loneliness, I messaged Levi and told him that I'd decided to let him be my tour guide. If Chase was with me, she would have said, "When life gives you lemons, you punch life in the face and take the strawberries. Then make a margarita, which is way better than lemonade." To anyone else, it wouldn't have made sense, but as I dried my tears, it was all I could hold onto.

Levi arrived on time at the hotel. I met him in the lobby with my trusty camera, a small notepad for taking down inspirations and notes, a scarf just in case it got cooler, a smile and a promise to myself that I would have a better time. I could tell that he noticed the puffiness under my eyes, but he didn't say a thing about it, and I appreciated him more for that. He kissed my cheeks softly, and he took my hand over his arm.

We didn't have much time, but he promised that he would make every moment count. Our first stop was the Eiffel tower. He greeted everyone on the way there like some celebrity, and they all greeted him back. Some women tried to catch his attention longer, but he just trudged on, talking about the history of the Eiffel tower, in case I didn't know.

Levi took pictures of me standing in the foreground of the famous landmark while we waited to climb it. He offered to take me to a different place where the view would be better, but I declined, confessing that being in the tower itself was high on my to-do list. Although, we couldn't go nearly as far as he hoped due to my fear of heights. Still, the view was incredible.

He asked someone to take a photo of us. The guy gave us a thumbs-up the first two takes, then asked us to kiss on the third. Why not? It could be quite a story to tell my future kids if I ever had them.

A soft breeze blew strands of my hair over my face. With the pads of his fingers, Levi gingerly brushed them off and tucked them back behind my ears. His blue gaze searched my face as he cupped it in his hands. His eyes slowly lowered to my lips. With tenderness, he captured my bottom lip between his. I closed my eyes, while my entire body trembled at first, then warmth flooded.

I opened my eyes to a flash, and to an adoring smile, soft lips hovering over mine. When Levi turned away to thank the man, I had to grab the side rails. The cold metal was a contrast to my burned skin. My lips continued to tingle even as I soothed it with my fingers. His taste remained in my mouth. A mixture of mint, cinnamon, and man.

Short on time, Levi promised that he would be my guide to the other landmarks that were on my list for the rest of the trip. Stopping at a charming *patisserie*, we picked up snacks and coffee before strolling along the Seine, hand in hand, and boarding a boat tour for the night. He'd only mentioned once that he had access to a boat, and we could do our own private tour, to which I replied that most tourists didn't have that chance.

I wanted to keep to my plan and avoid doing anything private with Levi until my heart settled.

Quietly we sat on the boat, the water softly rocking us, and I enjoyed the silent elation surging through my veins.

From a distance, the Eiffel Tower lit up, and it was spectacular. It revived the magic I thought it'd lost after seeing Sandrine in the dress. I leaned on Levi's shoulder as he wrapped an arm around me, and somehow carefully tied my scarf around my neck. He kissed the top of my head when he was done.

Anyone could easily have mistaken us for a loving couple. If only things weren't so complicated.

But I tried not to let those complications ruin the moment.

I was in the City of Love with a surprisingly tender man. Tomorrow could bring more twists and turns in our lives, but for a moment, with my head resting on his shoulder, and his arm around me, I felt cared for. For now, that was more than enough.

THE ENGAGEMENT

 $\mathcal{U}$ nexpected kisses were the best kinds. I had proof of it. While the coffee maker gurgled, filling my hotel room with delicious aroma, I admired the photograph displayed in front of me. They were connected, in more ways than one. His fingers lightly played with the edge of her jaw, while her hands were buried in his hair. Their eyes were closed. The backdrop of the city blurred around them as though nothing mattered but that the two of them and that kiss. Our kiss. My kiss with Levi on the Eiffel Tower.

I closed my eyes, and I could feel the rising of Levi's chest as he inhaled quietly but deeply before he kissed me. I licked my lips and tasted his signature mint and cinnamon flavor. It did funny things to my belly. The simple thought of it made the tiny hair on my arms rise, and my knees buckle.

I opened my eyes and saw us kissing. There we were, like lovers in the night, locked in a kiss that neither wanted to break. Levi's kisses were always unexpected. And memorable. Except for the times I'd had too much to drink. I couldn't live that one down.

After last night's boat tour, he walked me back to my hotel, and the entire time, he listened to me talk about nothing, about everything. After a light drizzle, a fog had set in and gave the city that ethereal appeal. The chill didn't faze either one of us.

It didn't matter what I was saying to him. What mattered was that I kept talking. He would ask simple questions, enough to encourage me to continue opening up. I told him stories about my childhood, growing up without a father, about my constantly broken-hearted mother and my innocent sister.

Levi kept me close to him, but he only held my hand if I was about to step over a puddle. When we reached my hotel, there was a moment when I battled with my own indecision—should I ask him up or not?

He made that decision for me, stepping closer, holding my frozen hands in his and lifting them to his lips. He blew warm breath onto them, while he peered at me through thick lashes. Levi flattened my hands together then rubbed his hands over them. Then he placed soft kisses on the tips of my fingers, one by one. There was a line of desire that tugged from my fingertips to the undeniable lust ebbing in my core.

"Good night, Sweet Veronica," Levi mumbled against my fingers.

I parted my lips to speak, but not knowing what to say, I pressed them together and turned it into a smile. When he let go, I turned on my heels and made my way up the steps of the hotel and into the lobby.

Chaz waved at me from his post by the desk. I meant to ask him what brought him to Paris, but I had no doubt in my mind that his answer was love.

The city had that magical effect on people. Strangers became lovers. Enemies became friends. What would happen to this bridesmaid and the best man?

That question kept me up until the wee hours of the night. When my eyes finally surrendered, all I could see behind my closed lids was the kiss on the Tower.

The memory of it instilled in me until I woke up that morning. I uploaded the photographs I'd taken the previous day on my laptop, and while I waited for Levi, the unexpected gentleman, to come so we could start another busy day trolling the streets of Paris, I stared at the photograph. Our photograph. Our kiss.

I groaned into my hand. What was I going on about? This was Levi. A player. Mister Casanova himself. Sure, he was charming, but I couldn't be part of his game. Frustrated with myself, I rolled out of the bed and headed to the shower. I wasn't expecting Levi until later, "closer to lunch," he had said yesterday. So when I opened the bathroom door and saw him standing by my bed, I nearly jumped out of my skin.

"Levi! You scared the behemoth out of me!" I bunched the fabric over the rapid heaving of my chest.

"Scared the behemoth out of you?" He tilted his head back, laughing at my expense. "Do you know how to properly swear when you're sober, Veronica?"

I rolled my eyes and harrumphed. "I know how to cuss, Levi." Walking over to the closet, I pulled out my sensible flats and a scarf that matched my dress.

He continued to taunt me, "Not cuss. Cussing is for mid-century women who wear bloomers, and I know for a fact that you're a lace kind of woman. So, I'm asking if you know how to curse, swear, say shit and fu—"

Ignoring his comment about my chosen style of underwear, I raised a hand and wagged a finger at him. "I know what you mean. I just choose not to say them. My mother always said it's unladylike," I explained, holding my head high as I expertly knotted the scarf around my neck.

"Then I shouldn't tell her that you swear like a drunken pirate when you're drunk?"

I grabbed for something—my brush—nearby to throw at him, but he caught it, his shoulders shaking with laughter. How could I have thought that he was a different person? A better Levi? That brief adoration I had for him melted away. I wanted to argue his point but the image on my laptop screen captured my attention. Had he been looking at it?

I rushed to it, diving on my bed and slamming my laptop lid shut. The hem of my dress rode up, and Levi had a lovely view of my pink lace undies. I turned to see him unabashedly gawking at my exposed behind. He wasn't laughing any longer; that was a plus. He had his hands stuffed in his pockets and he rocked back on his heels, but he didn't take his gaze away from me, even as he licked his lips. I sat up, brushed my hands over my dress, and pretended that my cheeks didn't readily flush.

Levi cleared his throat and extended his hands to me. "We should go. I have a big day planned for us."

Grabbing hold of his hands, I slipped off the bed and got on my feet, straightening my dress once again. "Big plans? What kind of plans?"

"It's a surprise. C'mon." He tugged, but I jerked my hands back.

"I don't like surprises."

"Don't be silly. Everyone loves surprises."

"Well, I don't," I said with a steady defiance in my voice, gathering my hair and began braiding it. "I'm a planner, Levi. I don't do surprises. Not for me, at least."

He scratched the underside of his jaw while he contemplated. Looking like he had come to a conclusion, he faced away from me, sauntered to the desk and picked up a picnic basket I hadn't noticed. "I guess I won't have any use for this."

"W-wait!" I stalked over to him and held onto the basket handle. "What's in it?'

Rubbing a hand over his mouth, he shook his head. "Nope. You can't look since you don't like surprises and this—"He lifted the basket "—is part of the surprise."

"What? No, I need to look. Let me see." As I reached for it, he hid it behind him. I had to hold onto his arms to get closer to it, at the same time, Levi circled an arm around me.

"Nope. No surprise. No picnic. No basket."

"Levi, let me look." His arm tightened around me, but he continued to pull the basket away from my reach. Worse, he began tickling my sides. I thrashed in his arms, forgetting the basket and focusing on getting him off me before I peed my pants. "Stop! Stop, please." My eyes welled up, and I couldn't stop laughing, which encouraged him more. I started kicking, slapping his arms away, anything to get him to release me. My left leg hooked around his and before I knew it, we were toppling down on the floor. Somehow, he was able to twist us around so that his back hit the carpet, and I, in turn, flopped right on top of him.

It was a graceful fall.

My nose grazed his. He exhaled heavily, and I inhaled his cinnamon-mint breath. Next thing I knew, I was nuzzling his nose, his cheek, and down his throat, basking in his masculine scent. Levi gripped my waist. I wiggled my hips against his, and he moaned and groaned, but not the happy, sexy kind. It sounded like a painful grunt. I raised my head and peeked through my messy hair. The pained expression on his face proved it.

"Levi? I…" I moved on top of him, and he produced another strained sound. "What's wrong?"

"You're on my…arrrghhh…your knee is on my crotch."

"Oh! Shoot!" Peeling myself off of him, I didn't realize that the knee I used to prop me up was the same knee that was in contact with his family jewels. Levi muffled his scream by covering his mouth with a hand. From a safe distance, I hid a snicker. "I'm so sorry."

Turning on his side, Levi curled into a fetal position, continuing to groan, grunt and mutter some colorful words.

"Levi?" I reached out a hand, but he held his up, halting me from touching him.

"Just give me…give me a sec." More grunts followed, with heavy breaths.

I sat, concerned until his moaning quieted down. "Do you need ice?"

Propping an elbow on the floor, Levi twisted around to face me. "I'll be fine. You may have effectively denied me having kids in the future, but for now, I'm okay."

Lips pressed together; I extended my hands again. "Let me help you up."

"No!" he said instantly. "I think I'm safer getting up on my own." Taking his time, he sat up first, lowering his head and muttering, "Serves me right…"

My heart began to hammer in my chest. It wasn't exactly clear, but I thought the rest of that sentence was "for wanting to kiss you." But I could be wrong. I didn't know if I should be disappointed that I wasn't right or that he didn't get to kiss me.

TO MAKE it up to him, I decided to let him continue with his surprise. It was the least I could do since for at least a half hour; he was limping as we marveled at the Notre Dame Cathedral. We stopped by a bakery for more delectable croissants.

Levi's grasp on the basket was so firm that I was increasingly nervous at what could be in it. Although I questioned if it even had contents since he picked up a baguette from the bakery. He did mention that he'd planned to rent bicycles for us, but as he was uncertain of his groin's condition at the moment, he opted to walk it through.

We strolled on the cobblestones of *Le Marais*, and he was patient enough to let me take photographs along the way. My camera clicked as Levi pointed out interesting architectural points and talked about the history of this part of the city.

While I was taking a shot of yet another ivy-covered apartment, Levi huffed and grabbed my camera from me.

I protested, "Hey!"

"You're doing it all wrong." He dropped the picnic basket by his feet and fiddled with my camera. "What? These are all..." Not finishing his sentence, he shook his head in frustration.

"It's beautiful. Hey, don't delete them."

"I'm not. Stay put. I'll do this for you."

I crossed my arms over my chest and tapped my foot. "Levi, give me back my camera."

He didn't argue, but he didn't give it back. Levi cocked his head to one side and without warning, he snapped a photo of me.

"Don't do that!"

"Why not? You said you wanted to photos of beautiful things."

My heart jumped to my throat. I bit down on my lip and hung my head low, embarrassed by his statement. There was another click. And another. When I looked up, he took another.

"Okay, stop. I think you've had enough fun with that." I asked for the camera back and after a few seconds of hesitation, he handed it to me. "Thank you."

We continued along, passing through massive doors that opened up to hidden gardens and courtyards. Every time we walked by a shop, Levi and I would pop in and he would slip his purchases in the basket after I'd tried different cheese samples or fruit.

"There wasn't anything in that basket, was there?" I asked when we arrived at *Place des Vosges*.

"There is now," he proudly replied.

He picked a spot in the garden and pulled a plaid blanket out of the basket. Then Levi spread out the baguette, cheeses, and fruits on it. He also brought out a bottle of sparkling water and wine, and glasses. For the finishing touch, he placed a few pink rosebuds in vintage apothecary bottles. He wouldn't let me help. All I could do was admire his handiwork once he was done. He was just as meticulous as I would have been with the entire process.

After rubbing his hands together, he stretched them out and asked me to join him for a picnic. For a real picnic at one of the loveliest gardens in Paris. It was a total cliché, proven by the fact that the place was full of couples, families and friends. But holy wow, was it ever romantic.

"So I told you all about my family yesterday, I think it's your turn to share," I said, about to bite a slice of Roquefort and quince jam on a baguette.

Levi's hair hung over his forehead. He raked a hand through his hair, brushing it back before he pinned me with his gaze. "There's not much to tell."

"Oh, c'mon. That's unfair. Tell me a little bit."

Pouring wine in glasses, Levi handed me one. He sipped on it and had a bite of Camembert and sliced pear. Clearly, he was uncomfortable with the topic. Who didn't have skeletons in their closets?

I was about to say that he didn't have to talk when he blurted out, "I didn't grow up with my parents. They sent me to boarding schools. Schools. Plural. I kept getting kicked out of them."

"Not much of a surprise there," I muttered, but regretted it by the way his face somber. "I didn't mean—"

"No, you're right. I was a hellion. I gave everyone a hard time. The best times of my childhood were going to Bordeaux, to my grandparents' vineyard. Martina let me work with her. She taught me everything about grapes and the wine culture."

"That's cool. You certainly know your stuff. This is amazing." I tipped the wine glass, taking a sip of the full-bodied red. His smile was almost shy. "You call your grandmother by her first name?"

"Yes, but I tease her sometimes and call her Onna."

"Onna? That's cute. What's she like?"

Levi looked straight ahead, as though he could see his grandmother in the near distance. He had chuckled before he said, "She's stubborn, really hard-headed, but brilliant and strong. She's an American. Was. She's more French than this cheese. Don't tell her I said that." He pointed at me, holding another slice of pear. "Martina and my grandfather met during the war. They lived here in Paris once the war ended."

"Did she ever go back home?"

"Once, I think. Although she's called France her home for decades."

"But you...you live in the US?" I couldn't figure out why, but there was a tug in my chest when I asked him.

"For now," he said quickly, then he worked the muscles on his jaw, deep in thought, as if he wanted to retract his reply but didn't know how or if he should. I couldn't help but feel a little disappointed at the thought of him leaving. Like Levi, I didn't want to say it out loud, nor did I know if I should be feeling anything like this toward him.

"Can you keep a secret?"

It was such a surprise that I almost spat my food out. Is Levi sharing a secret with me? I didn't think he was the type. "Someday, I hope to produce my own wine, one that would knock people's socks off."

"Is that how the sommeliers of the world measure the greatness of wine?" I teased.

"Oh yeah. All the time. If both socks get knocked off, it's a world-class wine." I laughed with him and continued on even when his laughter died down. Our gazes locked, and my giggles morphed into shallow breaths. A breeze blew past and pushed a wayward strand of hair to my cheek. Levi tenderly twirled it around his finger and tucked it back behind my ear. His delicate touch lingered, searing my skin with its warmth.

"I'm just like everyone else, Veronica. I'm just another dreamer."

I gaped. This was huge. He didn't only share his childhood memories; he told me his secret. He'd ripped the blinders off and made me see him. Levi.

"We better get going soon. According to your list-" He produced a piece of paper from his pocket, something suspiciously similar to what I'd carried with me yesterday "—You want to go to *Musee D'Orsay.* Unless you want to skip that and go to the Louvre."

"No. I want to save the best for last."

"Hmmm...don't we all?"

"What does that mean?"

There was a twinkle in his eye, maybe even mixed with mischief. Levi lifted his shoulder in a half shrug before offering me a pistachio macaron from Laduree, effectively ending that conversation.

After the picnic, Levi's phone rang. He said a quiet curse before he excused himself to answer the phone. He was agitated with his caller, pushing his fingers through his hair and tugging it. He spoke in French, so I had no idea what got him upset. I didn't want his phone call to ruin such a wonderful morning. Once I had his basket packed, I waited until he ended the call.

A few feet away, a man went down on one knee and proposed to the woman he was with. An opened blue velvet box sat on his palm. She cried the moment he presented the ring. Neither of them seemed to care if anyone was watching. It was just the two of them in the park. Just them and no one else.

"Do you want to walk or take the car?" Levi asked, taking the basket from me. "Veronica?"

I tilted my head and sighed. No surprise, I was a sucker for romantic gestures. "Isn't that sweet? That guy just proposed to her."

Levi scoffed. "Marriage is for idiots. Happy ever after is a tall tale."

It was like he wrenched my heart out of my chest. It stung so bad that my gasp could be heard at the other end of the park. "Do you realize what you just said?"

"Pardon me?" His brows knitted together. He was clueless.

"You basically just mocked what I do for a living, Levi."

He ruffled a hand through his hair and adjusted the collar of his shirt. "That's not what I..."

I interrupted, "Don't bother. I get it. Marriage is not for everyone, but I happen to believe there is such a thing as happily ever after. Because if it didn't exist, then the world would truly be an ugly place." His jaw dropped. I walked away, keeping the rest of my thoughts with me.

※

I DIDN'T LET that jab ruin the rest of the day. I acted as though his words didn't hurt me. He was distant at first, but eventually, he returned to the relaxed man who had no worries in the world. I didn't bother asking him who had called that made him upset. It wasn't my place to ask. We went through my personal tour taking numerous photographs and stopping at shops for souvenirs.

He called for our driver to take our bags and basket for us and continued on foot. As we headed to meet the rest of the gang for dinner, I thanked him for being a great tour guide with a chaste kiss on the lips and let him hold my hand until we entered the restaurant.

Everyone was already waiting.

Sandrine greeted us with kisses and the rest followed, except for Jake. He reluctantly gave me a quick kiss on one cheek, while nothing but a glare was offered to Levi.

I excused myself before sitting down to go to the washroom. When I returned, the atmosphere had changed. Levi was seething at Jake, and Jake was back in his usual happy mood. I wished I stopped missing conversations.

Like the last time we all had dinner, the conversations flowed, and so did the drinks. My mood changed every so often, and I fought to suppress the bursting, conflicting emotions in me. It had been a roller coaster of a day.

Watching Sandrine with Jake, old feelings resurfaced. I would remember the dress, the tears, and Levi's kiss and our conversations. I was a mess of happy and sad and jealous, and I didn't know what else.

Paris had brought out the good, the bad, and the ugly. What came next was anybody's guess.

I left a little after midnight, a little tipsy, confused, and alone.

THE MEN IN TUXEDOS

I used to believe in kismet. But it seemed the Universe was playing a cruel practical joke on me. At any time, Ashton Kutcher (the early years with Demi version) would pop out from somewhere and would tell me that I was being punked. Something was all too familiar when I woke up—the wide open curtains, the bright sunshine, the pounding headache, and the hand over my body.

Seriously, when would I ever learn?

Of course, the only difference was that I was in a hotel room in Paris and not my bedroom. I woke up next to the same naked man without meaning to in a matter of days. This time around, he was facing me, so there was no doubt it was, indeed, him and not some other random stranger. Did I mention he was naked again?

"What the hell, Levi?" I yanked at the sheets ineffectively.

He didn't move, just slowly opened his eyes into slits, and closed them again. "Don't tell me...you don't remember what happened again. Tell me, Veronica, do you make a habit of getting into bed with a man and not remembering him or what you did the night before?"

I smacked him hard with a pillow. He grunted but still kept himself almost glued to me.

"Don't be a jerk, Levi. How did you get in here? I left the restaurant by myself." I was pretty sure I did. Up until then, everything was clear.

"You called me sometime around two o' clock." He held onto the pillow that I had hit him with and placed it under his head. His sleepy eyes fluttered open. "If you don't believe me, check your phone."

My phone...where was my phone? I looked around but couldn't see it. What I did spot were two opened bottles of champagne on a sideboard. So much for not getting drunk again. I would get up to look for my phone, but there wasn't anything I could wear within my grasp, and I didn't want Levi seeing me naked, again.

Levi smacked the pillow he took from me, tried it again, and then sent it flying across the room. He then snuggled up to me, wrapping me in his cocoon. I could feel him wriggle under the sheets. The warmth of his body singed my skin. And it made me all too aware of something else hot, hard, and smooth, pressed against my hips.

"That better not be what I think it is." My voice was laced with warning.

"Relax, it's not like you haven't seen it before." He snuggled even closer, causing a bit of friction under the sheets. Even without looking his way, I could sense a smirk on his face.

I tried to squirm away, but he wouldn't let me. "Levi, please. At least point it somewhere else." That earned me a hearty laugh.

"You're so funny," he said, with way too much affection and adjusted himself under the covers. "Veronica," He

111

peered through his lashes. "Calm down. I won't do anything you don't want to do...but I beg of you, can we please go back to sleep? We still have a few hours before the tux fitting."

It was difficult to argue with those sleepy, sexy, bedroom eyes, and that gravelly tone, but I had to resist. He kept an arm locked around me, burrowing his nose into the curve of my neck. I tried not to get lost in a combination of his heady scent, the soothing flutter of his breath on my neck, in sync with my own pulse, and the tickle his day-old scruff was causing.

"Levi, I have to know what happened. Please." I pushed through my muddled thoughts.

He muttered something inaudible then said clearly, "I came here because you asked me to. You said you wanted to talk."

"Talk about what?"

"I don't know. We never got to talking. We drank champagne. We made out, and then fell asleep." The rumble in his voice reverberated in my ear.

"We didn't..." I swallowed the lump in my throat. "...we didn't do it?"

"Do what?" he asked quickly, a playful smirk on the corner of his mouth.

This jerk was going to make me say it. "Have sex?"

Levi groaned onto my shoulder. He pressed his body closer again, if at all possible, squeezing me tighter in his arms. "You feel this, Veronica?" He undulated his hip against one of mine.

Oh yeah, I could feel that. I had to close my eyes to avoid him seeing them roll back. I suppressed a sigh, not answering him, afraid that my voice would betray me.

"Don't you think if I had been inside you, you'd remember?" His lips were a kiss away from my ear. The timbre of his voice was too low and suggestive for me to ignore. It sent an almost painful cramp to my lower abdomen.

I heard a moan. When he snickered, I realized that the moan had come from me. He kissed the tip of my shoulder and proceeded to skim his lips gently on my skin.

Levi re-adjusted himself and released me, though not by much. "Let's get some more sleep, shall we? It's going to be a long day."

I nodded when he cupped the back of my head and kissed my hair, thankful that he didn't initiate anything else. Would I have been able to resist? I wasn't entirely sure.

But of course, I couldn't sleep. Not when he was naked beside me. Not when my head was threatening to implode. I needed to clear the cobwebs, so I could think.

Levi was snoring softly when I removed his arm from me. He had been sweet and gentle yesterday, except for that mishap at the park, and had promised to bring me to the Louvre today, which meant more walking. I decided he needed the rest.

Tiptoeing over to the closet to grab clothes, I noted the man's shirt on a hanger and the black overnight bag on the shelf. Levi had intended to stay when he came last night. If he thought I'd only wanted to talk, why did he bring extra clothes? Did talking, to him, mean something else? Unless I did call him that late. I didn't know where he was staying. Maybe he wanted to come prepared, just in case. Luck did favor the prepared, didn't it?

Walking into the bathroom, I locked the door, unlocked it, and then locked it again. And for safety measures, and to keep Levi from surprising me in the shower—something I foresaw him doing—I jiggled the handle, making sure it would stay locked.

Rummaging through my case, I picked out a travel-size bottle of painkillers, popped it open, and took two pills to rid myself of the headache threatening my brain. My glasses and contact lenses were in their respective cases, which meant that I had the intention of going to bed and sleeping. Alone. What was it that I needed to tell Levi that couldn't have waited this morning? Everything was fuzzy. It was unnerving. I'd never been this careless...twice!

There were a couple of bottles I didn't recognize when I went in the shower. Both labels were in French. I opened one and took a whiff. It smelled like Levi, and the intoxicating scent made me shiver. I placed it back on the shelf and didn't risk opening the other one.

Showering should have been a haven. A relaxing, soothing way to clear one's thoughts. It got me nowhere, except thoroughly clean and pruney.

The problem was clear. Levi had been too charming, but I had seen his M.O. before with women—kiss first, ask questions later. It disheartened me to think that not only could I not trust him, but I couldn't trust myself around him. After all, I still knew very little about the man.

I dried myself off, got dressed, and wrapped a towel around my head. Then I brushed my teeth, twice, because I wasn't paying attention to what I was doing.

The delicious smell of fresh pastries and coffee wafted in the room once I stepped out of the bathroom. My stomach grumbled at the aroma, but my mouth salivated over the man.

Levi was hovering over a cart of breakfast goodies, wearing a white robe and, I feared, nothing else. He brushed back his wayward hair as he sent a dazzling smile across the room.

"I took the liberty of ordering room service. You only

drink coffee after a drunken night, right?" He filled a white cup with freshly brewed coffee.

How did he remember that? "Yeah, coffee would be great." I didn't dare move closer to him. "Levi, why was I naked?" I couldn't help but ask.

He placed the coffee pot down on the tray. "You undressed yourself." He sniggered. "Actually, you stripped. With music and all."

I gasped. "No!"

"Yup, I'm afraid so, my sweet. Just like last time."

"Like last time? You didn't stop me?"

Levi regarded me as though I grew an extra head and sent me a cocky smirk. "I'm a man. I appreciate a woman's body, especially a goddess' body like yours." He inclined his head as stroked the stubble on his chin while observing me with a little too much interest than I was comfortable with. I swallowed a lump in my throat and ignored the flutter in my belly.

"Then why were you naked?"

He went back to preparing coffee, stirring in a couple of sugar cubes in one cup. "I always sleep in the nude." Of course, he did!

Wringing my fingers together, I asked him something that had been bothering me but had been too afraid to bring up. "We didn't do it last night, but...did anything happen last time?" I kept a good distance from him, only a couple of steps away from the bathroom door.

Levi stopped playing barista and sauntered over to me. His eyes were hooded. Brooding. I walked backward until I felt my back hit the vanity in the bathroom. He stopped at the doorway and leaned against it. Thankfully, his robe's sash was tied.

"What did I tell you? You would know, and you will remember when we make love, Veronica."

I tried not to focus on the words 'when' and 'make love'. I didn't think Levi 'made love.' Levi seemed the type to devour his lover. He was the 'rock your world' kind of guy, then leave his partner panting and waiting by the phone for a call that would never come.

"So, really? Nothing at all?" I tried again. Having witnessed the times he'd flirted with and played women in the past made me a non-believer. However, spending time with him had eased me into thinking that there was a completely different person standing before me than the one I thought I'd observed and avoided.

Suddenly a memory popped into my head: the clear memory of him with Sophie on the plane. There was pressure on my chest, but I ignored it. What he did on his plane was none of my business.

He deliberated before answering me, rubbing a hand over his growing beard. His countenance changed, and a smug smile made an appearance on his face. "Well, not nothing."

"What does that mean?" I gripped the edge of the vanity behind me.

Straightening and closing in on me, Levi stood a breath away. At just over six feet tall, he had to tilt his head down to talk to me. When he pushed off the doorway, he had untangled the sash of his robe. My grip on the vanity tightened, telling myself not to let go. That I shouldn't be tempted to lick the hollow of his throat or explore the planes of his broad chest. That I shouldn't check to see if he had put underwear on. But I looked anyway, and wished I'd listened to myself.

On his right hip, peeking out of the waistband of his low-rise, black boxer briefs, midway between the protuberance of his pelvic bone and the trail of dark hair that started below his navel, was the tip of a red and blue tattoo. My hand itched to dip in between his skin and the elastic and pull down the thick band so that I could see the rest of his ink. And other naughty bits.

His voice pulled me out of my dirty, dirty thoughts. "We fooled around a lot. But...and this better not leave this room..." Levi leaned in closer and titled his head to the side. "When I started going down on you, you fell asleep."

My mind tried to process the information. "What?" I looked up at him.

His gaze traveled from my eyes to my lips. "You're horrible for my ego, a threat to my manhood. That has never happened to me. And it won't happen again." Levi's voice was low and full of promise.

No man in his right mind would admit to something so embarrassing. I had to believe he was telling the truth.

His lips moved, but he didn't speak. His tongue darted out and wet a spot on his bottom lip. All I had to do was push up on my toes to experience what he had tasted. Or let go of the vanity and pull his head down to mine.

Choices. I had choices.

The spell broken when somewhere in the hotel room, a song played: Salt-N-Pepa's *Let's Talk about Sex*.

Note to self: change that blasted ringtone.

"Interesting," Levi said when it started playing again.

Cheeks burning, I stammered out a response, "That's... ah...Chase. She...uhm...put it on my phone. She never calls. Must be an emergency. I—I really should get that." Yet, I didn't move. The song stopped.

Levi took off the towel that was wrapped around my head and watched as my hair toppled down my shoulders. Then, with the towel, he pressed the ends of my hair, squeezing out the remaining water. He proceeded to dry my hair gently and slowly. His breathing was shallow. Setting the towel aside, he ran his hands through my hair, gently massaging my scalp. I kept my eyes open, but I relaxed in his touch. When he was satisfied, he pressed his nose against my hair and took a deep breath in.

The entire time I stared right at his lips, down the column of his neck, and up again.

"My sweet, sweet Veronica," he mumbled in my hair.

My knees shook. I was faltering. Levi was peeling my defenses away one piece at a time.

He placed his hands on the marble counter, trapping me against it and him. With a thrust of his hips against my belly, I felt him come alive. I guess he recovered from yesterday's knee-to-groin incident.

The ringtone played again, and I was ever so grateful that it did. I cleared my throat and excused myself, repeating that Chase called only at an emergency. He stepped away, his lips pressed together in a thin line. As I passed him, he gently stroked the length of my arm down to the tip of my little finger. I shivered at the subtle contact and continued on.

I found my phone tucked safely in my purse. I swiped the screen to answer. "Hi!"

"Why do you sound weird? Why are you breathless?" Chase asked after my greeting.

"I...uhm...I..." I looked over my shoulder.

"I told you, Nica, just because a hotel has a gym, it doesn't mean you have to use it. We'll do all the physical stuff when you get back. Your asthma attacks every time you push yourself too much, and I won't be there to help you. Just stop it." Chase laughed.

Squeezing my eyes shut, I hoped that I could clear all the other thoughts out of my head. "I'm fine. I didn't—I wasn't doing anything. Is everything okay? Is there something wrong?"

"Nothing's wrong. I haven't heard from you, so I got worried."

"Oh." How sweet of her! "I'm good. Working. Being a tourist. You know, the plan."

"Yeah okay. Well, I haven't hit the sack yet. I just wanted to see if you're okay." I knew what she was really asking. She wanted to know how things were with Jake and Sandrine, and how I was dealing with the couple in Sandrine's turf. She was more heartbroken than me when I told her that Diego and I had decided to stay friends.

"All good," was all I could say.

Chase sighed heavily. "Well, remember what I said."

"What's that?"

Her voice went down an octave lower. "It won't hurt to bed a Frenchman. I heard they're good in the sack." She guffawed into the phone.

I couldn't laugh with her. I shifted on my feet and glanced toward the bathroom. Levi had closed the door at some point and started the shower. I refused to think of him naked and wet under the hot spray. My breath became ragged. If only Chase knew how close I had been to accomplishing her suggestion.

AFTER HANGING UP WITH CHASE, I checked the time on my phone. Levi was wrong. We didn't have a few hours before the appointment with the tailor. We had fifteen minutes before the car arrived. I slipped the phone back into my purse.

I padded to the bathroom door, my hand poised to knock when I heard Levi singing. He was singing the lyrics of my ringtone.

Fifteen minutes. A lot could be done in fifteen minutes, I reminded myself.

With a deep cleansing breath, I rapped on the door. "Levi, we have ten minutes before the driver gets here."

He stopped singing. "Be right out."

My stomach made noises. I headed to the cart and took a sip of the black coffee, and debated which pastry I should go for. Eating more *pain au chocolat* in Paris? How could it be wrong? I was almost through the delicious treat when the bathroom door opened, and I nearly choked as something more delectable presented itself to me.

Fresh out of the shower, Levi had wrapped a towel around his waist. His torso was slick with water droplets, and his hair was dripping wet. He was rubbing his smooth, freshly-shaven jaw as he sauntered over to me.

Do not lick the water off his chest.

"Good breakfast?" He lifted my hand and nibbled at the last piece of croissant. A dollop of melted chocolate dripped on my hand. Levi's eyes flicked to it, wrapped his lips over my thumb and sucked and licked the chocolate off my skin. He moaned, and it struck me like lightning, tingling the nerve endings from my thumb to my center, where all the butterflies decided to take residence, and down to the tips of my toes. I stared at my fingertip, and then up to his face. There was something primal in his eyes, but the rest of his features remained neutral.

He released my hand, picked up his cup, and sipped, keeping his hungry eyes on me. "That's damn good breakfast." He tilted his lips into a crooked smile and drank his coffee again. All I could think was *lucky cup*!

I stood quietly, holding my cup with trembling hands, trying hard to focus on finishing my coffee. I stared out at the city while I listened to Levi moving around the room and singing that ringtone. My body silently hummed from that quick contact with him, and I refused to think of anything else.

"Ready?" I jumped out of my skin not noticing Levi behind me, his lips dangerously close to my ear. As soon as I was aware of him, all I could feel was the heat of his body burning me through my clothes.

I nodded, having trouble finding my voice. When I pivoted, Levi didn't move. We stared into each other's eyes, waiting for someone to close the gap. But my phone beeped with a message that my car had arrived. Saved by the bell had a whole different meaning to me.

The chauffeur might have been surprised to see Levi come out of the hotel with me, but he didn't show it. He greeted me with a polite nod and had a short conversation with Levi.

Once the ride began, I relaxed into the leather seat and focused on the day at hand. All the while, Levi was absently rubbing circles on my knee with his thumb. I looked his way when he gave my knee a mild squeeze, but his attention was focused outside the window. I took that chance to examine him closer. Something I had never thought to do before. My attention had been on the beauty of old architecture. Levi was something else to behold.

I traced a line with my eyes from his strong neck to his square jaw, lusciously full lips, and elegant nose, to deep-set blue-gray eyes that changed shades depending on his mood, graciously curled ear, framed by thick, dark brown hair, then back to his neck again. I had come to the conclusion that this man was beyond gorgeous. He even looked younger after getting rid of the beard. I stared back at his lips and imagined what they felt like on my entire body, wishing I could remember something this important.

He turned to me with amused eyes.

He was about to speak, but something over my

shoulder had caught his eyes. As Levi reached for the headrest of the seat upfront, he said some beautiful French words to our driver, who clearly obeyed him by pressing on the brakes, gently, without causing me to fly forward.

"Are we here?" I asked Levi and our driver.

"No, I want to make a quick stop. Claude will drive you. I'll see you at the tailor." Without another word, he kissed my lips hurriedly but sweetly and let himself out of the car.

I watched him cross the street and enter a shop. Before the car stopped again in front of a store, I had to admit to myself that I was already starting to miss Levi.

The other men were present, looking a bit tired when I walked in. Landon and Trent were goading each other, while Jake sat sullenly in a corner chair. My upbeat "hello" caught their attention. The cousins waved at me. Jake hopped up, smiled, but then he trained his eyes at the door as if waiting for something, or someone. I gingerly approached him, adopting the French way of greeting.

"Hi. How was your night? Did you get some rest?" he asked, not letting go of me right away.

"Yup. How was yours? You look tired." It was more of a question. Why did he look so forlorn? Maybe the stress of an impromptu wedding was finally getting to him.

"I'm fine." His tone told more than his words did; something was definitely bothering him. "I'm gonna start now. Levi should be here shortly," he said as he finally let go of me, then headed to the back room to change.

I would chalk up his weird mood to cold feet, but Jake was not the type of guy to get cold feet. Hopefully, we would have time to talk later on. One big part of my job was to always make sure that both parties were on track and feeling the same way about the wedding, (otherwise all the planning would be moot).

Levi walked in, appearing in a better mood than anyone

at that moment. His smile brightened his eyes. He greeted the cousins with hard taps on their backs before standing beside me.

Jake came back in a white tuxedo, followed by a very old man with wild hair and Coke-bottle glasses. "Nice of you to join us, Levi," Jake spat without even shooting a glance toward his best friend. I sensed a bit of vitriol.

"Yes," Levi smirked at him. "I slept in. You would too if you had a night like I did."

I stilled and blushed, praying that nobody noticed. I couldn't help but notice the evil glare Jake shot him through the mirror, which Levi, of course, merrily ignored.

When Jake went back into the changing room, Levi sidled up closer to me. I was still writing down as much information as I received from the tailor, as interpreted by Levi. "I have something for you," he whispered in my ear.

Looking through my lashes to make eye contact, I asked, "For me?" I was nervous and excited at the same time. He nodded, presenting me with a small boutique bag. I couldn't contain my excitement as I ruffled through the bag, finding a beautiful, elegant, soft as a baby's bum, silk Pucci scarf. "Levi, wow. This is too much. You didn't have to."

Taking the scarf from my hand and wrapping it around my neck, he told me, "I wanted to. You didn't wear one today and look; it even matches your dress."

There was a glimmer in his eye, and for a moment, I thought he was going to kiss me, but he stepped away, so quickly that I almost fell forward. I regained my composure from his sudden distance, although my mind was reeling as to why it even happened.

Jake replaced his presence beside me, but it wasn't quite the same. It was...different, uncomfortable. This wasn't right. This was Jake. My Jake. Well, my ex-Jake. We had spent so much time together, planning, going through every single detail, and when we weren't together, we'd been sending texts or emails to each other or talking on the phone. But as days passed, whether it was because of my sense of obligation as a planner or ability a saint to forgive, I had been feeling less and less like the woman who had fallen for this man, regardless of the memories that often invaded my thoughts. Was spending time with Levi enough to make me change my mind?

I was sure Sandrine had a lot to do with it too. After having spent some time with her, and talking to her via email, I had gotten to know Sandrine well and found what enticed Jake in the first place. She was beautiful, inside and out, unselfish (just don't ask Chase), kind, intelligent and one hell of a drinker. My dad would have loved that last part. She had been nothing but good to me.

When the boys—judging by how they behaved— finished with their tux fittings, we stood outside. Jake put his arm around me, a little too snugly. "Let's go have lunch. I'm starving," he suggested to us all.

"I can't. Levi and I are going to the Louvre. I won't have much time before dinner tonight. We'll just grab something on the go." I tried to ignore his tightening grip on me. "Shall we?" I smiled up at Levi.

"*Allons-y*. Let's go!" His arm already curved for me to hook into.

Jake, after a few seconds of hesitation, loosened up and brought me in for a tight hug. After kissing the top of my head, he finally let me go. On Levi's arm, I bid goodbye to the rest and let him guide me.

A few steps away, I turned and looked back to where Jake was still standing, the sullen expression back on his face.

❧

HEAVEN. I was in heaven! Tourists were milling about in the packed museum, but for an Arts major like me, it was a sanctuary. It might sound sacrilegious (to my Catholic mother) to say so, but it was sacred. We had enough time to see perhaps a quarter of the museum, so Levi and I agreed to visit only my favorites. How I wished that I'd brought my sketchbook instead of just my camera.

Levi paid attention to what I yammered on about the entire time. Whenever we entered a new room, he kept close, placing a hand on the small of my back. I had a feeling he had been here often enough. I was glad I'd declined—only slightly—his offer of a private tour, and that hundreds of people were around us at all times. I was giddy being in the Louvre, but I was burning inside being so close to Levi, having constant contact with him.

In the sculptures room in the Denon wing, I spotted Corradini's *La Foi* and was admiring the details when I realized that Levi wasn't behind me. I glanced around the room, walked past the sculptures and back to where we had entered, stopping mid-stride when I saw Levi studying a marble sculpture. He looked absolutely captivated. I couldn't help but take a photo. Sidling up to him, I touched his arm to make him aware of my presence.

"*Psyché ranimée par le baiser de l'Amour,*" he told me, without taking his eyes of the marvelous piece.

I was familiar with the Canova sculpture, having seen the plaster version at the Met in New York City, but this marble version was a breathtaking masterpiece.

He continued, "People come in here to see the *Mona Lisa, Venus de Milo* or Michelangelo's works, but this...this is my favorite. To me, it's the perfect symbol of..."

"Love," I finished for him. Levi surreptitiously glanced

my way, with a hint of shyness in his eyes, and then he returned his gaze to the lovers carved in stone.

"Are you familiar with the allegory that served as the inspiration?" He didn't wait for my reply. "When he first saw how beautiful she was, Cupid immediately fell in love with Psyche, defying his mother's orders. Venus then demanded that Psyche bring a flask from the Underworld. Psyche, out of curiosity, opened it, and out came the Darkness of Styx, which sent her into a coma. Cupid saw her laying there, seemingly lifeless, and pricked her with his bow, awakening her from the deep sleep." He waved his hand toward the sculpture. *"Psyche Revived by Cupid's Kiss."*

My eyes darted to it. Eros, the god of Love, enraptured by the goddess of Soul. Her arms were reaching out for her lover. His embrace was cradling her. Their eyes were searching one another.

I glanced askance at Levi. If I recalled correctly, Cupid had been Psyche's mysterious lover, visiting her in a palace in the dead of the night and making love to her. She had only known it was him when she lit a lamp to see his face, causing him to leave right away.

Life imitated art.

It was twice now that I'd woken to see Levi beside me. Who was this man before me? The man who had elicited reactions from within me through his words and actions.

Levi turned to me with a bright smile. "Shall we continue?" I nodded, and he led me through the crowd, our hands intertwined, and a constant current was flowing through my body.

❦

MY SHOES BEGAN to bite into my toes and heels as I stepped off the elevator after hours upon hours staring at works of art I had studied years before. We'd stopped at a cafe for a quick snack, but it hadn't been enough time for me to rest my feet. Levi, noticing that I began to limp, swiftly picked me up, with an arm under my legs and one behind my back. My knee-jerk reaction was to wrap my arms around his neck. I was terrified of falling, in more ways than one.

"What are you doing?" I protested.

"Reason number four. I will give you a piggy back ride when your feet get tired." His eyes lit up when he smiled at me, not even straining with the heavy weight, which I thought I must be. "Is this not a better way? Do you want a piggyback instead?"

I shook my head and tucked it into the crook of his neck. He smelled delightful, and it tugged at a muscle deep in my center.

Taking out my keycard as we reached my door, I opened it to let us in. He gingerly sat me on the edge of the bed and got down on both knees. Levi smoothed his hands over my right leg all the way down to my foot before taking off my shoe. Shivers ran up my spine and heat ebbed in my stomach and continued on when he did the same with my left leg.

After placing both my shoes aside, he rubbed the soles of my feet and up my calves, working out the ache of my muscles. Goosebumps followed the trails of his fingers. All I could do was moan and enjoy the rapturous sensation his touch elicited. If he had gone any higher up my thighs, I would have been powerless to stop him.

When he was done, he kissed the top of both my knees before clasping his hands over them, then propped his head on top. "Would you like a bath?" He gazed right up at me through long, dark lashes.

Did he mean with him? "That would be great," I answered with a breathy voice.

He stood up and strode toward the bathroom. A moment later, I could hear the gushing water, and the scent of lavender filtered into the bedroom. He reappeared with the sleeves of his white shirt rolled up, showing off the sinewy muscles of his tanned arms.

"All set for you." *Just for me?* I wanted to ask, but he added right away, "I'll meet you at dinner in a couple of hours."

My shoulders relaxed. As I stood to head to my luxurious bath, I leaned against him, and not knowing what to say, I placed a kiss on his soft lips. That made him smile, a smile that almost made me pull him into the bath with me.

"Your bath is getting cold. I'll see you later," he whispered against my ear before turning around.

How was I so wrong about him before? This guy had so much restraint. I had to let him go, because if I didn't, we wouldn't make it to dinner.

THE PARENTS OF THE BRIDE

*D*inner was at the Saint-Croix, at Sandrine's parents', home in Neuilly-sur-Seine, what Parisians called an *arrondissement*. I learned earlier on that it was how the city of Paris was divided. There was a mélange of centuries-old manors, contemporary apartments, pristine parklands, tall trees jutting past high stone walls, and iron gates. French architecture at its finest all around. I thought it fitted that Paris' 'suburbia' would look like this. I had to kick myself for not bringing my camera, or worse yet, forgetting my stupid phone.

The Saint-Croix stone-faced manor was tucked inside one of the towering walls and through an intimidating iron gate complete with ornate scrollwork. My mouth went dry at the thought of having a magnificent, dream-like wedding here. Why hadn't Sandrine and Jake considered this?

The heels of my faux-snakeskin mules echoed throughout the wood-paneled foyer as I followed the elderly butler who greeted me at the door. My eyes wandered and widened at my surroundings, much like they did upon seeing the garden out front.

The intricate veins of the marble floor were paralleled by the curves and glint of the grand chandelier hanging high above me. Through one of the open arched doors, I spotted what was—I could only assume from afar—an original Doré or an extremely well-done copy. At another door, the butler stopped, waited for me, and announced my arrival to the party waiting inside.

What should have attracted my eyes first were the large carved-stone wood fireplace and the antique tapestries on the wall, or the glittering, tiered chandelier lighting the space. Instead, I noticed—no, felt—the palpable tension hanging thickly in the room, and the invisible line that separated the people in it.

On one side were an elegantly dressed couple, and a hotter-than-hades man decked out in a three-piece suit. On the other side of the fireplace were Isobel and her cousins. All three waved at me without smiling. Right smack in the middle, facing the fireplace, and in the heat of it all, were Sandrine and Jake.

I sauntered over to the quiet couple, with my work smile on my face. A smile that I wore during 'shitstorms', as Chase would have said. Sandrine smiled back at me, but it failed to appear in her eyes. She was distressed. She greeted me customarily and muttered, "Welcome."

Jake, holding a crystal tumbler, half-filled with amber liquid on ice, hugged me tightly and kissed my cheek, lingering a little too long. I could feel the tremble of his body, and hear the grinding of his teeth.

I switched immediately to 'solver-mode'. There was trouble in paradise. I could see it in the lack of glint in Sandrine's eyes. I could smell it emanating through Jake's pores. I felt it through the slump of his hard shoulders.

"This is a beautiful home, Sandrine. I'm in complete

awe." Uncertain of what was going on, I tested my words carefully with her.

She beamed warmly at me, as Jake snorted at my compliments, which Sandrine and I merrily ignored. "*Merci.* Thank you. My parents are very proud of it." She visibly gulped down her nervousness. Was she uncomfortable in her own home? "Let me introduce you to them."

Jake scoffed. "Like that's what Nica needs right now."

"Jacob, I beg of you." Sandrine's voice was almost a whisper. She took my hand in hers, turning away from her sulking fiancé. It struck me how odd it was he'd been doing a lot of sulking lately.

I gave Jake a questioning look before moving away. Sandrine led me to the three elegant people on the right side of the room. The woman was seated in a Louis XIV chair, her décolletage covered with diamonds glittering with the light of the chandelier. The closer I got, the more familiar she looked. Sandrine resembled her. The bride-to-be should thank her lucky stars that she might inherit the slow-aging process her mother seemed to have.

"*Maman*, I would like to introduce you to Veronique. She is my planner for the wedding. Veronique, this is my mother, Vivienne Antoinette Saint-Croix." I didn't know whether I should curtsy, or wait for her hand to extend so I could kiss the top of her ring.

Vivienne Saint-Croix held her chin high, appraised me with calculating eyes, and most likely found me lacking. She said nothing to me and turned to Sandrine, speaking in rapid French. Sandrine, in return, retorted in the same language. I couldn't understand what they were saying, but I knew an argument when I heard one.

The older man in the trio spoke up, instantly quieting down the mother-daughter squabble. Then he faced me, his eyes crinkling a bit at the corners. He walked around the chair Vivienne was seated in and stretched out his hand.

« My name is François-Luc André Saint-Croix, Sandrine's Papa. Welcome to our home, Mademoiselle Veronique." I extended my hand so that I might shake his, but he turned it palm down and placed a kiss on my fingers.

"Oh! Well, it's such a pleasure to meet you." I glanced at Vivienne as François released my hand. "Both of you. I was just telling Sandrine how lovely this place...your home is."

"*Merci beaucoup, mademoiselle.* Thank you very much," François said, nodding. "You must forgive my wife. She does not understand the American way of putting together a very important event such as a wedding."

Oh, so that was what the argument was about? She didn't want a wedding planner?

Vivienne tilted her head up higher and spat out words in French at her husband. Sandrine joined in, and the three of them argued amongst themselves. All I could understand were the names I knew—Jake, Sandrine, even my name (or the French version of it) and Olivier.

Speaking of whom, I briefly looked around, almost expecting to see Levi seated at a corner, with a drink in hand, laughing merrily at the cacophony in front of me. But he wasn't present at all. A clearing of the throat alerted me. I turned to the source and stared right at the gorgeous man in a bespoke suit.

He oozed charm, his teeth as white as the smooth limestone busts out in the hallway. He had a masculine, strong jaw, eyes as blue as the ocean, and thick dark hair combed back. Debonair was an understatement for this man. He was Jake and Levi put together. I never thought it was possible, but there he was, in the flesh.

"I suppose I should introduce myself." Beaming smile. "My name is Gaspard des Rochers. I am...a friend of the family."

Weakened by Gaspard, I offered my hand and just let him do what he wanted with it. When his soft lips pressed against my fingers, goose pimples covered my entire body. He glanced up through lashes I would kill for, a smile hovering on my limp hand.

He straightened up when a hand clapped over his shoulder.

"I see you've met the enchanting Veronica."

Levi.

"Indeed, I have." Gaspard was still holding my hand, but when I caught Levi's glance, I jerked it away and kept it behind me.

"Levi," I squeaked out.

He stepped forward and kissed my cheek. "Hello, my sweet. Glad you made it."

Under Gaspard's spell, I didn't notice that Sandrine's argument with her parents had stopped. Sandrine stood aside, pouting, almost in tears, and her parents were murmuring to each other. Gaspard whispered something to Levi, who then responded by smirking and shaking his head. I sensed an evil plan in the making, as they both trained their eyes on me and simultaneously smirked. My cheeks burned like I was standing right in the fireplace.

"That's it! Nica, may I talk to you for a second?" Jake grabbed my arm and started to pull me aside.

For whatever reason, it ignited something vile from Sandrine's mother. In return, Sandrine started yelling at her mother, her voice echoing in the grand room. "Just leave him alone, Maman! He is my fiancé, and I am marrying him."

Vivienne returned fire. This time, she spoke in accented

English. How I wished she had stuck to French. "He is not good for you! He is a peasant! He is an *Americain. Mon Dieu!* Why couldn't you return to Gaspard and marry him as you were born to do?"

Uhm, what?

All was lost after that. The shitstorm of all shitstorms began.

Sandrine shouted back, pointing at Jake and Gaspard, and her parents. Her eyes filled with tears as her voice increased in volume. Vivienne pointed her dainty fingers at Jake, while also yelling at Sandrine, her husband and anyone nearby, including me.

Gaspard blurted a few comments at both women. When he reached out for Sandrine, Jake, who had been just an observer, shoved Gaspard, making the latter step back and knock an antique vase resting on a side table.

"Don't you dare touch her!" Jake shouted. When it wasn't enough, he bunched his hand into a fist, and it met with the other man's beautiful face.

Shock and fear rolled into the room. My voice was thick in my throat. I sucked in a hiss.

Trent and Landon came rushing to support their cousin. Levi and François helped Gaspard back on his feet. Isobel stood back, her hand clasped over her mouth. Vivienne gasped. Sandrine visibly shook, and she shouted when Gaspard retaliated.

The two men, in all their suited glories, returned punch after punch, crashing against chairs and pushing more vases onto the floor, and spraying blood on the rugs and the tapestries. Trent and Landon tried to hold Jake back, and Levi stood between him and Gaspard, who was lying on the floor, wiping blood off the side of his mouth.

"This is the man you want to marry? Look at what he

has done!" Vivienne yelled at her daughter, sobbing on the sidelines.

Sandrine, trying to swipe any and all of the tears off her face, took a step forward. She knelt down to check on Gaspard's bloodied, split lip and the cut on his nose.

"Sandrine?" Jake's quiet voice echoed loudly as he witnessed what his fiancée was doing. "You're choosing him?"

Sandrine hiccuped and sobbed. *"Non, mon amour.* 'e is hurt." She looked up at Jake, eyes pleading.

Jake took in what was happening before him—Sandrine's hand on Gaspard's arm, and one on his lip. "What about me?" Blood dripped from the corner of his mouth.

"Jacob, please," Sandrine begged him to understand.

"Screw this." Jake pulled away from his cousins' holds and stepped toward Sandrine and Gaspard on the floor. Then he stared at Vivienne. Everyone was ready to pounce, but he squared shoulders and lengthened his spine. "You've got your wish. Marry your daughter off to her childhood sweetheart."

"Jacob," Sandrine gasped. She stood, reaching out to Jake with her hand, smeared with Gaspard's blood.

Jake narrowed his eyes at her, but they widened, first in disbelief morphing into anger, as he stared at her hand. "Wedding's off."

THE WEDDING PLANNER

I stood at the threshold, mouth agape, unwilling to believe what I had witnessed. I didn't even remember walking away from the fight. If there was a patron saint of wedding planners, I would've prayed to him/her by now. A tug on my hand jolted me.

Isobel glared at everyone in the room, while she kept pulling on my hand. "Nica, c'mon. Let's leave this circus!" Her voice wasn't soft at all, and it echoed throughout the room.

I had broken up fights before, but I always had security (Chase) around. And never had it involved people I deeply cared for. I turned toward the hallway where Trent and Landon were trying to keep up with an apoplectic Jake. A loud cry brought my attention back to the room.

Sandrine had collapsed back on the floor and was sobbing her mascara off. Her shoulders shook as she mumbled into her palms. Her father knelt on one knee beside her, rubbing his daughter's back. Vivienne stood proud and incensed, glaring in my direction with pure hatred in her eyes. Hadn't she realized that, like her, I was only a witness to this whole debacle? Was she blaming me for this?

Gaspard stayed seated on the parquet floor, carefully rubbing the blood off his lips and chin. An egg-sized contusion had started to form underneath his left eye. Jake had done some damage on this man's beautiful face. Gaspard's perfectly regal nose was twisted. I had no doubt it was broken.

"Nica, let's go." Isobel tugged again.

In two strides, Levi stood before me. "Go with him. Make sure he doesn't pull any more stupid stunts. He's done a hell of a lot of damage here. I'll check on you later." Levi circled a hand around my arm. For a moment, I thought he'd pull me into an embrace and tell me that everything would be okay, but he didn't. He stared into my eyes with what seemed an apologetic look and walked away.

I turned and gave into Isobel's pull. I'd taken a couple of steps when some unknown force made me turn back. I wished I didn't. Levi stood, facing Sandrine. Her face was buried in his chest. His arms were wrapped around her, and his hand was rubbing her back. His lips touched the top of her head.

Levi had chosen Sandrine over Jake. He had chosen her over his best friend. Moreover, he had chosen her over me.

I bit my lip when at the unexpected stab of jealousy. I had no claim on Levi. He wasn't mine. We had no relationship.

With no other choice, I walked forward until the cool night air greeted me. I tried and failed to erase that last image in my mind.

Jake had left with his cousins. Isobel and I were left to take the car that had brought me to the manor. The ride back to my hotel was unexpectedly quiet.

"Can we get something to eat? I'm starving," Isobel asked when I made the move to step out of the car.

I wasn't hungry, and I feared that anything I ate would eventually make its way up again. But I gave in like I always did with the Benjamins.

She chose the first restaurant that suited her, just south of my hotel. It had old world charm with red velvet curtains and gilded chandeliers. It, unfortunately, reminded me of the manor and made me wonder what could be happening there at the moment.

Without looking through the menu, I asked for soup in plain English, without a care whether our server understood me or not. I patiently waited for Isobel to decide and attempt to order her dinner in French.

As soon as our server left, I couldn't help the questions from spilling out. "Who the hell is Gaspard? And why was he there? What was it about him that made Jake explode?"

Isobel pursed her lips and raised her eyebrow. "Don't they tell you anything? Gaspard was Sandrine's ex-fiancé. I don't know what he was doing there. I think Sandrine's parents invited him to piss off Jake."

"They were engaged? For how long?"

"Years. Decades. I don't know." She waved a dismissive hand. "It was arranged, of course. I'm sure money had a lot to do with it. That's why I didn't trust Sandrine. How could anyone break a long-term engagement like that and then turn around and get engaged again to someone she met less than three months ago?"

" Jake knew about the engagement?"

Isobel looked about the room. "Yeah. He told me about her previous engagement to Gaspard. It's shitty. But hey, at least you don't have to sabotage their wedding." She smirked at me.

I popped open my mouth and was ready for a

rebuttal when our waiter came back with Isobel's drink and poured me a glass of water. As soon as he trotted off, I spat out, "I never said I was going to sabotage their wedding. I had no intentions of doing so."

But Isobel was unaffected. "Oh well, it's over now."

"Aren't you at least a bit upset for your brother?"

With her eyes rolling, Isobel tsked at me. "Nica, I'm glad that it's come to this. She was going to take Jake away from us!" She reached for my hand.

Her outburst garnered a few uncomfortable looks from other diners, but unaware, she continued, "They were going to move to some third world country and join Doctors Without Borders. Like, are you kidding me? That's my brother! Hell no. I'm not letting a little French twit take him away from me."

Selfish as Isobel might have been, at least I knew she cared for her brother.

Was this Jake's plan or was it Sandrine's? Jake had never shared that he wanted to work abroad, but he had always been a philanthropist.

"It was Jake's choice. It's what he wants to do," I mumbled.

"Nica, don't be ridiculous. Jake would never be caught with such a stupid idea."

"It's not stupid. It's commendable..."

Isobel interrupted, "Second of all, it doesn't matter because the wedding is off." Thinking our conversation had finished, she leaned back with her arms crossed over her chest.

Our server came back to give us bread, which neither of us touched. Isobel struggled to keep quiet. And when she couldn't anymore, she blurted out, "Gaspard was hot, though. Well, until Jake did a number on his face."

I took the bait. "I never thought he could be so...violent." I used to think he couldn't hurt a fly.

With a glass tilted to her lips, Isobel snorted. "Right. He's been getting into trouble since college. Jake and Levi even formed their own fight club. A couple of dingbats. You should have seen my mom's face when Jake came home with a black eye for the first time."

"Fight club? That's a little far-fetched, don't you think?"

"Not at all. How do you think he and Levi met? Levi was in business, and he was pre-med. Not even the same fraternity. They became best friends because of that stupid underground club."

I didn't know. I only knew that Jake and Levi met during undergrad.

Isobel was in a sharing mood, and she kept telling me things I should have known but was too naïve to have asked. "They got into all sorts of trouble. Jake was such a player back then, too. I guess it came with the bad boy vibe. He dated skank after skank. My parents were so worried that one of them was going to get pregnant or something. Then Jake went to med school. We had no way of knowing if he'd stopped his shenanigans or not. Mom just hoped he did."

Jake? A player? No, not the Jake I fell in love with. I would never have thought that with how amazing he was with me. I stayed silent, waiting for her to continue, but our waiter chose that moment to appear with our meals: a creamy soup for me, an artfully plated dinner for Isobel. She dug in right away, not bothering to appreciate the skill presented to her. She was blind to the beauty. Was I blindly in love with Jake?

"You have to imagine my mom's relief when he brought you home." I gave her a curt nod. I distinctly remembered how sweet Jake's mother had been when we had dinner at their home. I had been so nervous, and she was so welcoming. Now I knew why. "Then months later, he brought Sandrine home. We didn't even know you guys broke up until that night. Mom took a liking to her, of course, because she's pretty, a doctor, and French."

Had it come from any other person, I would have broken down and cried, but Isobel was with me, and I doubted she could handle it. I didn't touch my soup. I waited until Isobel finished her meal. When she asked if I wanted dessert, not checking if I even ate my dinner, I excused myself and told her that I was going to walk back to my hotel.

I had a lot of questions—some only Jake could answer, others, I was afraid, were all up to me to figure out.

Taking my time, I trudged through familiar streets. The city had a certain allure. Lovers held each other out in the open; friends celebrated. This was the city where Jake fell in love with Sandrine. And tonight, this was where their relationship came to a sudden end. Paris kept their secrets. I'd adored Jake this whole time, wanted him to leave Sandrine for so long. Now that it happened, I was starting to question my real feelings for Jake. How could I have fallen in love with a man I barely even knew?

Once I returned to my hotel, the lobby was buzzing, despite the late hour. I took the first available elevator to my floor and held onto every vestige of courage I had left. I was unsure of myself more than I had ever been in all my love life. I couldn't let myself fall apart in front of strangers in a confined space. Turning the corner toward my room, I readied myself for the onslaught of panic, confusion, and tears that would undoubtedly come.

When I saw the tall figure leaning on my door, my heart stopped.

THE EX

"*I*'ve been waiting for you. Where have you been?" Jake asked. I stood there, head lowered, chewing on the inside of my cheek. I was afraid to show my emotions to strangers in the elevator, unknowing that I would be faced with the most unfamiliar man of all. "Aren't you going to invite me in?"

"Oh, yeah, of course." Fishing in my clutch for the key card, I unlocked the door and held it open to let him pass through. I didn't know why but something made me I crane my neck around to see if there were any shadows lurking in the hallway. There was nothing but silence and semi-darkness. Feeling desolate and dejected, for reasons unclear to me, I closed the door and turned to face my ex-boyfriend.

He chose to sit on the bed, shoulders rolled forward, looking beaten. I hesitantly moved toward him. When he tilted his head up, I could see he hadn't even cleaned his wounds.

"Jake, your face." I placed a hand under his chin and

moved his head from side to side, taking in the broken features of a broken man.

He let out a little chuckle. "You should see the other guy."

I raised an eyebrow and flattened my lips together, unimpressed. "Really? That's what you're going for?"

His lopsided smile disappeared, and he lowered his eyes. "Sorry, Nica."

"We'd better clean it up before it gets infected." I didn't wait for his answer. I walked to the closet to take out the mini first aid kit.

I gasped as I opened the closet door. The scent of *man* hit me with full force. A mixture of sandalwood, musk, and bergamot evoked feelings and conjured up memories. Levi's shirt was hanging in the closet, and his overnight bag was sitting underneath it on the floor. All I wanted to do at that moment was to take that shirt and press it on my skin. My breath hitched. What was going on? Jake was here...with me. Not engaged. This was what I wanted, right?

I inhaled a cleansing breath as I unzipped my luggage to take out my kit. Even as I closed the closet door, Levi's scent had infused into me. I had to clear my head. Jake was in the room, needing my help. I needed to focus. I turned to the bathroom to get him a wet towel.

The scent of lavender and vanilla in the bathroom almost did me in. I was teetering precariously on the edge of crazy town. Levi had been sweet and thoughtful enough to run me a bath earlier that day. I wished I had pulled him in with me. I wished I hadn't gone to that dinner. I wished. I wished...

When I returned from the bathroom, Jake had flopped down on the bed. The lights of the city coming through the window illuminated his face. His arm was propped over his forehead as he stared out into Paris at night.

Sensing my reappearance, he turned his head. "Beautiful view." I was sure he meant the city, but my stomach flipped by what those words could have meant, coupled with that agonizingly sexy look on his face, despite the cuts and bruises.

No, he only meant that the cityscape was beautiful. Nothing else. My mind tamped down any other possibilities. I was beginning to tire of this game.

I went around the room, turning on every single light source there was. I wasn't afraid of the dark. I was afraid of what could happen in subdued lighting with my ex. "I need to see better." Jake hadn't asked for an explanation, but I felt the need to give one anyway.

After zipping open the first aid kit, I ordered Jake to sit up. He pushed himself up with both arms until his face leveled mine. I swallowed the lump in my throat. I had been this close to him since we broke up, but not when it was just us two, and it hadn't felt this intimate. Or improper.

Using the now cooled face cloth, I grudgingly rubbed off the dried blood on Jake's face. He hissed at the friction.

"Are you trying to wipe my entire face off?" Jake complained.

"Hush. You, of all people, should've known how to care for this. You're a freaking surgeon, for Pete's sake," I chastised him, but eased on the rubbing.

Once I rid his cheeks, lips, and chin of any crusted blood, I picked up a cotton ball and doused it with peroxide. I lifted my hand up to his face and gave him a warning, "This is gonna hurt like a bitch." Without hesitation, I dabbed at his cuts. Jake let out a few choice words, but he let me clean his wounds.

"Thanks, Veronica," he murmured while I placed a couple of small Band-Aids on his face. I hummed upon hearing him say my name. It sounded off. I'd only been Nica to him. He'd never called me by my first name before. Only one other person had done that every single time.

I shook my head. It was both a part of a reply to Jake and a way to rid my mind of another man, and the confusion that came with thoughts of him. "It's nothing. I just wish you'd cleaned it sooner."

When I looked back up to Jake, I couldn't help but get drawn into him. This was Jake after all, and once upon a time, I loved him, but this was entirely for a different reason. *Once upon a time*...why did it seem so long ago, even though it had only been less than four months since he and I broke up? I gazed into his eyes, and I found him lacking. He was and wasn't my Jake. Something in him had changed.

Or was it me?

My heart didn't speed up from the sound of his voice. Although I still thought of him as a good-looking man, it there wasn't a flutter in my stomach from the way he smiled at me. If we had been alone like this weeks ago, I'd be laying claim on his lips again. I'd make sure that he'd forgotten any other woman's name. He'd only know me. Nica. But I wasn't just Nica anymore. I was Veronica. I was whole without him.

Jake touched the side of my cheek. "You're so good to me." He leaned forward, eyes connected to mine, and a tickle of warm breath hit my lips.

As I tuned in to what he was about to do, I jumped off the bed and put space between us. My hands flew to my chest, as I tried to slow down my breathing. "What do you think you're doing?"

Jake seemed confused. He tried to stammer out a response, "I –I thought...I was just thinking..."

I knitted my brows together and pointed an accusatory finger at him. "You were about to kiss me!"

He looked away, fiddled with his hair, and rubbed his jaw as though I had smacked him. I should have. "I thought it's what you wanted."

My eyes rolled up to the high heavens, and I muttered a silent prayer to whoever was listening, "Give me strength."

"I'm sorry, Nica. I didn't mean to..."

I stopped him from further embarrassing the both of us, lifting my hand, palm toward Jake. "Please, don't say another word," I snapped, pacing the room.

"Nica, can you please sit down? You're making me nervous," he pleaded.

I stopped a foot away from the bed and glared at him. "I'm making *you* nervous?" I scoffed.

He shrugged. I chose to sit on the chair by the window, refusing to make eye contact with the man sitting on the bed.

Heaving out a sigh, I began, "A few weeks ago... No, even a few days ago, I would probably have loved nothing more than to let you kiss me. I will admit that I've thought of us getting back together again...but things change. I thought you'd changed. I've only recently learned so much more about you than when we were together. So I suppose it's not really you changing, it was just me not knowing."

"I don't know what to say." His voice was full of hurt and uncertainty.

Looking up, I could see how lonely he must feel. Everything—his engagement, his love life—was up in the air. "I still love you. I care about you." And it was the truth. I couldn't change what had happened to us. I could never erase what we'd shared. "But you broke up with me and got engaged to someone else. To someone who unmistakably loves you back. You're not mine to kiss anymore. To be honest, I'm not entirely sure if you were mine even before." I massaged my temples like it was going to help clear the cobwebs inside. "I was acting like a forlorn lover, and I didn't see." I stared at him straight in the eye. "You don't belong to me. You belong to her. To Sandrine. I've witnessed it. I've seen with my own eyes."

"It's too late now. It's over." He looked away, but not before I saw the gripping pain in his eyes.

"I don't believe that. I can't possibly accept that, and neither should you." I stood and walked to him, wrapping my arms around the man I once thought completed me. "We all make mistakes, Jake, but you have a chance to fix it. Go get your girl back. I can see how much you're hurting without her."

Jake leaned his head on my shoulder and hugged me back.

We stayed like that for a while, leaning against each other, listening to our breathing, to the thumping of our hearts. His beat for Sandrine. And mine beat for someone else.

❧

I KEPT my sunglasses on for the entire flight back from Charles de Gaulle to San Francisco International Airport. After Jake had left, I didn't bother with sleep that I knew wouldn't come. I used earphones to ignore the noise around me rather than listen to music or to whatever was playing on the screen before me. My head was turned to the window of the aircraft, peering out but not really seeing.

Flying coach wasn't as comfortable and glamorous as it

would have been if I'd flown back on a private jet, but I couldn't stomach facing anyone I knew that morning. When Jake left, I had packed my belongings hurriedly, while frantically booking the next flight out. The hardest part had been getting Levi's stuff together. I'd waited all night for him to call or text. To see how I was doing. If I was even alive, but it was clear now, I was no concern of his. But I couldn't just leave his bag in the hotel. The only solution had been to pack his things and take them with me.

Every time I had inhaled, his scent saturated my senses and brought flashes of memories to mind—the boat tour on the Seine, the hand-holding around the city, the kiss on the Eiffel Tower, the discovery in the Louvre, the picnic, the tease of his tongue on my thumb.

My face was dry, and my jaw felt locked, possibly from all the gnashing and gnawing and grinding of teeth, as I picked up the single piece of luggage I brought with me on the trip and the leather bag that didn't belong to me. My body was bone-tired. My head pounded. My heart ached. I was more of a mess now than when I left.

I'd laid in bed, thinking of a man who had shown interest in me because it was convenient. Levi had needed a plaything while we were in Paris and I was too naïve to realize what he was doing until it was too late and I began feeling something for the man. Out of sight, out of mind. It stung like a bitch.

How did one get over a heartbreak that shouldn't have been?

I stood and lined up for a cab, moving automatically, not really thinking about what I was doing. Once I got inside one, I blurted out a destination. It wasn't until I stopped in front of my office that I noticed what address I had given.

Jewel saw me right away and darted toward my office. I stood for a good minute or two before feeling the bite of the luggage handles on my fingers, and so I released them drop on the floor. Jewel might have said something to me, but I didn't hear it. When I turned around to see her, I was faced with someone else. Chase.

"What the hell are you doing here?" Chase took a step toward me, concern written all over her face. "You weren't supposed to be back until later tonight."

I felt for something solid around me, weakness claiming my body. The cool solid glass-top desk met my hand, and it was what I held onto.

"Nica? Are you sick? You look like you're about to..."

Stepping back, I fell into my chair. The events of the past days and the emotions that came with them burst out in forms of tears, sobs, and hiccups. Heartache wracked my entire being.

"Oh shit." Chase ran to me, pressing my face into her undoubtedly expensive designer dress. "What did they do to you?"

My reply was an incoherent mumble. Chase patted my head.

"Tell me, who do I kill first, Nica," she demanded. "Oh, sweetheart, don't cry over those assholes." She tilted my head up and removed my sunglasses.

I cried even harder, reaching for the box of tissues on a shelf. "I...He...So messed...I didn't know..."

She led me to the two-seater by my office door. After ensuring that I was comfortable on the sofa, she grabbed the tissue box and placed it on my lap. "Tell me everything."

And I did.

The look on Chase's face was indescribable when I finished. Clumps of wadded up tissues lay on the floor by my feet. I blew my nose into another one and threw it on the pile.

"So that's it. Now I'm here." I sounded hoarse after having just poured all my emotions out.

"I just...I can't..." Chase straightened and stared right at me, with disbelief in her eyes. If my heart wasn't wrenched from missing him so much, I wouldn't have believed it either. "Levi! Who knew?"

"I know, right?" I hiccuped. "I didn't see it coming. Had I known, I would have prepared for it."

"Nuh-uh. I don't think so. There's nothing you could have done to prepare for this. For him! I mean, it's Levi."

"Yes, I get it. I know. I was there."

Chase rolled her eyes to the left, then narrowed them. She bit her lip. "So... I know you're feeling confused and all, and I don't mean to be insensitive, but...out of curiosity..."

I mouthed a 'what'.

"Was he..." Chase lifted her hands, palms facing each other, then moved them apart a good foot away. "...big?"

I coughed and snorted. "Chase!"

"What? I'm just curious. Wouldn't you want to know if I had seen it instead of you? You know you would."

"That doesn't even warrant an answer." I crossed my arms over my chest.

Chase bit her bottom lip again. "Can you tell me at least if he's hooded?"

"Goodness gracious, Chase!" I chastised my friend. "My heart is exploding here."

"I don't mean to be insensitive. You know how I feel about uncircumcised men." She winced as if she had tasted something vile.

"You are a horrible best friend." But I had to admit, Chase had her ways of dealing with uncomfortable situations, with her best friend's belligerence. And she was a huge proponent of laughter, or at least an uncomfortable chuckle, being the best medicine, even for heartbreak. Most especially from heartbreak.

"I know." She clapped her hands together. Her eyes widened. "I have the best solution." She twisted her body to open the door she had closed earlier, and hollered outside my office, "Jewel, can you grab my emergency kit?"

I groaned. Almost too quickly, Jewel came in and handed Chase her 'emergency kit': a bottle of liquor, two crystal tumblers, and packages of Reese's Peanut Butter Cups. Every month the liquor changed. Today, we had whiskey. It never made sense to anyone but Chase. And, at a certain point, when I had downed more drinks than her, my mind was numb enough not to think of anything else but the ensuing hangover and bloating the day after.

For the moment, I was willing to do just about anything to keep Levi out of my mind, even though I knew nothing would completely eradicate him from my thoughts. Because my heart wouldn't let it.

THE CONTRACT

"Wake up, sleepy head," Chase's not-so-soft voice pulled me out of a deep slumber.

Fluttering my eyes open, I groaned. I tried to lift my hands to cover my face. Then I realized how much of a mistake that was. Everything ached. Even my eyeballs were too painful to move.

It had been almost a week since I'd returned from Paris. And during the week, Chase had turned me into her number one project. She had accused Jake and company of under nourishing me. She claimed that I had wasted away. The scale in her office had proved her right. I didn't understand it at first. Cheese, wine, and pastries were the staple diet while I was in Paris. However, with the whirlwind of excitement and stress, tension and pain, I managed to lose a few pounds. It wouldn't have been horrible if I had done it properly.

I garbled a response at Chase's intrusion.

"What'd you say? Come on, up and at 'em. Diego waits for no one." She bounced on my bed.

Her movements caused trembles that my body did not appreciate. "Go to hell, Chase!"

"Oh, so we're getting cheeky now! I like it."

I hoped she relented, but hope was for the weak and those not best friends with a hellion.

"Use that anger and get your ass out of bed. Let's go!" She got on all fours and bounced harder.

There was only one way to get rid of her. Unfortunately, it was to go with her.

"Can I at least sleep for another ten minutes? I promise I'll skip lunch to save calories."

"What? No way! Today is pizza day."

It sounded counterproductive, and truly, it didn't make sense. Chase's motto was to 'exercise brutally and eat excessively'. She might even have a shirt with that on it.

"I can't anymore. Just leave me here to wilt and die," I begged her, stuffing my head under a pillow.

"You're so melodramatic. Get up, let's go see Delicious Diego, and I'll tell you about our newest, biggest contract on the way there." She nonchalantly added that last part. Wench.

It got me up. "Newest and biggest?" I scrubbed sleep out of my eyes, squirming at the soreness with every movement. Even the muscles that had no business being sore were sore.

Chase nodded. She hopped out of my bed and held out her hands. I grabbed them, and she helped me up.

"It will blow your mind." Chase loved to exaggerate, but she also knew what kept me going. I thrived on big events. The countless possibilities. The numerous ideas. The glamor in the details. The rush of adrenaline with the planning. I could use an upper from being so down in the dumps these past few days.

After a few more protests from my body, I managed to

head to the bathroom to change, grabbing an old college shirt, sports bra, and shorts along the way. I faced myself in the mirror and ignored the dark circles under my eyes while I brushed my teeth. It might have been partly the jetlag, but since Paris, I hadn't gotten a decent sleep. Too many memories. Too many thoughts of him.

I refused to take short cuts and drink my brain cells away or take sleeping pills that weren't prescribed for me. I would get over this. I would get over him. I only wished it would happen sooner rather than later.

Chase was standing over a floral box that sat on the living room floor when I came out of my bedroom, tying my hair up in a ponytail. There was no sense in putting on makeup or doing my hair, since, in an hour I would look as disheveled as a homeless man.

"What's all this?" She sipped on her green smoothie and handed me my tumbler.

"Jake's stuff." I chugged the thick concoction. It was like drinking sweet snot, but Chase promised it contained the vitamins and minerals I needed to survive Torture.

"A breakup box?"

"Yup."

She bent down to rummage through it. "He left an awful lot of crap here."

I leaned over, remembering what I had thrown into the box. "A few personal effects for when he stayed over, and some clothes, just in case he got called in for emergencies at night." Jake had left three sets of clothes, an electric shaver, an electric toothbrush (which matched mine), a phone charger (which possibly had been actually mine at one point), three books I would never read, and a couple of DVDs I would never watch. Jake might be a world-renowned surgeon, but he had an appalling taste in movies.

Most nights Jake had been too tired to read or watch, and would spend the night just sleeping beside me while I read or worked in bed. In retrospect, Jake and I hadn't had much time for each other. We both worked crazy hours and often received calls to go back into work to fix or mend something (in his case, someone). We ate takeout a lot. We made love often; but in hindsight, it had been more like an obligation—something a couple had to do to prove to each other that they were in a relationship.

Jake had still been loving in his own way. If our relationship had gone longer, I would have gotten to know him better, and either loved him more or liked him less, knowing what I knew now.

The trouble was, compared to a good chunk of women my age, I was still fairly inexperienced. Before Jake, there had been two other guys. Mavin, the guy I went to prom with, whom I had lost my virginity to (uncomfortably and laughably), and who promptly told me the day after we slept together that he was gay. It had caused me a lot of confusion back then. I had wondered if my callowness had affected his sexual orientation.

Thankfully, I became smarter and knew better. Marvin and I remained good friends. Just last year, I had attended his wedding.

Then there was Tony in college, who was shy, sweet, and polite. He had constantly assured me that my sexual performance was okay, that he had been satisfied, and who had profusely thanked me for it, post-coitus. After two months of comfortable dating, he'd enlisted in the army, got shipped to a war-torn country, and broke up with me through a tear-soaked letter. His tears, not mine.

I believed in love, true love. And I had loved all three of them.

I picked up the box and hitched it over one hip. "Let's go get Tortured." Chase grinned.

❧

ONCE CHASE HAD GIVEN up on her attempts to force me to ride behind her on her death machine/motorcycle, we rode in my car to Delicious Diego's Torture. I couldn't contain my excitement about finding out what the big event was, asking her the 'what' and the 'who' as soon as I car engine turned over.

"Lautner and Brimley fired their planner. I found out last night, made a few phone calls, and got us an appointment. And by us, I mean you," Chase proudly announced.

The Lautner Evans and Brimley Brixton Nuptials would be the wedding of the century. They were the Brangelina of the Bay Area. Wealthy, lavish, pretty people marrying. Anyone who was anybody in this universe would be on that guest list. This could be our ticket to the top.

"When is the meeting?" I bounced happily on the driver's seat, taking a sharp left and barely missing a man walking his dog.

"This afternoon, at the Brixton Estate, for tea," Chase replied...a little too quickly. And, she sounded way too ecstatic. She was hiding something from me.

"Spill it," I said in a flat tone.

"What." She didn't even form it into a question. She knew the jig was up.

"What aren't you telling me, Chase?"

She hesitated, and waited until I parked the car. "It's the same date as Jake and Sandrine's."

"What? Chase!"

She waved her hands wildly. "They're done, aren't they?"

I pouted. I hadn't heard from either Jake or Sandrine. I had no idea if they had patched things up. What I did know was that doing the Lautner and Brimley's wedding would be the opportunity of a lifetime.

"Think about the media coverage, Nica. It's the big league. After that wedding, there will be no stopping us. They're desperate too, I could tell. The gossip mill was buzzing yesterday. Apparently, the saintly, supposedly virgin bride-to-be is expecting a little something-something." Chase patted her flat stomach. My eyes widened.

I should do it. I owed it to myself. I'd pull out the big guns. Lautner and Brimley wouldn't know what was coming at them. But a little niggling thought punched me in the gut—my inherent sense of responsibility. We had a binding contract with Jake and Sandrine, something Chase had insisted on. I would have to review it and find a loophole.

"I know what you're thinking. You don't need an out. They broke up. The wedding is not happening." Chase opened the car door, ready to face Torture.

Considering everything that had happened... "Okay," I began. Chase's made-up eyes brightened. "But we'll have a look at the contract. I don't want to deal with a lawsuit."

"Yes, I'll get on it, right after Delicious Diego...who is staring out the window right now. Shit, we're late!" Chase jumped out of the car, as did I. No one wanted the wrath of Delicious Diego.

❦

AFTER THE GYM, we head straight to work. As soon as

Chase and I were in front of our office building, Jewel burst through the main doors, huffing and puffing.

"I've been trying to reach you, both of you!" She was clearly spooked.

I shot Chase a worried glance. She waved a dismissive hand. "I guess I forgot to check my phone. We were at the gym. What's going on?" I took out my purse and the floral breakup box from the backseat of my car and carried them with me.

"They're here," she stated, trying to catch up with my usual fast pace and Chase's long strides.

"Who?" We asked simultaneously, but we didn't need an answer as soon as we were inside and spotted the couple waiting in my office.

Chase grabbed my arm, carefully twisting me to face her. "Are you going to be okay with this? I'll be there with you the entire time."

I touched the hand on my arm, keeping my eyes trained at my office. "It's okay, Chase. I'll be fine on my own. New me, right? And the new me isn't a pushover." Even though I heard the words come out of my mouth, I didn't believe them.

I stepped forward, but Chase hadn't let go. "Wait..." My gaze met hers. She was concerned, and rightly so. Heaving out a sigh, she continued. "Whatever your decision is, I will support you one hundred percent." Exhale. "All right, fine." She threw her hands in the air. "Maybe not one hundred. A good ninety-eight percent at least."

I patted her hand, trying to reassure her I was more than capable of handling whatever hail and brimstone were coming my way. Having her support was enough to encourage me. "That's more than I could ever ask for." She finally released my arm. Taking deep breaths and squaring my shoulders, I braced myself to meet the guests waiting for me.

They both turned around when I swung the door open. Sandrine was seated on a chair facing my desk, and Jake stood behind her. His hands were on her shoulders, and one of hers was on top of his. From the door to my desk, I took in the mood.

I set my purse and the box aside, placed my steady hands atop my desk, and threaded my fingers together. I hoped they didn't notice my knees trembling as I sat. With a deep breath in and a slow breath out, I greeted the picture perfect—well, nearly perfect—couple in front of me.

"Jake. Sandrine...I see you've managed to patch things up." It hurt to smile, physically and emotionally, but I did it anyway.

They both appeared nervous. Sandrine squeezed Jake's hand before speaking. "Yes, we 'ave. We apologize for intruding. We know 'ow busy you are..." This was usually the time when clients tell me that my services were no longer required. In a way, I was relieved that they were doing this now. I still had the chance to present to another possible, and much bigger, client later in the afternoon.

"I don't mind at all." Smile. Smile. Little nod. Smile.

"We're just gonna come right out and say that we appreciate the work you've done for us, and fully understand and accept your decision. In light of things, we are wholly grateful for the dedication you've shown..." Jake started to explain.

"Oh, for Pete's sake, just say it." My porcelain exterior cracked. I flattened my hands on the desk and inclined toward them. "Are you guys getting married or not?"

They were shocked at my outburst, and frankly, so was I. Hey, new me, right?

"We are getting married," Sandrine answered with a smile.

"Well, good." Brushing my dress over my lap, I settled back into my chair. "Now, I am more than happy to pass on the reins to whoever you're going to hire. I will keep the deposit, of course, and send you a detailed invoice on expenses that weren't covered. The vendors will also keep their deposits, and I can..."

Jake interjected, "Wait...Wait! Are you breaking up with us?"

That was one way of putting it. "Well, I thought you two were..." I waved a hand at them.

Sandrine and Jake shared a look. "We fully intend to continue with you."

I stared at the both of them. "Why didn't you start with that?"

"You were kind of intimidating when you came in," Jake explained as he took a seat beside Sandrine. "I've never seen you like that before." He almost sounded proud.

"Oh, well, I'm trying out a new health regimen." I pursed my lips, deep in thought while catching the surreptitious glances these two were shooting each other. Clearly, they were still very much in love. They wanted to get married. And they wanted to retain my services. All great things.

But it also meant I wouldn't have the chance at the big leagues. I would have to pass on Lautner and Brimley. I searched for Chase beyond my office door and found her standing by Jewel's desk, staring right at me, arms crossed over her chest. We shared a look. Her previous words rang right through me. She wasn't clairvoyant, but she was smart, and I could tell that she had guessed that something like this would happen. Shrugging, I returned my attention to the couple.

They kept quiet the entire time, letting me make my decision. Their hands were intertwined between them, as they gave each other silent support.

I didn't know Lautner and Brimley personally. I had no way of knowing if they were truly in love and in it for the long haul. These two in front of me clearly were. And the romantic in me couldn't ignore that. And I couldn't ignore the prospect of a wedding meant for true lovers. I was a twenty-five-year-old woman who believed in fairy tales.

"Alright, let's do this." My answer wasn't merely for them, but also for myself.

"Ç'est fantastique! Thank you! Thank you!" There was a tear in her eye.

I raised a finger, stopping them from saying anything else. "Provided you guys tell me everything, and I mean everything there is to know. I don't want any more surprises. No more ex-fiancés lurking about." I looked pointedly at Sandrine. "And no fighting of any sort." I squinted at Jake. "I'm all for it, but I don't like getting blindsided."

"I promise nothing of the sort will happen again." This came from Jake. He had a faint bruise under his left eye and a small scar near his lips. The scar might stay forever, a token of his love for his future wife, for the one he had fought for.

"Are we keeping the date?" I flipped open my MacBook. They nodded, and I proceeded to read through their wedding checklist. "Venue is still good. I will contact the vendors and check in with them, confirm any other appointments we have. Have you received a lot of responses from the invitations?"

Again, they nodded. This was going to be easier than I thought. "I'll have my assistant confirm any flights and reservations for that weekend. I'll contact you directly. We have less than a couple of weeks left. It will be a gong show from now on."

"We understand," they said simultaneously.

It was freaky. I couldn't help but think if there was something else going on. This was way too easy. They were too eager and willing to do what I asked of them. They could still find a decent—not as great as me, but functional enough—new planner, considering they were willing to drop a large amount of money into this wedding.

Keeping my fingers hovering over the keyboard, I stopped typing and gave them my full attention. "Is there anything else you want to add?"

"Yes. My parents are no longer attending," Sandrine said.

Her parents not coming to her wedding was a big deal, but I let it slide. "Anyone else?"

Jake shook his head. Sandrine opened her mouth, closed it, and opened it again to speak. "My Papa might still try to attend. It will depend on 'ow he can 'andle my mother, but everyone else we've invited is still going...as far as we know."

"Good." I typed out the details in their file.

"And Isobel is still our maid of honor. I hope you haven't changed your mind on being a bridesmaid." Was Jake kidding me? After all the hard work I'd been through this week with the boot camp and drinking a green smoothie? I intended to rock that dress! The only reply he received from me was a small nod. "And Levi is still the best man. But don't worry, you won't see him much since he's still in France." Now it was their turn to look pointedly at me.

I continued typing, but I bit my lip. Damn. His name hadn't been mentioned around me for a while. I exhaled slowly, trying to keep my wits together. So he wasn't even in the US yet. I wondered what was keeping him in Paris. Or maybe he was in Bordeaux with his grandmother. My heart ached thinking of him.

The wedding, I could handle. Levi, on the other hand, was an altogether different story. Keeping my eyes on my screen, I managed to pretend that Jake's revelation hadn't affected me.

"All good, guys. You can go on your merry way. I'll shoot you an email of upcoming appointments with the florist, and a final walk through at the venue. I'll check in with the photographer and the band. Sandrine, you still have to send me your stylist's info, and I will need to know when the dresses and tuxes are coming in." A long breath out gave them time to take it all in. "Now go, before I change my mind."

We all got on our feet. Sandrine thanked me profusely, showering me with kisses. Jake gave me a great big hug and told me I looked fantastic and healthy. Before they left my office, I picked up Jake's box and shoved it in his arms. We shared an unspoken understanding.

He was happy. He looked relieved. Jake leaned over and gave me another parting kiss on the cheek. "Thank you, Nica."

I bade them farewell and reminded them that I would be keeping in touch.

Chase traipsed in as soon as they left. She slouched on the sofa, and I sat ramrod straight beside her.

"Sorry, I couldn't say no," I told her.

Chase crossed her long legs and leaned back. "Nica, if you had said no to them, it would mean you've completely changed. I like the little changes in you; you're much stronger. You're fiercer. You kick ass in your own ways. The rest...well, you're who you are, and I love you no matter what."

"Now, you're scaring me," I joked.

"I'm well capable of love. I'm not all android in here." She tapped her chest with a finger. "What I am worried about is how you will handle being around you-know-who."

I sighed. "Me too, Chase, me too."

THE BACHELORETTE

Sleep had been impossible these last few days. Work began to pile up, and it was starting to take a toll on my body. Levi had taken up residence in my mind night after night. I contemplated calling him, but I changed my mind. I did that several times last night when I received a one-line text from him.

Tu me manques.

A quick search translated it to "I miss you." My heart clenched, but his absence since the fight at the St. Croix's home remained in my mind. Where had he been? Why did he disappear? By the time I had enough courage to grab my phone, it was four a.m. I didn't even know where he was, whom he was with. What if he wasn't alone? What if he made a mistake and didn't mean to send me that message? I groaned at the unknowns.

When Chase came to join me to head to Torture, I was waiting in the car. She was surprised by my readiness to exercise, but she could tell that I wasn't in the mood to talk and kept quiet the whole drive. When we arrived at the gym, she reached over and gave me a hug. Chase was not a hugger, and this freaked me out. Without a word, she stepped out of the car.

Diego looked like his usual delicious self that morning. His greeting was short and sweet. I, of course, returned a 'g'morning' and walked to my spot at the back of the class where I could look like a fool in gym shorts and a yoga top, away from the rest of the more limber girls.

After another rigorous workout, I stepped out of the locker rooms; Diego was chatting with Chase.

"There she is! Ready to go?" She handed me a smoothie.

"Yup." I turned to our tantalizing trainer. "Great class today. Did Chase tell you we won't be able to make it Sunday? We have an event."

Diego nodded. "She did. I hope you ladies have a great time." His expression turned serious when he leaned closer. "How are you doing? Any progress with…" Brows furrowed, I wondered what he was going on about. I waited 'till he continued, and the breath was sucked out of me when he said, "Levi? You're with him now, aren't you? Chase said you were in Paris with him."

I glanced at Chase, who suddenly was too busy to join in on the conversation. "There's nothing to say, Diego," I told him, sipping my smoothie.

"That's surprising. Are you sure? It seemed to me that you were on your way to having a great relationship with the man."

"Nah." I lowered my eyes to the floor. "I would know if I was in a real relationship." I think.

"But he told me…"

I stepped back and raised a brow. "Told you what?"

Unexpectedly, Diego stepped closer gave me a soft kiss on the cheek. "You'll figure it out soon."

THE REST of Friday and Saturday found me running around like a lunatic in four events, including one I wasn't even supposed to be involved in (thanks to a slightly disorganized Chase). And thanks also to my convoluted, anxious self, my normally structured timeline and systematic methods went bye-bye.

No, this was all Levi's fault. Levi and all the things he did to make me feel for him, want him, miss him.

"I miss you, my butt!" I screamed in my parked car, shaking the steering wheel out of frustration, after another busy Sunday, and another day that there was no word from him.

I came home a bit after three a.m. and didn't bother changing out of my clothes. In a few hours, I would be picked up and brought to a spa as part of Sandrine's bachelorette party. At least I had that to look forward to.

At exactly seven a.m., I was shaken out of bed by the magnanimous Chase. I knew it was seven because she repeatedly yelled it at me. "Nica, I am not missing out on this free luxury. I heard it takes months to get an appointment at Sense. These bitches reserved the entire place for the day, and I don't want to miss a second of it."

"You're a real brute, Chase. The car won't come around until eight." I rolled back on the bed, pulling the blanket over my semi-naked body. "I'll get up when it's here."

The mattress dipped beside me. She began combing my hair with her fingers. "Nica, Nica, Nica, I don't think you understand, sweetie. They're known for the most luxurious baths and scrubs. Armageddon cannot stop me from enjoying every blissful moment," she said the words so soothingly that it made me very, very afraid.

I peeked out from under the blanket. "I know, but I'm

so tired. I kept waking up because Levi's face wouldn't stop popping into my head."

Chase sighed, her shoulders slumping forward. "Do you want me to call them and say we're not going?"

"No! Of course not. I just don't know how to move forward." I sat against the headboard. "I wasn't like this with Jake. I thought of him, but I managed to work and sleep and eat. With Levi..."

"It's not the same kind of relationship. Jake was your boyfriend. You guys had exclusivity. You dated, you slept together, you broke up. With Levi...you just got felt up." Chase patted my hair.

I leaned my head back and regretted it once it slammed against the wooden section of my headboard. "Do I get over him? Do I pursue him? What do I do?"

Chase walked to my dresser and pulled out a light sweater dress, bra, and panties, and handed them to me. "You'll get dressed. Then you'll get pampered, and after that, you will throw the most spectacular wedding the darling couple paid for. Levi will find his way back to you, if he wants to, and if you let him."

"He sent me a text message a few nights ago."

"Good. What did you say back?"

"Nothing." I pouted. "I didn't know what to say."

"Okay...What did he send?"

"I miss you." Her brows raised. "Well, in French." I grabbed my phone from the side table and showed her the text.

"You know I don't know French, except for the curse words. But I know what that means." I waited for her to continue. She held my hands and looked me straight in the eyes. It freaked me out when she went soft like this. "It doesn't just mean 'I miss you.' It means 'you are missing from me.' That shit is deep."

"What does he mean by that?" I yelled.

"Only he can tell you. Next time, you see him, ask."

SANDRINE APPROACHED us as soon as we came through the doors. The smell of eucalyptus and peppermint, coupled with the ambient music immediately relaxed me. "Ah, bon! You are 'ere! I'm very glad." Sandrine greeted us, kissing both my cheeks. She turned to Chase, but she stopped her with a finger shake. Sandrine immediately backed away.

A woman with wild orange hair, in a white sports bra and yoga pants, approached us. Her hands were in a prayer position. "Namaste. Since everyone is here, we should get started."

"*Oui, merci*. Yes, 'owever, my friend is not dressed for it, I'm afraid." Sandrine waved a hand my way.

I shot her a questioning look. "Dressed? Oh, I can head to the locker room. Are there robes there?"

"You will need yoga wear for the class," the lady in white answered me in a monotone voice.

"Yoga?" I looked at Sandrine, and back to the lady. "Nobody told me there would be yoga."

"That would be my mistake!" Chase produced a pair of yoga capris and bra from her bag, an exact copy of what she was wearing, although the outfit would look different on me (due to smaller tatas and rounder hips). "I packed them for you when you were changing." She didn't even pretend to be sorry. "What?"

"But, I thought..." What I thought was that I would have rest from exercising for the day. It was only then that I noticed what Sandrine was wearing: Yoga pants and a top that were like a second skin. Sometimes I disliked tall people.

Chase thrust the clothes at me. "Here, take them. It's only an hour and a half of Bikram. I received the email at work yesterday. If I told you about the yoga class, there's no way you would have come. Look on the bright side, and you've done worse with Diego." But at least Diego was great to stare at.

I supposed I had no choice. I took my workout clothes and followed the woman, who I assumed was the instructor, to the changing rooms.

As I was trying to fit into my capris, I heard a knock on the door. My pants were midway up my hips. "Yeah?"

"I am so sorry, Veronique, may I come in?" Sandrine asked from the other side of the door.

"Sure, why the heck not?" I suppose the French didn't understand sarcasm, as she burst through the door of the dressing room barely a second later. I yanked the pants up too quickly, the friction causing a mild burn on my thighs. "What's going on? Is everything okay?"

"I 'ave some great news!" She paused, but I only stared at her, waiting for her to continue. "My friend Natalie is here. Isn't that wonderful?"

Natalie? Natalie...Natalie...Natalie...I dug through the recesses of my mind trying to figure out who Natalie was, other than being Sandrine's friend. Sandrine didn't wait for me to answer. "She just flew in last night from France, surprising us all. I cannot wait for you to meet 'er. She 'as lost some weight from being quarantined, but she is well and healthy."

"I'm glad she made it." I pondered the information for a bit. "Wait, does this mean she'll be your bridesmaid and I don't have to do it?"

Astounded, Sandrine grasped my shoulders. "*Non*! That is never going to 'appen! You 'ave been vital in our lives.

More useful than Isobel, if I may say so. I've convinced Jacob that Natalie can be the new maid of *honeur*, and 'is sister will be a bridesmaid as well. Everything works out." She raised her right hand, displaying two fingers. "Two groomsmen, two bridesmaids. That will work, *non?*"

"Yes, I guess." Good thing I waited to have the programs printed until two days before the wedding. Changes like these always happened. At one particularly memorable affair, the bride replaced all of her bridal party! "Will she have anything to wear?"

"That is nothing to worry about. Isobel and Natalie 'ave the same physique," Sandrine assured me. "I've called Crâyon and 'e sent another dress for Isobel. Levi and Natalie brought them back last night."

Oh? Was Levi back home? I wanted to ask. My finger itched to check my phone if he had called or left another message, but I kept my cool. "Perfect then. It's all going smoothly. Shall we go? That yoga teacher looks mean."

Sandrine stopped me from moving forward, squeezing my left arm. "There is something else."

"Of course, there is!" I couldn't control my mouth. I was tired, hungry, and the hopes of skipping anything laborious for today had gone out the window.

Hesitation marked her expression. Her forehead wrinkled, and in the dim lighting of the changing room, Sandrine looked momentarily older, less put-together. "Since you requested that we tell you everything... Natalie and Levi are former lovers."

Whoop-tee-doo! Just what I wanted to hear.

My throat clogged up with emotions. This was like having chicken pate as icing on a cupcake.

"Wonderful." I kept my voice neutral, but I was quaking inside. Why would he send me meaningful French text message but not tell me that he'd be back home with his ex-girlfriend? Unless if my previous theory was right and he sent it to the wrong person. I wasn't French. Natalie was. Could he have meant to send her the message, instead of me? Perhaps it was his way of telling he wanted her back and they'd since patched things up. Then they traveled back to San Francisco, together. These unanswered questions were giving me heartburn. Or heartache. I couldn't tell.

"Thank you for telling me. Shall we go? I'm itching to do some stretches since I skipped my boot camp class this morning." Only parts of what I said were true.

Sandrine had hugged me before we left the changing room, and she gleefully traipsed down the long hallway to what I assumed was the yoga studio. Along the way, as I followed her, I wished that Natalie was a hideous beast. Much like I did before meeting Sandrine for the first time. As I walked into the large room lit with various candles, I greeted everyone I knew, including Jake's mother (nothing awkward there) and Isobel. Natalie wasn't present.

Our instructor introduced herself as Ariana and directed us to choose mats spread out on the floor. Naturally, Chase was up front, and so were Sandrine and Isobel. Jake's mother, Cynthia, took the spot to my left. Before Ariana started chanting, a Brazilian model walked in and claimed the mat on my right.

She beamed at me. She could be a Brazilian model— tall, had a perfect body encased in a nude halter unitard. She had sun-kissed skin, voluminous chestnut hair, a flawless face and perfect teeth. Right away, I knew that was she Levi's—to quote Sandrine—former lover. Who else could it be?

The possible model waved her fingers. "Hi, I'm

Natalie." I knew it! A fit of giggles burst out of me. Natalie was entertained. "You must be Veronica. It's a pleasure to finally meet you. I've heard nothing but great things."

"Of course, you are." I meant to say something that sounded less sarcastic. Everyone turned my way, and Ariana shushed me. Natalie made a face and stuck her tongue out at Ariana once the other woman turned her back.

I could probably have handled another Ophelia. But Natalie was stunning, and worse, she seemed pleasant and down to earth.

Why couldn't the universe work with me for once?

I was panting and wheezing halfway through the fifth round of sun salutations. I had to excuse myself. Tempted to leave this so-called spa altogether, I made my way back to the changing rooms where I'd locked my purse in a locker. I retrieved it and carried it with me to the front entrance, burst through the doors into the thick fog that lay over the city and inhaled the briny smell of the ocean.

I dug in my purse for my cell phone and stared at it for a while. What was I about to do? Had I pushed past the precipice and was now willing to call Levi? For what? Or should I give him hell for making my life a misery these past few days?

My phone buzzed in my hand. A slight disappointment kicked me in the chin when I saw that Deigo sent a message:

I hope you're having a well-deserved break. I kept looking toward the back of the room, expecting to see you during class, but you weren't there.

How thoughtful of you! I responded.

If nothing else, that gave me a surge of power. Why was I pining for someone who couldn't make heads or tails out of our situation? There was this Adonis sending me well wishes and telling me he missed me (yeah, I read the text that way!). Why couldn't my life be this easy? I sent a quick reply back telling Diego that I was having a fantastic time and tucked my phone back in my purse, ignoring the other messages and emails that came through while I was doing downward dog.

Taking a deep breath, and slowly letting it go, I walked back into the spa and returned my purse to the locker.

When I returned to yoga, my body complained, but I pushed through to the end. I paid no heed to whoever was around me and how much better they were doing. I was my own woman.

Right after the class, we were given herbal teas and led to separate rooms to change out of our yoga clothes and don fluffy white robes. Then we all gathered in a circular room, seated facing each other, while estheticians soaked, filed, and scrubbed our feet.

Across from me were Chase and Natalie. They seemed to be getting on swimmingly. I pouted as I observed them. It was one thing for Natalie to have had relations with Levi; it was another for her to take my best friend from me.

After mani-pedis, I was taken back to my treatment room for a scrub, a massage and a bath. After the scrub, my skin felt raw. I didn't think my esthetician appreciated it when I called her Helga. Her massage techniques were angry, and I had more tension in my body afterward than when she first started. I was grateful for the end of the treatment. Helga (her name might have been Susan) got a bath with essential oils ready for me, complete with rose petals, jets, and lights in the tub. Then she left me to soak in tranquility.

I only sighed when there was a knock at the door.

"Go away," I muttered, knowing full well that they

wouldn't hear me. I should have shouted, but it was too late when Sandrine came in.

"Sorry if I'm bothering you again. Oh, petals! 'ow lovely." She sat on the edge of the tub.

Didn't she know I was naked? I'd like to keep my private parts private! I tried unsuccessfully to gather all the petals closer to me.

Sandrine wasn't fazed. "I wanted to speak to you one more time."

I gave up. I lolled my head back and let her see whatever the petals wouldn't cover. "With regards to?"

"Levi." She sensed my hesitation right away. "I 'eard about his little gaffe at the bakery. Why didn't you tell us before? Chase told us."

"Little gaffe? It was the Mac Daddy of tactlessness."

"Mac Daddy?"

I waved my hand, encouraging her to continue.

"I apologize for 'is behavior. 'e was never one to get into that much trouble when he was little." She laughed shyly, with a look in her eye that said she remembered an old memory.

"You knew him when he was younger?" I lifted my head, keeping eye contact with Sandrine.

« Ai, Oui. 'e is mon cousin. »

I narrowed my eyes, repeating that last word in my head. "Ku-za? What does that mean?" I sat straighter, splashing water over the lip of the tub.

"'e is famille. 'is mother is my Papa's sister."

"Oh, he's your cousin? So that's why he stayed with you afterward...at your parents'... after the fight?" That answered one niggling question.

Sandrine nodded. "There are things that you should know, but I'm afraid it isn't yet the time to tell you. I do 'ope you give 'im another chance." She laid a hand on top of mine, the one gripping the edge of the tub.

"Another chance? What do you mean?"

"As it sounds. You two were lovers? N'est pas? Correct?"

I sputtered a choking sound and returned to looking her straight in the eyes. "No. Nothing happened! What about Natalie? They came back here...together. Wouldn't she want to be with him? Maybe there's a chance for them." When in doubt, divert attention elsewhere, even if it caused an insurmountable pain in my chest.

Sandrine shrugged. "I am not too sure. They were together for a long time. They seemed 'appy. We thought they would marry, but Natalie decided to leave France. Levi 'asn't been the same since." She gripped my hand harder, forcing me to stare into her hope-filled eyes. "That was until you came along." Her voice turned soothing. "He is flawed, in many ways. There's something missing in 'is life. I think you might be the one to fill it."

&.

WHILE WE WAITED for the rest of the women to come out of their treatment rooms, I contemplated on what everyone had told me. Diego, Chase, and Sandrine had pretty much said the same things. It would be nice to hear them from the horse's mouth itself. Everything was pointed to a direction, to us being together. All I had to do was figure out if it was the right way.

Isobel plopped herself beside me on a lounger not a moment later. Her skin glowed, but she glowered. Bad news was written all over her. Before I could escape, Isobel asked me, "Nica, is there something going on with you and

Levi?" Was this the theme of the day—poke at Nica's love life?

I swung my feet over the other side and stood quickly. How fast could I get away from her and her meddling? "Why would you ask that?"

Isobel leered at me. "I hope you know what you're doing. I wouldn't trust him if I were you." She studied her nails, ignoring my discomfort. I opened my mouth, but only a frustrated sigh came out. "He's the reason you're not with Jake anymore."

"What do you mean?" I tried to play that I wasn't too intrigued, but I failed.

A touch of mischief played at the corner of her lips. "He introduced Jake to Sandrine."

My body numbed.

When Jake returned from his trip to Paris, he'd only told me that he had met someone and had fallen in love with her immediately. Levi had never mentioned that he had anything to do with it. I held onto the back of the lounger when my surroundings started spinning. My chest heaved, as I gasped for air, trying to push the heaviness away. I had to get out.

I stumbled toward the front of the spa and pushed open the door. I welcomed the salty breeze. My mind was full. My heart was heavy. Tears set to drop.

I thought of the days I spent with Levi. Of the tenderness that he'd shown me. Of the promise of something beautiful that I held onto. And of the betrayal that I now felt.

Levi had been around Jake and me a lot during the months we dated. I'd been aware of his presence, but I ignored him. He knew what I felt for Jake, and what Jake had felt for me. And he had no qualms breaking us up by bringing Sandrine into the picture.

What of the unexpected feelings I'd had for him these past weeks? Had I been blinded all this time? After spending a few days with him in Paris, I had seen him in a more convivial light. I was enamored by Levi's beautiful side. Was it all a ruse? All this time, had he been using me? But for what purpose?

What sick game was he playing?

THE SINGLE GIRL

*D*eep breath in...then out...And a couple more times...

Maybe one more for good luck.

Hand hovering over on the handle, I prepared for what waited on the other side. I could simply turn back and hide in my office. There was still time.

There was a crash, followed by a shriek beyond the door. Dang. I wondered what broke this time. Pinching the bridge of my nose, I slid a foot into my apartment, but I was not looking forward to the ensuing chaos. The mistake was—and always would be—that I gave my mother a copy of my apartment key. Whenever she'd feel like coming to the city, she'd make herself feel at home without my knowledge. However, today the request had come from my half-sister, Maggie. Apparently, our mother had another heartbreak to deal with. Mom was constantly in on-again-off-again relationships with various men. I didn't know which one was the culprit this time.

With one foot in the door, my subconscious screamed

me that they hadn't seen me, yet, that I had time to leave my place. The city. The state. Head to Canada!

"Oh, finally you're here!"

Too late.

"Maggie, your sister's home," my Mom yelled into the kitchen. Her petite body was halfway past its threshold and the living room. She had a glass of wine in hand. I suspected it was the bottle a grateful client had given me, a vintage Bordeaux. I didn't know much about wine, but Chase told me that that particular one was worth a good amount of money.

I narrowed my eyes to the glass while slipping inside my apartment. "Yeah, I had a meeting that ran a little too long." Not completely true. The meeting was short, but I kept Chase talking longer after it, knowing full well what was waiting for me at home.

"Is that my cake?" Mom tucked the wineglass between her boob and her upper arm and stretched out her hands for the Divine Delights cake box.

Eddie baked Mom's break up cake, a dulce de leche cheesecake, every time she came over. Trying to avoid any more breakage or unfortunate spills, I grabbed the wine glass from her and handed her the box. "Eddie sends his regards." I dumped my gym bag and purse on the floor.

"What a sweet man." She'd met him once, and since then, he'd been only known as the 'sweet man.'

I followed her into the kitchen, where the sixteen-year-old Maggie, was lip-locked with a boy named June (His twin sister was called May). "Hey, Mags. You've got something on your face."

Maggie chuckled while June was still sucking face with her. Oh, young love! When she was finally free, she jumped off June's lap and wrapped me in the tightest hug. "Hey, sis! Ooooh, your hair smells like caramel."

"Same shampoo, Mags," I told her as we let go of each other. "Hey, June. I didn't know you were coming." I shot Maggie and an inquisitive look.

She grinned, walked back to her boyfriend, and draped an arm over his wide shoulders. "You don't mind, do you? He's never been here before." Cue puppy-dog face.

I rolled my eyes to Mom, who was too busy sampling the cheesecake. "He can't sleep in the same bed with you." If I wasn't getting any, no one else in this house should. Plus, they were both sixteen, and last I heard, Maggie was still a virgin.

"Of course, they're not sleeping in the same bed. June can sleep on the couch," my mother said, tilting the vintage bottle and pouring the expensive wine into her glass. She was a special-occasions-only drinker since my father died of liver cancer. Oftentimes, she worried about me and my so-called "life" in the city. Sometimes, I worried about me too.

"That's fine. It's a comfortable couch. I'll take out bedding for you." I stared pointedly at June, who was a boy-man of very few words. I thought I heard him grunt, and he gave me a one-shoulder shrug.

Taking a glass from the cupboard, I placed it beside hers. Mom looked my way and smiled as she poured wine into it. We'd never shared a drink together, but as soon as I directly looked at her in the eyes, I knew she was hurting. Could she see the same in mine?

DINNER, as usual, was Chinese food at my mother's favorite restaurant, The Lucky Gato. And it was not real Chinese food, but American Chinese: lots of grease, salt, and shiny sauces. I felt bloated, my ankles swollen, right after. Then we headed back to the apartment for cheesecake and tea. Good thing I had Torture tomorrow or I couldn't forgive myself. There was still a wedding I had to stand for, and a dress I had to fit in.

I sat on my refurbished wing-back chair across from June and Maggie, who were on the couch, twisted together in some canoodling position. They'd been dating since sixth grade. They still seemed very much in love now. I supposed Maggie was lucky to find love at an early age. The older I was, the harder it got. I could barely figure out what was going on with my so-called love life at this stage. I glanced at Mom, wondering if she was still heartbroken for that man who sold her a new set of tires.

Maggie and June were feeding each other cheesecake, which made me think of Levi during the cake-tasting (minus Oh-feel-yah). Gosh, I missed him. I missed the time we had in Paris. I equally missed the little and deep conversations that we shared about the City of Lights. I longed for both his subtle and heart-stopping kisses. And boy, what I would give to wake up next to him again, even though those couple times before had been accidental.

"We best get to bed." Mom jolted me out of my thoughts. "We have an early day tomorrow." She stood and walked straight to my guest bedroom, where she and Maggie would be sleeping.

I gathered the dishes and brought them back to the kitchen. Maggie joined me at the sink, and we washed up, just like back home.

"Thanks for letting him stay," Maggie said, handing me the last dessert plate.

"I wasn't going to kick him out. Where else would he go?"

"Yeah, but I'm still glad you didn't freak. I know I

should have asked when I called, but I was afraid you'd say no." She leaned both elbows against the counter.

"Not likely. I know June. I used to babysit him and May, remember?" I laughed at the memory of little Maggie, May, and June running around my mom's garden in their diapers. "It's nice to see you guys are still going strong."

Maggie glanced back into the living room. "Yeah, he's great." Then she turned her sights back to me. "How about you? Got over Jake?"

I laughed. And laughed. I doubled over, trying to get my bearings back.

"Shoot, are you okay?" Maggie was concerned, probably thinking her older sister had gone mad.

"Yeah, sorry. Sorry." After wiping the tears from my cheeks, I reached for the kitchen chair in the corner. "I guess I haven't talked to you in a while." I recounted the whole wedding thing to Maggie. Needless to say, she was shocked and awed. I did skip the parts with Levi. My heart was still raw, my mind a jumble of confusion.

"Something's missing, Mags. I didn't know it was missing until someone tried to fill it."

I WAS CHECKING out handmade jewelry in a small open-air shop at Ferry Place Market when Maggie sidled up to me with a look of concern on her face.

"Hey, I think you have a stalker."

"Hmmm?" My attention was on a sterling silver cuff with intricate patterns.

"I said, I think you have a stalker," Maggie repeated. I looked up at her, and she pointed to my left. "There!"

I squinted. It was a hot, cloudless summer day. Perfect

day for stalking. "I don't see anything out of the ordinary."
I tuned back to Maggie.

She had a hand on her forehead, blocking her eyes from
the sun. "I think he left. Or maybe he's hiding. I saw him a
few times a while back. I didn't think he was following us
because there were a lot of people here, but he kept staring
at you. Like really staring."

"A man? Staring at me?" Maggie had way better vision
than I did. I tried to focus past the stores and stalls we
passed but still didn't see anything or anyone who stood
out. "What did he look like?"

"Tall. Hot. He was wearing a button-up shirt and jeans,
I think."

I dropped the cuff back on the table and moved away
from the shop, pulling Maggie with me. June and my mom
were looking at some metallic items across the way. "What
do you mean hot? Details." I urged her with a wave of
my hand.

Maggie contemplated before answering, "Hot, like good
looking. I dunno. Brownish hair."

"Long?"

"Ish."

"Beard?"

"Clean-shaven."

My heart started that quick tattoo that often happened
when I thought of a certain someone.

"Sunglasses?"

"Nah, just regular glasses."

I pressed my lips together, letting my mind wander.
Levi didn't wear glasses. "Are you sure?"

Maggie lifted a brow at me. "I think I can tell the
difference between sunglasses and not. Do you
know him?"

Did I? I wasn't too sure. I thought I did. Sure, Levi had

opened up to me while we spent time in France. But he'd been out of my life for more than I was comfortable with. Yet, I couldn't stop thinking of him. That he broke up my one great relationship, one that had promise, and played with my heart while I still ached for Jake?

What could I tell Maggie?

"Should I be worried?" she asked and chewed on her bottom lip.

"Nope. It's probably not even who I think it is." I waved a dismissive hand, but my heartbeat stayed errant. "Mags...was he with someone?" Like a tall, brunette, possibly Victoria's Secret Angel?

"No, just him. Are you sure you're okay? You look a bit flushed." Maggie scrutinized me with her hazel eyes.

Tight-lipped, I didn't reply. I glanced the way she had pointed again, just in case the stranger befitting the description decided to appear once more. No one looked familiar, but as I turned away, the hair on the back of my neck raised and a shiver ran along my spine.

He was here. I could feel him. He was watching me. Why wouldn't he talk to me?

Ignoring my own feelings, I pointed at our mother who was picking up a round item that resembled a shield inside the shop across the way. "We better get Mom away from that." Maggie hurried to them, stopping Mom from paying the man for the shield. Because I was stubborn, I let myself glance back, thinking it wouldn't cause any damage. Wrong.

Even though it had been days since last I'd seen him, I spotted him right away. Levi, in his relaxed strides, was heading my way, looking like a sin I'd like to keep doing over and over again.

"I PANICKED." I heaved into the paper bag again before trapping my phone between my ear and shoulder. "I panicked, so I left. I ran."

Chase groaned on the phone. "Why would you leave?"

"I said I panicked!" Heave. Heave. Heave. "I told Mom and Mags that I had a meeting with a client. I sent them back home because I didn't know how to deal with this."

"You've been waiting to see him all this time, and now that you've finally seen him..."

"I was afraid!"

"What? Why?"

"Hold on, the light changed." I threw the paper bag beside me and pressed on the gas. I tapped on my phone and spoke to Chase wirelessly. "I didn't know what to do. I didn't know what I would say to him. He's been gone for over a week, Chase. Our communication was next to nothing, and I couldn't...just couldn't...I was afraid."

"Of what?"

Sighing heavily, I replied, "I don't know." Lie. I remembered what Isobel told me at the spa, about Levi's involvement in Sandrine and Jake's relationship. I didn't understand why he would do that. I flicked the turn signal and parked in front of my apartment. "I'm afraid, and I don't know how to deal with this. I didn't plan on feeling this much for someone I barely knew. Someone I didn't even like in the first place."

"What are you going to do? You'll see him later this week at the rehearsal dinner, and at the wedding. What's this really about, Nica?"

After turning off my engine, I threw my keys into my purse and unfolded out of the car. "I'll figure it out. I'll be in later tonight. Make sure Jewel doesn't stay too long. We'll need her working overtime at the wedding."

"Where are you?"

"I'm ho—" I couldn't finish my sentence. My breath hitched as I saw Levi standing at my doorstep.

Head down, hair falling on his forehead, his rapt attention was on the phone he had in his hand, swiping his thumb over the screen. Whatever he was staring at caused him to tilt his lips into a crooked smile. That adoring look created a flutter to my stomach, much as it had done before. But I had a feeling of uncertainty in facing him.

With my right toe behind my left foot, ready at the go to pivot and run before he could notice me, I waited. As though he sensed my hesitation, he brought his head up, his hand brushing off the hair that had fallen on his face, and the crooked smile morphed into something tender and full of affection.

His blue eyes sparkled like the clear blue sea reflecting the sun's rays. They revealed more than he might have intended. "Hi." Levi languidly straightened, pocketed his phone, and strode over to me. A quiver on his lips expressed a tinge of something I couldn't put my finger on.

Unsure of what to do, I busied myself by ending my call with Chase. She'd be pissed off about it, but when I explained why she would understand. Fishing in my purse for my keys, I kept my head down. "How do you know where I lived?" I tried to keep my voice steady, and it came out flat and robotic.

I had the keys in my hand, but made no move to open the door. Instead I basked in the heat of his body as he leaned toward me. Avoiding looking him in the eyes this close, I was frightened of the possibility that my own would reveal the chaos running through my head and the mixture of emotions that came with it—affection, jealousy, betrayal, hurt, indignation. Could a person die of too many emotions?

Ever so gently, he cupped the side of my face, making

me tilt my head up, my breath hitching. My eyes shuttered closed as he placed a warm kiss on my lips. I froze at the connection. When he removed his hand, I moved past Levi and unlocked the door to my apartment, afraid to even breathe. Stepping inside, I released the jagged exhale that he tried to steal from me.

"You ran away from me," Levi stated as he followed me in, his voice sounded distant.

The conversation with Isobel was suddenly fresh in my mind, and the most prominent feeling jumped out. The feeling of betrayal. Anger surged through my body, numbing my fingers and toes. I refused to face him. I blurted out a reply, "I was busy with my family."

"Veronica, why did you walk away?"

How could he ask me that? Isobel's revelations had been running through my mind since I saw him at the market. And I couldn't help saying, "You chose her over me." Balling my hands into fists, I challenged him. Levi tilted his head, worry, and confusion on his features. I pushed a lock of hair from my face and stabbed a finger in his chest. "You...Jake met Sandrine because of you. You introduced them." When my eyes met his, I made sure he saw only one emotion. I was livid. He had ruined the perfectly happy relationship I had. "He met her through you."

"Yeah, I heard you the first time." He chuckled nervously, rubbing a hand over his chin. "I was in Paris for business when Jake came. I'd made plans to meet Sandrine, and he came with me."

A laugh spurted out of my mouth, dry and humorless. "I can't believe you did that. We were so happy together."

"Happy? What?" He seemed confused. He took a step forward with a hand stretched out. I stared at it and stepped back. He continued, finally understanding, "Are you insinuating that I had planned to...You're blaming me for your breakup?"

"Yes!" The word was out before I could stop it.

"Now, that's unfair, Veronica." He kept his voice low, but it had an edge to it. Worry lines appeared on his forehead, and his lips pressed into a thin line.

I waved his hand away and closed in on him. "Jake broke up with me because of you. Because you brought her and introduced her to him. And he was happy. With me. We were great together. You took that away." I jabbed my finger at him; tears welled in my eyes.

"I had nothing to do with that." Levi, looking like he was holding onto a very fine line of patience, grabbed hold of my hand and kept it on his chest. His heart thumped madly against my palm. "I was as surprised as you when he decided to pursue a relationship with Sandrine. Don't forget, Veronica, if he was as truly happy as you adamantly claim, he wouldn't have left you. He wouldn't even have looked at another woman if he was as enamored with you as you claimed."

Bile threatened to rise in my throat. "You don't know that." I struggled away from his hold, but I was too weak to fight him off.

He tightened the grasp on my hand and held my body to him with an arm around my waist. "I do know. I've known Jake longer than you have. He's never stayed long with just one woman. If he hadn't met Sandrine, he would have left you eventually. I did you a favor, Veronica."

"And I should thank you?" My voice rose with the rage boiling inside me. All those times we'd spent together, the times I thought I'd finally seen something good in him was peeling away from me. I was broken from Jake, but Levi's betrayal was something I didn't know if I could survive. "So you decided to what? Swoop in and take over for him? Is that what you've been doing with me?"

Complete disbelief colored his expression. "Is that what you really think of me?" He released me like I was on fire and I'd burned him.

Steadying back on my feet, I scoffed. "Please, Levi. We both know what a snake you are." I looked him up and down, judging the man. "You parade around with different women in your arms, night after night, and still, constantly flirt with others."

"Are you calling me a cheat?" I raised my head, challenging him to prove me wrong.

Shock painted his face. His eyes lowered, matching my glares. "You had me fooled."

Me? I fooled him? He was prancing around, acting like my knight in shining armor in Paris. I might have been a damsel in distress, but he wasn't the knight I wanted to rescue me.

He rubbed the nape of his neck. "I never led people to believe I was something I was not. The women I'd been with knew the score. They chose to be with me because of my social standing. They knew the possibilities that could open up for them just by being seen with me."

"Don't be so high on yourself, Levi!"

He smirked. I could almost see a new thought forming in his head. "I get it. All this time, you still have feelings for Jake. You're trotting around with his fiancée planning a wedding, taking everything that's thrown at you in hopes of what? Winning him back? You thought that if you spent more time with him that he'd change his mind? Talk about the pot calling the kettle black. Like I said, Veronica, I was always honest with my women, and I've never tried to steal someone else's fiancée."

I had no rebuttal.

With our back and forth, Levi ended up an inch away from me, and my head was tilted up, his head hung down. His breath tickled my lips. Not one part of our bodies touched, but I felt the sizzle of current running through us. It wasn't the warm, thrilling electricity that I'd felt before. His fire had reached the same level as mine.

He glanced down at my lips, and I trembled at the surprising thought of him kissing me. Wanting him so badly that I was ready to admit defeat. My mind didn't know which way to go. Out of nowhere, I recalled his little dalliance with a flight attendant and blurted it out, "You screwed Sophie on the plane."

My words powered through. It took him a moment to understand what I said. He stepped back from the bite.

"Sophie?" he began, "you think I did what?" He searched my eyes, possibly waiting for me to explain, but I stood my ground. "Next time you're going to accuse me of something, get your facts straight."

"I saw it with my own eyes," I hissed at him, indignant.

"You saw nothing," he gritted out. "What you saw were two people in an embrace. I couldn't have done what you think I did. One, I'm not even Sophie's type."

I scoffed. "Like that's ever stopped you before."

Levi narrowed his eyes at me. "Sophie's been a good friend of mine for a number of years. She and her longtime partner, Charlotte, have been going through artificial insemination for a couple of years. They just found out that she's pregnant. Sophie just happened to be sharing the news with me, and that's what you saw."

I blinked furiously, forcing my mind to replay that exact moment when I'd caught Levi and Sophie in *flagrante delicto*. Had I been wrong? What had I seen? Levi and Sophie in that bathroom, wrapped in an embrace. Had I thought they were kissing?

They were completely dressed. Her head laid on his chest, his arms were around her, her eyes were closed, and...a tear had rolled down her cheek. That was the moment I'd opened the door.

I bit back a gasp at the memory of that embrace. It had been simply that—two people in each other's arms.

I'd surmised Levi as a slithering player, and all this time I'd held my head high, sure of my assumption that he took every chance he could get to bed any woman who threw herself at him. And he possibly had, but I couldn't have known what the deal really was.

Tonight, I had managed to convince myself that he had betrayed me and that he had used me for his own entertainment. I could fault no one but myself. I bit my lip at the probability that I was the one who threw myself at him. I was one of those women who had used him for their own benefit. He'd been nothing but a sweet, gentle, and caring man. Was he right about me?

"I see in your eyes that you've come to your own conclusion. It wasn't my intention to hurt you in any way, in fact, I wanted the opposite, I wanted you to give me a chance. I wanted you to love me just like you did Jake," Levi declared, his voice softening. "Clearly, you're still very much in love with him, but Veronica, you're not the one he wants."

He didn't move. We stood on edge, both of our bodies humming, trembling at everything that had been said. I wanted him to touch me. I wanted him to kiss me, even if it was for the last time. I sucked in a ragged breath as he closed his eyes and turned away.

Levi rubbed his chin, scraping his hand with the stubble on it. "I was wrong about you."

As soon as he left, I went straight to my guest bedroom's tiny closet where a box was hidden. I knelt and pulled it out, lifted the lid, and let the scent of its contents hit me.

I bawled, my head dropping on Levi's overnight bag, the one he had left in my Paris hotel room. It smelled of him. Strong, yet gentle. I pulled out a white button up shirt and inhaled. Undressing, then slipping into his shirt, I crawled onto the bed.

I made a massive miscalculation.

I wanted him.

I loved him.

He'd wanted me.

He'd wanted me to love him.

Our time together was short. Too short. I needed to make things right. I clenched the fabric of his shirt in my hands and thought of ways to get him to give me another chance.

One way or another, I had to return what was rightfully his.

THE REHEARSAL DINNER

*T*he Benjamins opened their beautiful mansion in Pacific Heights for Jake and Sandrine's rehearsal dinner. I'd had one chance to stay in this vast property when Jake and I dated. I loved it then, and it still awed me now.

After parking my car, I took some items from the trunk that I would need for the night.

"Hello, Nica!" Jake's mother greeted me from the portico. "Do you need any help?"

I waved at her while stacking my things. "I'm fine, Mrs. Benjamin."

She didn't listen. She grabbed my purse and the dress I brought to wear tonight. "How many times do I have to tell you to call me Cynthia? Is this what you're wearing tonight? How beautiful!"

"Thank you." It had been an impromptu purchase just two days ago. It was the most expensive dress that I now owned. When I had shown it to Chase, she had agreed that the overpriced dress would be the perfect thing to wear (and wow) on the night that I would come face-to-face with Levi again.

Cynthia directed me to the library where I could store items. After that, I went into the large kitchen where people of all shapes and sizes were running around like maniacs trying to get everything prepared.

I tapped Jewel's shoulder to get her attention away from the tablet she was holding.

"Thank God, you're here!" She handed me the tablet and, in one breath, said, "Flowers just arrived. Mateo and Gerard are setting up the bars, two in the terrace and four in the yard. The lights should have been strung up last night, but they weren't, so that's happening now. I just found out that at least six people are allergic to seafood. And the string quartet just called to say their cellist has the stomach flu."

"Jewel, breathe. You've done a great job. I'll take over. Chase is waiting for you at the office."

Jewel had been working for us since the startup. Chase and I agreed that as soon as we expanded, she would be offered a partnership. But that was a long way off yet, and Jewel still had a lot to learn.

She nodded. "Yes. You're right. Jake asked that you see them as soon as you came in. He and Sandrine are in the parlor."

"Thanks. I'll check in with the chef; then I'll go and see them. Now, go! Bye!" I pushed her toward the door.

The chef assured me that Jewel had told him (at least six times) about the seafood allergy. We both agreed that once those particular guests were informed of certain ingredients, they could stay clear of any food offerings containing seafood.

He let me try some of the hors d'oeuvres, and they were delightful. After checking in with the staff in the terrace and the yard, and knowing that everyone was on schedule, I made my way to the parlor.

"Nica, you're here!" Jake gave me a tight hug as soon as I entered. "Everything looks great."

"It will be, once it's all done. How are you guys holding up? Remember that this is only the rehearsal. A practice for tomorrow." I moved over to Sandrine, who was waiting to greet me as well.

"We know that we are in good 'ands." She turned her eyes away from me and glanced at Jake. The two shared "the look", the one that only a couple who truly understood each other had mastered. "We were wondering if we could talk to you about something."

"Does it have to do with your rehearsal dinner?" They both shook their heads. "With your wedding? With the two of you?"

"No, not exactly," Jake answered. "But Nica, we..."

I stopped him with a raised hand and a warning look. "Jake, you know me. I have to focus on this." I tapped on my tablet, referring to work. "Tonight. Tomorrow night. And only the two of you. Anything else beyond that can wait. I will ask you again: does this thing you need to talk to me about pertaining to anything that I have mentioned?" More head-shaking. "Good. Now, if you'll excuse me, I have to make some calls."

I took my phone out of my jeans pocket as I walked out of the parlor. I had a feeling I knew what they would want to talk to me about, but I didn't have the guts to deal with it at the moment.

Finding the number from my contact list, I connected with the best cellist in the city. This I could handle.

❧

I TRIED to stay hidden for most of the afternoon, and when the first guests started arriving, I was either in the kitchen, in the library, or in one of the four bathrooms on the mansion's first floor. Hidden and still professional. I had a Bluetooth device in my ear to make sure I could keep in touch with the staff, and go to them whenever and wherever they needed me.

I chastised myself in the black and white bathroom by the foyer where I ran the moment Levi arrived. I saw him park his car through the library windows, and step out of the convertible in his signature button-down shirt, dark jeans, and sunglasses.

He looked different. Was that an extra spring in his steps? He seemed happy, calm, and relaxed.

The next time I spotted him was when he greeted and shook hands with one of my sub-contracted staff, Mateo in the backyard by one of the free-standing bars. I didn't even know they'd met before. Their interaction was like watching two old friends chat.

Once I was dressed in my pricey garb and painfully high-heeled shoes, I fixed my hair up into a messy French braid that I once saw on Pinterest, and added pearl studs in my ears. I'd have to let the dress shine. A little mascara, blush and a touch of gloss on my lips and ta-da! I was all set. I'm going to get my man back.

After ensuring that the kitchen and staff were prepped and ready, I searched for Jake and Sandrine. I found them in the library with Jake's parents and told them everything was set.

Jake and Cynthia introduced me to several relatives. Isobel, who had drunk a couple of flutes of champagne, air-kissed me and told me that she loved my dress. Two little girls, the flower girls, and Jake's cousins' daughters, came up to me and also complimented my attire.

"We can rehearse in here, if you'd like, before heading out to greet the masses," I offered Jake and Sandrine. "I'd have to get the rest of the bridal party in…"

"Rehearse? I don't think we need that, do we?" Jake turned to Sandrine. "I thought it was just one of those terms."

Cynthia explained, "Traditionally, yes, we have to figure out what we're supposed to do tomorrow. But Nica, do we really have to?"

All eyes were on me. I swallowed the lump in my throat. Why would they listen to me? I was just the wedding planner. I was just the person responsible for the comfort of every guest attending their wedding, as well as making sure the bride and groom were satisfied. What did I know?

"Well, as long as everyone's clear about what they need to do. We're not following any tradition for the ceremony. As long as Jake and Sandrine have their vows prepared?" The couple nodded. "Chase and I will be around to guide you. I suppose…"

"Good! Let's party!" Jake wrapped an arm around me and kissed the top of my head before leading the group out of the library.

Clients. They could be difficult sometimes. Was it too late to back out of this deal?

While walking toward the terrace and the yard, where most of the guests were already eating and drinking, I chatted with the flower girls, and they assured me that this wasn't their first rodeo. Being the only two little girls in the family, they were asked to do that "job" so often that they'd become "professional flower girls." Good, I had nothing to worry about. Right?

Then why did my heart start to hammer against my chest?

Levi.

Even without trying to look, my sights zeroed in on him as soon as I stepped out. He was standing beside Natalie, a few guys in suits I didn't know, and Trent and Landon.

Natalie had all their attention. She was beautiful and elegant. And tall. She and Levi fit nicely together. There was familiarity whenever they touched—a hand on his upper arm, on his shoulder, on the small of her back, leaning toward each other, the laughter shared. One would think it was their rehearsal dinner.

Jealousy punched through my gut. I looked away when Jake and Sandrine joined their group and went to see Gerard, my bar staff and Mateo's husband, at his station.

"Hey, G, how's the night?" I flattened my hands on the bar.

"Nica, look at you, hot stuff! Mateo told me about the dress. Va-va-voom, honey!" He was pouring a drink for a guest, who I greeted with a silent 'hello' and a nod. When he passed her the drink, she walked away, leaving me with Gerard (and to gripe). "What d'ya wanna drink?"

I shook my head. "No drinks tonight. I have to keep my head straight."

Gerard pursed his lips. "You sure about that?"

"Yup. I am running this show, you know. Who cares if no one listens to what I say? It's just my butt on the line if things go south."

He leaned forward, placing his forearms on the bar. "That's not what I meant. I want to know if it has anything to do with a certain tall, yummy Frenchman?"

I rolled my eyes. "Not you too." Mateo and Gerard were another couple who made relationships look effortless, and in turn, they wanted the rest of their friends, including me, in wedded bliss.

"I met him earlier. Doesn't look like anything to write

home about." Gerard winked, squared his shoulders, and placed a tumbler in front of me.

"Well, since you've snagged Mateo, the rest of us have slim pickings. And, no, he's not the reason why I need to stay sober." He poured an amber liquid in the crystal glass.

Then he passed it to me. "You better change your mind and drink up now..." I raised my chin, shooting an eyebrow up my forehead. He leaned forward and whispered, "because in five seconds, he'll be standing beside you."

Goshdarnit! I reached for the drink and gulped it in one go, puckering my lips as the liquid warmed my tongue and sucking in a hiss when it burned all the way down my throat.

"Veronica." There was no mistaking that voice. I pushed the glass back to Gerard and signaled for another. So much for staying sober.

I slowly turned to the source of that deep, warm, velvety voice. My knees buckled as I realized how close he was, so I gripped the bar for support and stretched my lips into a smile. I wasn't too sure how my voice would sound, so I kept my mouth shut. For now.

"You look—" his eyes traveled over me with a look of unmistakable admiration, making my stomach clench "—amazing. Beautiful."

I curled a lock of my hair and tucked it behind my ear. "Thanks." I glanced at my feet then let my eyes move slowly from his shiny black shoes to his dapper black suit, and then up to his magnificent face. When did he change? "And you...cut your hair—and shaved." There were no signs of those prescription glasses that made him even more appealing.

Levi raked his thick hair with his fingers. "That, I did."

Gerard nudged my drink toward me, and asked Levi what he wanted.

"Scotch, neat." He trained his blue eyes on me. "Make that a double."

Interestingly enough, I noted that Gerard had given me the same drink. Gerard poured him what Levi had asked for, and slid it across the bar.

Levi lifted his drink, and we clinked glasses. The liquid warmed my throat and my stomach, but it didn't squash my anxiety.

I thought I was ready for this. I thought I had prepared enough for the time we met again.

As I let the alcohol warm the rest of my body, I calculated ways to escape this uncomfortable situation. I touched the device that was still stuck in my ear and was about to open my mouth to excuse myself, pretending that I was getting a call when a hand clapped over Levi's shoulder.

"Laurent! I thought I'd find you by the bar." The man grinned at me. "What do we have here?"

I couldn't ignore the lascivious look the other man gave me. I furrowed my eyebrows, but I was still working, and he was a guest, so I plastered my pro-smile on.

The muscles on Levi's jaw tightened. "Monroe, I didn't think you were coming." He crossed his arms over his chest. His entire body was angled in a protective stance, almost blocking me from the guest.

Monroe either ignored Levi's spite, or he wanted to piss him off. He grinned. "And miss Jake's wedding? Nah, man." He pushed past Levi with a hand stretched out to me. "I don't think we've met. I'm Tristan Monroe."

I shook Tristan's clammy hand. "Great to meet you. I'm Veronica, one of the bridesmaids." This information made him grin some more. As I tried to pull my hand away, he ogled my cleavage. "If you'll excuse me, I have to talk to the couple."

Tristan loosened his grip. "Catch you later, Veronica." He winked.

I sent him a polite smile, then turned to Levi, "I'll see you later, Levi."

A muscle in his jaw twitched. "I'll find you." It sounded like a promise. "I'd like to have a quick chat with you." Sure, a quick chat, like we were chums.

I nodded once and started walking. Before I could get away, I overheard Tristan saying, "I heard you're moving back to France for good."

I managed not to trip over my own feet, but my legs had turned to jelly. Too afraid to hear Levi's response, I kept going, fighting the tears from falling down.

Finding my way to the kitchen, I checked in with the staff to see if I was needed. They were too busy to notice that my eyes were red. The chef pushed me away in an instant and ordered me to have fun. Yeah, like that was possible.

My head throbbed. My heart was about to burst. I wanted to be needed, and useful. I didn't want to be just another guest. But between the chef and Jewel, who had returned as per Chase's order, the event was running like a well-oiled machine. I should have been proud of this moment. This was one of my creations. But I was drowning in a different emotion.

I made another stop at a powder room, just so I could stare at myself in the mirror. My cheeks were flushed—most likely from the crying and the alcohol. I'd like to have another if only to dilute the many different things I couldn't stop thinking of. Levi, being at the forefront.

I spread my arms and fanned my underarms—I didn't stink, but I felt I was sweating profusely—when the knob on the door jiggled. Time to move. When I opened the door, Natalie gripped my wrists and pushed me back into the bathroom.

"I've been looking all over for you," she said. "We need to talk."

Yeah, join the club. This night was turning into a let's-all-talk-to-Veronica event. "We do?"

"I went out with Chase last night, and we bumped into your trainer. Did you see Diego this morning?" Her eyes twinkled when he said his name. Diego and Natalie? Why not?

"I did. I had boot camp."

Natalie bit her lower lip before asking, "Did he say anything? About me?"

"I'm..." She looked hopeful. "...sorry, but I was in and out. Should he have?"

Natalie released my wrists and leaned against the marble countertop. "It was just... amazing. He is such a great guy. And he's so beautiful. We spent the rest of the night talking, just talking. Getting to know each other."

"Well, did you exchange numbers and make any more plans to meet?" It was easier to deal with other people's relationship issues because mine was sucking the life out of me.

Natalie turned shy. "He knows where I'm staying." Oh, no she didn't!

"Did you sleep with him last night?" My voice rose.

"No! Well, we...I asked him to come up for a nightcap. We talked a lot. Made out a little. The sun was starting to rise when he left." No wonder Diego wasn't so peppy during this morning's boot camp class. "So, he didn't say anything?"

"Natalie, I don't know what to say. He's my boot camp trainer. I go in, and he kicks my butt, then I leave. I didn't even know you guys were together last night. I would have asked."

She nodded, but she looked worried. "No, I understand."

"What did you tell him?"

"We talked about everything. I told him about work, about Paris, about possibly going back to Doctors Without Borders again."

Diego didn't believe in long distance relationships. I was about to impart that information when the door handle jiggled again. There were three other bathrooms on the first floor and three more elsewhere in the house!

"We better go out there. Jake and Sandrine have to do their speech. I'll talk to him tomorrow," I promised her, although, I didn't know how my talk could possibly affect his decision.

"Veronique? Are you in there? I can 'ear you." It was Sandrine on the other side of the door. I opened it for her, and she jumped in, locking the door behind her. "Oh, Natalie, good, you are 'ere too!"

"I think we can talk outside," I commented, but both Natalie and Sandrine grabbed my arms. Was I being initiated into some kind of secret sisterhood? "Or, we can talk here."

"You can't go out there yet," Natalie said.

"Not until you let us say what we need to," Sandrine added.

This could take forever, so I sat on the padded bench against the wall. "Alright, talk. What's up?"

The two friends stared me right in the eyes. "Did you think about what I said? About Levi and giving 'im a second chance?"

"What?" I looked at the two of them, sure that they'd

gone crazy. Or, it might be a French thing. "I'm not going to..."

"No, Veronique, you must tell me." Although she said the words hurriedly, she sounded very concerned.

"I..." I turned to Natalie, then to Sandrine. "I can't talk to you guys about this, about him. You're his cousin." I pointed at Sandrine, then switched to Natalie. "And you're his ex." And back to the bride again. "This is your rehearsal dinner. People are waiting out there for you. Levi and I can wait."

Although I liked Sandrine, and Natalie was pleasant company, they weren't the people I needed to talk to about my heart breaking into pieces.

"But..." they both started.

I stopped them immediately. "Please. It's simply not the time." I heard a beep in my ear, and it took me a few seconds to realize someone was calling me. "Hold on. I have a call... Veronica."

"We need you out here," Jewel said. "The parents are about to give their speech, but we can't find the bride."

I stared at Sandrine. "She's with me. We'll be right out." I signed off. "Natalie, Sandrine, it's really great that you're both concerned, but tonight is not the right time, nor tomorrow. Whatever it is I have to deal with, I'll deal with it in my own time, and with Levi."

They opened their mouths to speak, but I didn't let them. "Please."

Sandrine nodded. "You're right, of course, you're right. I'm sorry." She sighed and leaned over to hug me. Natalie joined in on the hug.

The three of us filed out of the bathroom afterward, garnering a questioning look from a passing server.

Sandrine joined Jake and his parents on the terrace, and Natalie hooked her hand around my arm and grinned like we were besties. During their speeches, I scanned the crowd, and like a magnet to true north, my eyes fell on Levi standing by Gerard's bar. As though he'd waited for me to return. Back to him. I couldn't see his facial expression from afar, and I was hoping he couldn't see mine.

The longer I stared at him, the faster my heart beat, and the tighter my core clenched. My mind urged me to pretend he wasn't there, but I couldn't, particularly when he started making his way to where I stood, never once taking his eyes away from me.

The applause broke the trance of his gaze. I released a shaky breath, clapped, and sauntered back into the house. I told the chef I was retiring for the night to prepare for tomorrow's big event. I called Jewel and informed her of the same, and asked her to let the couple know I'd left.

I'd had enough for tonight. My false confidence to face Levi was simply that. False. And if...when...when he left...no, I couldn't think about that. Not yet. Lips trembling, hands shaking, I unhooked the device on my ear while I walked to the library to gather what I'd brought with me. Among them was Levi's bag.

My heart fluttered as I picked up my bag that contained my clothes and personal items and slung the strap over my shoulder. I could just leave his here. I hadn't checked for tags, but someone was bound to find it and figure out that it belonged to Levi.

I warred with myself. It was a simple move, a simple decision. I owed it to myself to at least do it in person. Getting over him, once he left, would be difficult. Couldn't I hold onto something of his for a little longer? Something to remember him by? But I didn't want to just remember him. I wanted more than just memories. He wanted me. I wanted him. Why couldn't it be as easy as that? I picked up the bag and felt the heaviness of it in my hand, a heaviness that I felt all the way to my chest.

When I opened the library door, there he was, muttering to himself and seemingly lost in thought. Levi paused his soliloquy when his brooding eyes reached mine. I closed the door behind me, tugged and adjusted the strap of my bag. Holding onto it like an anchor.

"You're leaving." He might have meant it as a question, so I nodded. So was he.

"You left this." His eyes dropped to the leather bag I'd brought. "I've meant to return it to you." He made no move to take it, only continued to stare at it. "You left it in my hotel room...in Paris. I stuffed everything you owned in there." This was harder than giving Jake the breakup box.

I brought it up higher, and he reached for it. His hand covered mine over the handle. That zing to my center was back, in full force. Levi electrified me.

My body trembled. I tried to slide my hand away and let him take the bag, but he held me tighter.

In a faltering voice, I said, "It might be of good use when you leave for France." Tears threatened to escape my eyes, but I held it in and steadied myself.

"Veronica..."

"Please take it." My lips quivered. His half-lidded eyes darted on them. He knew what this was doing to me. He had to know. This was causing me pain. He knew what I had overheard. He knew what it could mean to us.

When he freed my hand from his grasp—enough to hold on to the bag—he lowered his head, and looked down at his feet. "Thank you," he said in an apologetic tone. "I'd completely forgotten about it. Thanks for bringing it back."

A breathy, "Yeah," was all I could muster.

"Veronica, I just want to say..." He rubbed the back of his head before bringing his gaze up. His eyes were the bluest I'd ever seen them. It would be easy to get lost in them, to pretend that we had a chance. To think that he would change his plans for me, to be with me. "What I want to say is..."

"What? What do you want to say?" I didn't want to sound angry, or hurt, but I was, and it took him by surprise.

"I'm sorry." Levi paused to bite down on his lip, and work his jaw with one hand, but he didn't take his gaze from me. "I'm sorry for the stupid things I've done. For that time with Ophelia. For leaving you in Paris. For not having the guts to talk to you sooner." I wished he'd stop talking now. My fragile nerves started to fail. "I want you to know that I appreciate everything that you've done, and for putting up with me these past weeks." He laughed, mirthlessly, but his eyes lit up. My chest tightened at that sight. At him. At the honesty in those blue depths. "You've been very patient with me, even when I didn't deserve it."

"Yeah, well, part of my job." I hadn't meant to say it, but I couldn't take it back. "I better get going. Big day tomorrow. I'll see you?" I knew I would, but like everything else—how much I felt for him and what exactly he thought of me—I wasn't too sure.

I motioned toward the door, at the same instant he stepped toward me, grazing my arm with the tips of his fingers, causing goosebumps to rise on my skin. With a pleading gaze, I begged of him to let go. My pulse thrummed in my ear. My heart skipped a beat. He dipped his head, down to mine, and his lips touched the edge of my lips.

So softly...

So tenderly...

I closed my eyes as I inhaled his scent—committing it to memory—together with the feel of his lips, and the warmth of his body this close to mine.

This close I could feel the rise and fall of his chest.

This close I could hear the tremor of his heart.

He ghosted his lips along the line of my cheek, stopping just below my ear. I tilted my head, granting him more access. With his fingers, he curled the hair that had loosened from my braid as he silently...

...and deeply inhaled.

In a gravelly, trembling voice that would shatter me for eternity, Levi breathed out, "Sweet Veronica."

My heart exploded. I was filled with hurt. Pain. Love. And affection. I forced myself to back away from him, as the tears rolled down my cheeks, and whispered, "Goodbye."

THE BIG DAY

I parked my car right outside a heritage building, where Chase stood waiting on the front steps. She ran over when I looked up with tear-soaked eyes, and practically ripped the door open to get to me.

Even though I thought I didn't have any tears left, they wouldn't stop pouring out. And she just let me ugly cry on her shoulder.

She didn't make any snarky comments. She didn't offer any words of comfort. She didn't have to say anything.

Once I quieted down, Chase said she would drive me home. It was for the best, considering I could barely keep my eyes open from the heaviness. When we arrived, Chase walked me to my bedroom and helped me into a sleep shirt. She led me to my bathroom, and while I stood there like a mindless zombie, she brushed my teeth for me and dabbed my face with a wet cloth. I was exhausted like I'd been sucked dry.

Tomorrow would be the end of it all. Jake and Sandrine would be married. They'd go off on their month-long honeymoon. And Levi...he'd walk out of my life, and I'd find a way to move on.

I'd been through this before, and I thought my heart would be used to it by now. But it wasn't. Tonight, before I left, he had to do that. He had to make me feel again.

"Get some rest. Don't worry about getting to the club early tomorrow. We don't have to go to the gym. Diego knows." Chase undid my messy braid, and untangled my hair with her fingers. "I'll take care of everything. You can trust me on that." This was why I had her in my life, as my best friend. She understood. "I'll sleep in the other room. If you need me, you know where I'll be." Before she stood, she hugged me through the blanket.

I nodded and closed my dried-out eyes, hoping that when I woke up, I would find that everything had only been a senseless dream.

I DRIPPED the eye drops into my eyes, blinked a couple times, and replaced my glasses. I'd forgotten to take out my contacts the previous night, in addition to all the crying, and my eyes had suffered.

Hopefully, the makeup artist could do better with the red splotches on my face and dark circles under my eyes than I had. The used tea bags I placed on them while Chase drove us to the club hadn't made much difference.

The theme of this afternoon's event was old Hollywood glam with a Parisian flair. Glitz, glamor, gorgeous. With a hundred or so flower arrangements placed strategically inside and outside the tents, the glint of ten crystal chandeliers hanging above the square tables covered with purple silk cloths, the gold chivari chairs with purple velvet upholstery surrounding them, and the elegant stage—

which would hold the eleven-piece big, sound band—in front of the dance floor, the reception area was close to completion. I could have been a vindictive ex, listened to Isobel and sabotaged the event, but I would never be able to live with myself if I chose that path. I stood at the back and admired my handiwork. I was good. No, I was great. I was a fantastic wedding planner, giving the couple just the fairy tale wedding they wanted. Any other time, I would have been ecstatic about my creation, but it served as a symbol of more heartbreak to come. When would I get my happily ever after?

I heaved out a sigh. This wedding was going to happen. This wedding would go on even without my presence. Run. Run before you see him. I rubbed my temples in a futile attempt to erase the thought.

❦

MY PHONE BUZZED on the counter as soon as I zipped my dress up. I leaned forward to check who was calling. It was Chase.

"What's up?" I answered, bypassing the cheery greeting.

"I need you. Come down to the kitchen." An unusual panic laced her voice.

"Leave Chef Laupin alone, Chase."

"It's not him. Just come down, okay?" She signed off.

After replacing my flats with the new gold peep-toe Louboutin's Sandrine had given her bridesmaids and MOH, I hurried to see why Chase wanted me. I stopped short when I saw the older, yet still, quite a good-looking man standing beside her.

"Monsieur Saint-Croix?"

Chase sighed with relief. "So, he is Sandrine's dad."

"Is Madame Saint-Croix with you?"

The man hurriedly shook his head. "*Non,* she is back 'ome in Paris. I couldn't possibly miss my only daughter's wedding. I will deal with Vivienne when I return." He squared his shoulders.

I smiled widely at him. "I see you've dressed for the part." My eyes wandered over his tuxedo-clad form. Even at his age, he could give the single men in the party a run for their money. "How about I take you to your daughter?"

"*Oui,* that would be lovely." He turned to Chase and nodded once. "*Merci, mademoiselle.*"

We walked arm-in-arm out of the kitchen, swerving around staff until we reached one of the smaller back rooms that the club had allowed us to use for the bride's preparations. I smiled at François before knocking lightly on the door and opening it a smidgen.

Sandrine, beautiful as ever, sat languidly on a chair facing the window. The train of her gown pooled around her feet. Natalie stood beside her, pinning the vintage veil on Sandrine's hair. A click sounded from the photographer's camera.

"How are things here?" They all turned to me, as I slowly slipped inside, still holding onto the door.

"Ah! Look at you, Veronique! So lovely."

"Thanks. And you, wow, I've never seen a bride more beautiful." I smiled at the photographer. "May I have a moment with Sandrine?"

"Yeah." She looked at her camera. "I have quite a bit here. I'll go see the groom again." She signaled to her assistant, and they both gathered their kits and left the room.

Now, for Natalie. I looked at her with pleading eyes.

"Oh, me too. Yeah, of course." Thank God, she was smart. She leaned down to place a kiss on Sandrine's cheek and muttered a few words in French. I hoped she'd keep quiet when she saw François outside the door.

I lifted my index finger, gesturing for her to wait, then opened the door wider to let the father of the bride in.

Sandrine let out an audible gasp, her hand flying to cover her gaping mouth. Mr. Saint-Croix had tears in his eyes.

"Papa!" Sandrine stood and opened her arms wide to welcome her father.

I stepped out of the room, leaving father and daughter alone to have their moment.

I leaned against the closed door upon realizing that I would never have such moment with my Dad on my wedding day. If I ever had a wedding day.

❧

"GIVE IT TO ME." Chase stretched an upturned hand to me. "You don't need that. I've got it all covered." I hesitated. "Nica, trust me. If not, trust Jewel." We both glanced at Jewel, who was being followed by Trent and Landon.

I averted my gaze, knowing full well that Jake and Levi were right behind. I plucked the earpiece from my ear, gave it to Chase, and pouted.

"Why the pout, Nica?" Jake wrapped an arm around me. "It doesn't become you."

"Because she's no longer in control." Chase showed the Bluetooth device to Jake, grinning wickedly. She twisted on her heel. "All right, ladies and germs, it's show time!"

Jake gave me a little shake. "C'mon, Nica, cheer up! I'm getting married today." I rolled my eyes at him but offered a weak smile. He leaned down to whisper, "You've done a fantastic job. I will forever be grateful." Then he kissed my temple before taking his spot.

A warm breeze whispered past me, and I felt the jolt of electricity from the person that brought the warmth. Levi sent a surreptitious smile my way as he joined Jake. It was so fleeting I had no time to look away, but it had been enough to affect me. My legs turned gelatinous. He was so handsome. Dapper. World-class heartbreaker.

Chase touched the side of her ear, spouting off orders, "Cue music... Men, move your asses."

Not exactly how I'd word it, but her way worked. The men lined up and strutted down the aisle. I forced my eyes to stare somewhere other than at the best man.

He was tempting in that tux. All I had to do was close my eyes, and I could see him clearly, just as I'd seen him when he tried it on at the tailors in Paris. I kept my eyes closed as the memory of our wonderful time together clouded my mind.

Chase forced me out of my daydream, calling my name, "Nica, your turn, babe."

Clutching the bouquet in my hand, I walked down the petal-strewn aisle, smiling sweetly, and staring straight at the officiant. Only at the officiant.

I stood on my spot on the right-hand side of the altar, facing the guests, and watched Isobel strut down the aisle, followed by Natalie. The two equally beautiful women stood at their places beside me. I took a furtive step forward, so I could get a better view of Sandrine. There was a uniform gasp when she came out with her father. Heads turned, all eyes were on them, on her. Her eyes were directed only at her groom.

There was a niggling that I always felt when I thought someone was watching me. Taking a chance, I glanced toward the opposite side of the altar and sucked in a sharp breath when I found Levi gazing at me with unbridled interest. I blinked away when the officiant spoke, and refocused on the wedding at hand, ignoring the numbness in my fingers and toes and the rapid tattoo of my tired heart.

When the officiant asked the crowd if anyone thought the couple should not wed, I stiffened. How peculiar the way life had me turned around.

Just a little over a month ago, I'd been wishing that it was me standing beside Jake. That this would have been my wedding (although, a lot smaller, more intimate, and less extravagant). That I would have been the one saying 'I do.'

Thinking of that now, everything felt surreal. My relationship with Jake had felt like a prelude to something more promising, something real and tangible. Through my lashes, I glanced at Levi.

There was serenity on his face. The corners of his lips twitched up slightly, and a secret smile reached all the way to his eyes. Was he thinking of someone? A happy memory perhaps? Was he thinking of me?

His eyes darted to me as if I had called his name aloud, and because I didn't know what to do with myself when he looked at me like that, I lowered my gaze and studied the sparkling crystals on my shoes. I was such a coward.

"The couple has prepared their own vows," the officiant said, and took a half step back, as Jake and Sandrine faced each other.

Jake spoke first. "My darling, Sandrine, my light. You came into my life when I was unprepared, and you brought clarity, peace and pure love into my heart. I promise to cherish you and love you until I take my last breath. I cannot promise you a life that is perfect, but I promise you that I will strive hard for it. Sandrine, my love, my beauty, my all, this I vow."

His words should have hurt. It would have caused me a

great deal of pain if I hadn't agreed with him. Somewhere along the way, I'd figured out that he didn't belong to me, that we hadn't been right for each other. And I was happy to witness him marry the woman who *did* own his heart.

"*Mon amour*, Jacob..." Sandrine inhaled, pressing her lips together as her eyes watered. She spoke in French, words that were so beautiful that I wished I understood. But from the look in Jake's eyes, he did. The words were meant for him and no one else. She finished off in a slightly shaky voice, "I vow to love you forever and always."

I daintily brushed the tears off my face. I didn't doubt— not now and not after experiencing what I had with them; they would fight adversity—together until the end. They would fulfill their promises to each other, loving one another every step of the way.

Jake and Sandrine accepted rings from each other and sealed their vows with a kiss. The officiant declared them 'husband and wife', and the guests stood and applauded. Shutters from cameras clicked everywhere.

Even though my mind was full of cluttered thoughts, I was pleased. If it hadn't been for this moment, for Jake and Sandrine, I wouldn't have experienced the indifference that morphed into desire and lust, which blossomed into love.

The newlyweds walked hand-in-hand as their witnesses hooted and hollered and threw petals and heart-shaped confetti in the air. Levi offered his arm to Natalie. Although I knew who Natalie ached for, I couldn't fight off the green-eyed monster within. And I wondered if Levi had walked down that aisle with me, would we have looked as perfect and as happy?

As I curved my hand in Trent's arm, with Levi in my thoughts, I replied to my own question: a resounding 'yes', and walked with my own secret smile.

THE SPEECH

I massaged the skin in front of my ears and along my jaw line as I claimed a spot on a bench under a mature weeping willow tree, slipped my shoes off my feet, and rubbed my aching calves. It seemed Louboutin stilettos weren't the best footwear on grass.

The photographer, Roan, her assistants, and the videographer wanted photos of only the newlyweds in another part of the garden, thus, giving the rest of us time to recover. The two flower girls had been given their passes to return to their parents. Lucky girls!

Jewel drove in one of the golf carts to bring us much-needed refreshments. By now, the wedding guests would have proceeded to the separate cocktail-hour areas we'd placed around the main tent, or in the rotunda of the main club building, enjoying delicious canapés and choices of three customized drinks for the event.

"Did you have the tartare?" Jewel asked when she approached me, carrying a tray of champagne flutes.

"Hmmm, yeah, so good...what were those chips?"

"Taro chips. Laupin's a genius. Champagne?" she asked, handing me a flute.

I shook my head. "Nah. Gotta keep my head straight. Did you bring water?" She nodded. "How's Chase doing?"

Jewel rolled her eyes, and for a second, let her shoulders sag. "Freaking out because she can't drink or make out with anyone." We both chuckled. "She's really taking this seriously. We don't want you worrying about anything, and you shouldn't."

"I'm not." Disbelief was written all over her face. "I'm not!"

"You're not what? Oh, champagne!" Natalie grabbed one of the flutes and sat beside me.

"So thirsty." I gave Jewel a puppy-dog pout. "Water please?"

"'kay, I'll grab it." As she walked toward the cart, Isobel stopped her to grab one of the crystals from the tray before making her way to us.

Scooching aside, Natalie cleared space for her on the bench. "What up, bitches?" Isobel chugged the champagne, settling on the spot.

"Someone's thirsty." Natalie laughed.

"When is this photo shoot going to end? I think I dislocated my jaw with that last shot." Isobel rubbed her cheeks, opening and closing her jaw.

I knew why she was antsy. I happened to trip over her and her new boyfriend making out in a corridor inside the club earlier. She wanted to return to her new 'baby love'. His name eluded me. All I remembered was that he was young, good-looking, probably rich, and horny.

"Won't be long now," I replied, sagging against the bench. Not very lady-like.

From my vantage point, I watched Levi approach Jewel.

She titled her head back, laughing at something he said, and he took the two bottles of Perrier she offered.

Levi joined Jake's parents and cousins and François by the large pond and handed Sandrine's father one of the bottles. While they continued their conversation, he stole a glance in my direction. Keeping in mind that there were three people sitting on this bench, one of whom was his model-esque ex-girlfriend, I ignored the stammering inside my chest. He nodded a reply to what François said, slipped his phone from his pocket, and made a call.

"You must be exhausted." Natalie tapped my arm, garnering my attention. "I don't even know what time you left last night."

"Much earlier than you guys did. I had to be here first thing this morning."

"Yeah, and I can see how much work you've done. You like your job, huh? It really shows."

I beamed at her. "I wouldn't be doing it if I didn't like it. That's for sure. Do you like being a doctor?"

She leaned back and rested her hands on her lap. "I do."

"You've always wanted to be a doctor then?" I was resigned to trying to understand how Levi's mind worked, and if I could do that by asking his ex a few questions, then so be it. Only, I had to make sure I did it with finesse.

"My father was a doctor. I wanted to follow in his footsteps, regardless of how much my mother hated it."

"She did?" If I'd decided to become a doctor, my mother would have announced it to the entire world! But science and I did not meet eye-to-eye.

She lifted the corners of her lips and nodded. "Absolutely. I grew up with Sandrine. Our mothers are, were best of friends. They're not anymore. Long story." She rolled her eyes and waved away whatever thought she had. "They both believed that all we needed were to keep

our looks and figure intact and marry rich, powerful men."
Much like Levi.

"Trophy wives? Well, you are beautiful. Ever thought of modeling?"

Natalie scoffed. "I did it in my teens. I was terribly bored. I did it to appease my mother. Some of the girls were nice and sweet, but others partied too much, got into drugs, and had way too much sex with wealthy men old enough to be their fathers. I got yelled at too often for eating real food during shoots or before shows. Sandrine did it too, for a year, for the same reason, and quit when I did."

I pressed my lips together before continuing my interrogation. I eyed Isobel, who was keenly focused on her cell phone. "I guess that's how you met Levi?"

Natalie's smile stretched wider. "I was wondering when you'd ask." She stared at him across the expanse of grass. "I didn't meet Levi until after med school. My mother introduced us. I knew he was Sandrine's cousin, but I never really saw him before. He spent most of his childhood at his grandmother's and boarding schools. Then he moved here to the States. He doesn't like living in France much." Then why was he moving back? I wanted to ask the question, but we were interrupted by the very person who was the topic of our conversation.

"Excuse me, ladies. Sorry to interrupt." Levi had his phone pressed against his ear. I didn't even notice he had made his way over, which was weird since lately, all I'd been too keenly aware of was him. He sent me an apologetic look and turned to Natalie to ask, "Nati, seven p.m. takeoff on Tuesday fine with you?"

It was always shocking to hear him talk around me. The times I'd thought of him and of the things he had said to me before, I'd often imagined a different timbre in his voice. My memories did not do it justice. It was smooth and as tempting as melted dark chocolate.

I tried to ignore his words, but couldn't help feel that kick of jealousy. He had called her Nati, a nickname only those closest to her would have used. Like how he had called me his "Sweet Veronica." There was a punch in my gut. Were they leaving together? Back to France? On Tuesday?

The restriction in my chest tightened.

"That's good. Is François flying at the same time?" Natalie asked. Levi gave her a curt nod, then returned his attention to his phone as he walked behind the bench.

Roan saw the three of us sitting on the bench. I could tell she appreciated the background of the rich greenery and sparkles from the pond. She waved Trent, Landon and Levi over to stand behind us.

I slipped my shoes back on, sat straight and pressed my lips together. Even smiling was too much work. The other two girls kept their relaxed posture. I felt a presence behind me. By the way, my skin hummed, I knew it was Levi.

❧

THE TAP on the microphone brought my eyes to the podium. Levi was setting up for his best man's speech. I leaned back in my seat, trying to make myself invisible, too weak to let myself to even catch glimpses of him.

As he spoke, I could almost picture him. By the glazed expressions of most of the women—and some men—in the crowd, and the timbre of his voice, he had full-on charm.

I couldn't help but smile at his anecdote of the first time he met Jake and had gotten into a minor fight with him.

"Finally, I'd like to share a little bit of poetry..." The women swooned. A handsome guy who read poetry, how could women resist? "I don't want to screw this up, so earlier, I wrote it down."

The rustle of paper made me take a peek. As I did, Levi unfolded a small note on the podium, then reached into his pocket, brandishing a pair of glasses—not sunglasses—and pushed them high up on the bridge of his nose. Could he look any sexier?

Levi cleared his throat, and his lips spread into a megawatt grin. "This is from the famous artist and writer, Khalil Gibran:

LOVE ONE ANOTHER,
>   *but make not a bond of love:*
>   *Let it rather be a moving sea*
>   *between the shores of your souls."*

CUE WOMEN SIGHING. Levi reached for his champagne and raised it. "To two special people in my life, who have found and completed each other, Jake...Sandrine, salut!"

I raised my own flute and took a small sip of the champagne. Jealousy stabbed at me—not for Jake finding Sandrine, but the two of them finding and completing each other.

I found myself asking once again, *Where was my happily ever after?*

❧

ONCE THE GUESTS were invited to the dance floor, I took the chance to find a little escape. I walked into the bathroom.

Several guests stopped me and told me how pretty I looked. I didn't know any of them, but they assumed I was important.

"Care to dance?" Levi's question came from behind.

My lips parted when I quietly inhaled, afraid he would know right away that I was quaking in my shoes. My eyes widened at Jewel, who hadn't warned me that he was approaching. I captured my bottom lip between my teeth as I turned. His right palm was upturned as an offer for me to take it.

"Dance?" I looked beyond him at the dance floor. The band was playing a quick-tempo French song I didn't know.

I was tired and depressed, but curiosity got the best of me. I could vaguely recall him dancing that one time we had gone to the club—and promptly after, I had ended up in bed with him—nor had I seen him hit the dance floor during any of the events that I had planned, and he had attended.

"I guess one dance won't hurt." I tried for a smile, but my lips wouldn't cease quivering.

"Nica, your purse?" Jewel grabbed my clutch from me.

"Thanks."

I took Levi's hand, and he led me to the middle of the floor. As soon as Levi stopped and faced me, the song changed. A rendition of Marvin Gaye's *Let's Get It On* played.

Levi chuckled under his breath. If I wasn't so nervous, I would have too.

"Something funny?" I asked instead.

"I love this song," he stated, his eyes twinkling.

" Did you request it?"

He chuckled again. "No. I did ask if they could do a Salt

N Pepa cover, but it wasn't their thing. Relax, Veronica. It's just a dance."

Yeah, right, like I could relax when the dance involved him this close to me.

He placed one of my hands over his left shoulder, and his left hand warmed the small of my back. The fingertips of his other hand whispered over my left arm, and the resulting tickle caused me to lift it. Then he tucked that hand over his.

Our bodies were pressed against each other, but not as tightly as he'd probably wanted (judging by the way he was trying to pull me in closer). I steadied my breathing and stared at the boutonnière on his lapel to avoid his dreamy eyes.

We weren't moving much, but by the way he swayed his hips, I could tell the man had hidden talents. If only I could relax and just let him lead...

"Ready?" His sudden question had me looking up into his clear blue eyes. Yup, they were dreamy.

"For what?"

Levi quirked his lips into a grin. "Turn." He moved his hand from my back to the side of my hip, and with a nudge of his right hand, he made me rotate on my feet. My arms extended as I swung out.

I gasped and hadn't recovered when, with a quick flick of his right hand, he pulled me back into his arms. My behind ended up pressed against his front. My arms were tangled with his over my stomach. Our fingers were intertwined.

My legs had turned to jelly from the quick turn, or from the man —I wasn't quite sure. I instinctively leaned against him, convincing myself I had done it for support.

Levi changed his position, moving a leg forward between my legs. He tightened his arms around my stomach and splayed a hand over my hip. I could feel him against my backside as he undulated his hips.

White hot desire scorched within me.

I was dizzy with lust. I leaned my head on his shoulder, and Levi nuzzled my exposed neck. If he didn't stop, I would be tempted to rip his shirt off, push him down on the floor, and give the wedding guests a show they would never forget.

Levi's parted lips made their way up my neck and behind my ear. His hot breath scorched my skin and left me breathless.

I wanted him to stop, but I was doubtful that he would hear me, or that I would be able to form any words at all. All I could hear was the thumping of his heart and the whooshing of blood into my head. I silently pleaded for the self-control I had lost.

Levi took a deep breath, inhaling my scent. "God, Veronica, the things you do to me." He nipped at the edge of my ear, causing ripples of painful desire all over my body.

And he was the one to accuse me of the things I did to him?

I somehow managed to turn around and face Levi. My eyes focused on his lips. The world around me blurred. Levi and I ceased swaying. We just stood there, holding onto each other.

Kiss him!

Sighing out loud, I whispered, "I can't." I brought my eyes up to his. My lips held his gaze. He looked worried, unsure, afraid. "I just can't."

There were things I had to say, things I wanted him to hear and understand. My practiced discipline returned, and the noises and sounds around us came back.

"Veronica, don't." He kept my hands in his, pressing

them against the thumping of his chest. "Stay a little bit longer."

I could have asked him the same thing.

This wasn't the time nor the place. This was his best friend and his cousin's—my friends'—wedding. There were too many people around us. Too many questioning and curious looks. Too many witnesses to my impending heartbreak. I pulled my hands from him and stepped back. I sidestepped around the other people dancing, as I once again walked away from Levi.

❦

WITH ONLY THE moon to light my path, I made way to a small, hidden garden, taking off my shoes and carrying them with me along the way. The stone path was covered with arches of Pierre de Ronsard roses, which led to a lone wooden bench.

Sighing with relief as I sat, I steadied my breathing and listened to the ripples of water in the small pond facing the garden. In the quiet, my insight was clearer. It was about time I gathered up my courage—grew a backbone, as Chase said—and let Levi know how strongly I felt for him, regardless of his plans for departure, regardless of the ache he would inflict upon me.

I fiddled with the hem of my dress as I ran the words through my head, picking the right ones to say. I would have to tell him tonight, after Jake and Sandrine's sendoff. I sighed and promised myself: Levi would know how I felt, but I would not ask him to stay.

A soft breeze whistled past carrying the scent of roses. I hugged myself against the chill, but it stayed even as the breeze died down.

Under the clear night sky, as stars twinkled and the

moon shone, Levi stepped forward, with his hands fisted at his sides. His hooded eyes beckoned. My heartbeat sped as I waited for him to reach me.

This was the chance I had waited for, and this time, there was no running away.

THE SENDOFF

*H*is stride was slow and deliberate. His main objective was right in front of him: Me.

With shaky legs, I stood and waited for it to happen.

From a distance, I could hear the band play Etta James' *At Last*.

When he reached me, I breathed him in, much as I did when we were dancing. My memories of his scent had been lacking. Levi smelled more delicious, more achingly appealing, more masculine, sweeter yet sexier.

I dared not look him in the eyes as he pressed his whole body against my own. Shivers ran down my spine and heat flowed throughout my veins.

Levi's hands cupped the back of my head, and he threaded his fingers through my hair, making my head tilt back, and my lips part.

"Veronica." His voice was as soft as the wind, whispering a sigh against my lips, pleading.

I gazed into his azure eyes, and with the rays of the moonlight that slipped through the small spaces of the rose arch, I could see his pupils dilate, and I let myself get lost in them.

Levi whispered my name once more before his lips covered mine.

It was a kiss that claimed. An all-consuming, primal connection. A passionate caress. A touch full of promises.

My skin hummed. Desire flooded my mind.

I felt light-headed, dizzy from his spell, dependent only on the breaths we both shared. My hands reached for him of their own accord, tugging at everything that would deepen our connection—the collar of his shirt, the nape of his neck, the hair that curled around his ears.

I wanted more. I needed more. It was as though without him life would cease to continue.

Levi trapped my bottom lip between his lips, and his teeth nibbled lightly at it, causing a jolt of electricity down to my core before he let go.

Our labored breathing was in tune with the hammering of both our hearts.

I kept grasping at his shirt, afraid that if I didn't, my legs would fail me and I would fall flat on the ground.

My eyes were still closed as he nuzzled my nose with his, as he spoke against my lips, "You have no idea how much I've been aching to do that. My sweet Veronica, I have thought of you for so long."

I let out a choked sob. How could he say that, knowing that our time together would soon end? This little piece of heaven would soon cease to exist.

My head shook. "But you're leaving." I was afraid to open my eyes, afraid that I would see the truth in them.

Levi sighed, and once again, he kissed me. This time, his lips were softer, a simple caress against mine. "I thought I was."

My eyes popped open, and I found him searching mine. "What do you mean? Last night, I heard Tristan say..."

"I know what you heard." He touched my cheek with the back of his hand. Instinctively, I leaned against it. "And up until yesterday, my decision to leave was final. Then I saw you..."

A pained look replaced his emotions. "And you said goodbye."

I moved my hands down to his chest, feeling the errant thumping underneath.

"I thought it was the right decision. Every time I thought I'd see you, my heart filled with anticipation. And each time I did, all I received was cold indifference."

"You could hardly fault me for that," I protested.

"I know. I blame no one but myself." Levi scoffed at his own words. "That first time I saw you after Paris, I saw the change in you. It was so clear to me that you'd moved on. You didn't need me. You didn't want me. And I wanted to get away from that. I wanted distance from you because I felt there wasn't a chance I could ever be with you."

"With me?" My voice faltered.

"With you. To kiss you." He pressed his lips against mine. "To touch you." His hands feathered over my arms, creating a sizzle all the way down to the tips of my fingers and my toes. "To love you."

My heart swelled at those last words.

Levi cupped my face, making me lift my eyes to his. Not only did I see intensity, I saw hot passion, pure desire, and unfettered honesty.

"I love you, Veronica. I have ever since the first time I saw you."

He smiled against my lips.

"You can't possibly, Levi."

"I can. I have, and I do. Veronica, I meant every word I

said in Paris about wanting you to love me. I can't pretend to know how you feel about me, but know that what I feel now is what I've felt for a very long time."

"I..." My legs weakened more from his proclamation. "I have to sit down." Everything around me felt real: his touches, the smell of roses, the distant sound of music. But to hear him say those words was beyond my imagination.

He helped me lower myself down on the bench, and instead of sitting beside me, Levi knelt in front of me, his face tilted up to mine.

Levi touched my lips with a thumb, kissed them and touched them again. It felt as though he couldn't get enough of me. And I felt just the same.

"You're not leaving?"

"I am not."

"And you love me?"

"I do. Veronica, I do."

Levi closed his eyes and feathered his lips over mine.

"You want to be with me?"

"More than anything. If you'll have me." Levi opened his eyes, and we gazed at each other. My hands were clasped in his. "Life with me will not be easy. I cannot promise that it will always be smooth and perfect, but if you let me, I will love you more than I have ever loved anyone." His eyes crinkled at the corners with a smile. "I am far from perfect, but with you, I feel whole."

All those times, I had wondered what he had been thinking, what he had been feeling. And he had opened up and offered himself to me. Was I dreaming?

I lifted a hand to his face and felt the soft stubbles on his jaw. He was real. He was there with me. And he loved me.

My heart was so full. Elation thrilled me. I let out a soft

laugh. How did one respond to such an honest and unexpected declaration of love?

I pinned him with my eyes and nodded because I didn't trust that my words were enough.

"Is that a yes?"

"Yes." I leaned forward and kissed him with all the emotions surging through me. "That's a yes."

"I love you, Veronica," he whispered against my lips.

Levi straightened and reached up, plucking a rose bud from the arch. He tucked it behind my ear as he sat on the bench. He lifted me up by my waist and pulled me onto his lap. My arms wrapped around him as he continued to devour me with his lips. His hands roved all over my body. He held me and pressed me closer to him.

I could stay in his arms forever.

"You're shivering," he said, as he ghosted his lips from the tip of my shoulder, over my collarbone, and to the hollow of my throat.

I was, but not from the cold. Even so, he leaned back, took his jacket off and covered me with it. My head swam as his scent, and the warmth of his body, enveloped me. I rested my chin on his shoulder as he continued kissing me, nipping at my sensitive skin, and tasting me.

At the moment, there was nothing else to say. It was enough that we basked in each other.

❧

LEVI'S HANDS made their way to my back, lightly rubbing over my dress when I felt a buzz in his jacket pocket.

I kept my head leaning against his when I spoke, "I think your phone is vibrating."

He hummed, and it resonated deep within me. "I'm

sure it's nothing important. I'm here with you, and that's all that matters."

I smiled at what he said. And let it be.

"Tell me...when did you start wearing glasses?"

"When I was eight."

"You've always worn them?"

Levi made a noncommittal grunt as a reply. "Only when I'm reading. I don't like them."

"Why? Because they make you look like a sexy librarian?" I teased.

He chuckled, "Only you pull off that look, which I am a big fan of."

I felt the vibration against my chest, and it took a moment to realize it was coming from his phone again.

"Ignore it," he told me, as he flicked the tip of his tongue against the skin behind my ear.

"It's not my phone." The buzzing continued. "I think they're calling you again."

The real world had intruded, and I realized that there was still life outside our little cocoon. Friends who were most likely wondering where I'd gone, where he had gone. A couple to whom we would have to say our farewells.

"You want to go back now?" Levi read my mind.

I hesitated but nodded. "I suppose we should."

Before we faced reality, Levi hugged me again and kissed me senseless. I was breathless when he pulled back. It felt dangerous to let him have this power over me, but it thrilled me nonetheless.

He helped me slip my shoes back on my feet, rubbing my calves as he did before we both stood. We walked back with our hands intertwined. I was giddy, and I knew it showed. But I didn't care.

"Finally." Chase threw her hands up in the air as soon as she saw us, not batting an eye at our connected hands.

"I thought I'd have to send an army to look for you. Bouquet toss. You're up." She pushed me toward the dance floor. "Come on, bridesmaid."

"No, no, no." I tightened my grip on Levi's hand, looked back at him and pleaded with my eyes to not let me go. Levi showed me his achingly charming smile before placing a kiss on my knuckles.

"Go get 'em, darling," he said as he let go.

I gaped, and my eyes narrowed, but I could see the playfulness at the corners of his lips. I shrugged off his coat and handed it back to him before trudging my way to the middle of the pack awaiting that toss. I crossed my arms and shot a gaze at Levi.

Jake had joined him, and they were both grinning at me. The groom clapped a hand over his best man's shoulder and said something. Levi nodded, and they shook hands. I'd have to ask him about that later.

Later. The thought of having that conversation, any conversation with Levi later, warmed me. He was staying. He'd be with me. He'd tell me again that he loved me.

We still had a lot to learn about each other, but I believed that what I would learn would only make me love him more.

Levi waved and signaled for me to look forward. And, as I did, I saw the bundled bouquet of purple and yellow flowers in mid-air coming right at me. I didn't know what to do. I uncrossed my arms, lifted them, thought better of it and dropped them to my sides, but at the last minute, I lifted them again.

Before the bouquet hit my hands, two pairs of hands flew my way, grabbing the flowers. Isobel and Natalie wrestled for them. Eventually, Isobel won. She stood and lifted her hand in the air, with the bouquet as her prize.

I made my way back to Levi, and he welcomed me into

his arms. "Looks like you'll be planning another wedding soon."

"Let's hope not. They just met." I glanced at Isobel, grinning at her boyfriend, who seemed perturbed by the offending bouquet.

"My sweet Veronica, when you know, you just know." He held me tightly as he wrapped his coat around me once again.

❦

Levi and I joined the group in front of the main building to see the newlyweds leave for the night. The cloudless sky boasted twinkling stars. A breeze whistled past every now and then, but I was comfortable in the warmth of Levi's presence.

Jake spoke to Levi as Sandrine hugged and thanked me. She held me at arm's length and smiled. "I couldn't thank you enough for what you've done." She surreptitiously looked at Levi. "And I'm so 'appy you've finally made a decision." She hugged me again. "'E will take good care of you." I didn't doubt it one bit.

Sandrine kissed both my cheeks before switching places with Jake.

"Nica," Jake began, "I'm glad you're giving him a chance. You both deserve to be happy. Take care of him, okay?" Jake kissed my cheek. "We'll see you in a month."

They moved on to say goodbye to other people before getting into a classic Rolls Royce decorated with roses and a "Just Married" heart-shaped sign.

Levi hooked his arm over my shoulders, letting me lean my head against his chest, and I wrapped my arm around his waist.

"Would you like some champagne?" he asked as we made our way back to the main tent.

I shook my head, and replied, with pride, "No, thanks."

"No?" We paused in our steps. Levi turned me to face him. His eyes brightened with barely hidden excitement.

"I am staying sober tonight." I tilted my head up, pressed my palms on his chest, and planted a kiss with a smile on his lips. "I don't want to forget anything. I want to remember every single moment with you."

BONUS CHAPTER

THE BACHELOR'S CONFESSION

LEVI

I was mezmerized.

She might have had a lot to drink, but she'd loosened up and became the carefree Veronica I'd come to admire. She laughed out loud. She joked around with the guys. She danced without a care in the world, swaying her hips and wiggling her apple-shaped butt against my crotch. I gripped her hips and let a hand wander over the curve of her ass, and it was all I could do to contain myself from making love to her right on the dance floor.

Veronica turned to me, her irises darkening under the club lights, her lips pouting, her hands spreading all over my chest, my abs and down my pants. I could have exploded right there and then. When she raised her chin and licked the underside of my jaw, I lost my mind. I had to have her. I just had to. All those months of careful discipline not to make a move on her because she was my best friend, Jake's girlfriend, escaped my mind. Her fingers played with the lapels of my shirt when she said, "Take me home."

I was playing with fire, and I knew this when I took her hand and led her out of the club, ditching the rest of our group. Her hands continued to wander over my body when we settled into the car. Her mouth sucking on my neck turned me into molten lava. And I winced from the insurmountable discomfort when she palmed my erection.

We fumbled into her apartment, knocking over a lamp when she tried to undress me. She was laughing, giggling when I kissed the delicate pulse on her neck down to the swell of her breasts. Veronica's legs wrapped around me when I picked her up and carried her to her queen-size bed, while her fingers made their way behind my neck and over my shoulders. I wanted her. I needed her.

She practically ripped her own clothes off as I stood before her and undressed slowly. Her arms, seemingly glittering under the light of the moon through the windows, welcomed me. Her legs spread for me, her fingers clawed my back. I could devour her, all of her, but this was my first with Veronica and...I couldn't. Not yet. I wanted this to be more than a quick fumble in the sheets after a drunken night. I wanted it to be memorable. Special. Call me a pansy, but she was...Veronica.

I paused, my rigid body pressing down on her, my arms resting on her sides, my lips hovering over hers. Her hair was spread over her bed, creating a dark halo around her delicate features. I reached up to clear the short tendrils off her face. Ma belle, Veronica. Sweet and enchanting.

Her eyes held some kind of spell on me. A man could die happy under that gaze. Then she whispered in the night, "What's wrong, Jake? Why'd you stop?"

If my heart could scream it would have let out a wail of pain and defeat. It wasn't me she'd wanted. It wasn't me who was in the room with her at the moment. Frustration, guilt, and a palpable ache poured into me. Veronica played with the ends of my hair. She wriggled her hips under me and moaned.

With a deep sigh, I rolled onto my back and pulled her flushed against me. Her head lolled onto my chest and I felt the warmth of her breath over the thumping of my heart. With my fingers tangled in her hair, I said, "Let's get some rest, sweetheart. You've had a long day." I reached down and covered our bodies with her bed sheet.

Veronica hummed. "I'm so tired, baby."

"I know."

She snuggled in closer. "I missed you."

I could practically hear my heart tear into pieces. "I missed you too." There was so much truth in my own words, nothing she could ever imagine.

Not before long, she was asleep in my arms. I inhaled her sweet scent and let it soothe my heartache. Soon, she would realize who I really was, who I could be to her. But for now, all I could do was hold onto her and hold onto hope.

❧

I HAD KNOWN all along that Veronica was a morning person. She was too cheerful not to be. But I was hoping that she would make this day an exception. After all, she'd had more alcoholic beverages than I had the previous night. It was concerning, but with the way Jake was all over Sandrine, I could see why Veronica wanted to drown her sorrows away.

I had hoped to give her another solution to forget Jake. Well, let's just say it was a night that would forever be embedded in my mind.

When she started jabbing my skin with her sharp fingernails, all hopes of sleeping in shattered. I continued to pretend sleeping, burying my head into the pillow, basking in its sweet smell– Veronica's delectable scent–and keeping my right hand touching her. I loved the feel of her skin.

Poke. Poke. Jab.

I turned my body away from her, finding it difficult not to chuckle at the little gasp she let out when the sheet fell off my torso and exposed part of my buttocks.

Jab. Jab. Poke.

God, she had some talons on her. They sure felt different on me last night when she held onto my arms as I carried her into her bedroom, and when they dug onto my back while we made out on her bed. She wouldn't stop. At this rate, I'd need stitches from her nail scratches.

Giving up on sleep, I groaned out, "Please don't tell me you're a morning person."

It took her a few seconds to reply. I imagined her connecting the dots, or the voice to the person it belonged to. The bed shook slightly when she was about to get out of it. She yelled out my name, "Levi!" I felt a tug on the sheet and so I yanked it back. I heard her scrambling behind me.

"What the hell are you doing in my bed?" Why was she yelling? It was too early and I was too hungover for any of that.

With a quiet intake of breath, I sat up, letting the sheet fall off me. Veronica was naked beside me and all that had happened between us last night was still fresh in my memories. A particular part of me enjoyed that all too well, and was fully erect that morning. I glanced over where she stood in shock, then caught her gaze on me, and then away from the tenting of the sheet on my lap. She was beautiful, even with the mess of hair on her head and shoulders, and a few pillow creases on her lovely face. Her eyes were circled with smudges from her makeup, but I remembered how bright they'd look last night while I kissed her hungrily, while I held her in my arms. I wondered if I could persuade her to continue what we couldn't.

"Veronica, please don't yell. My head is going to explode." I gripped my temples for added effect. "Why is it so bright in here? Don't you believe in curtains?" I was an ass. I knew it. But I couldn't help getting a rise out of her at times. She was too adorable whenever she tried to appear tough.

"Just tell me why you're in my bed." I looked over at her. Yup, adorable.

I flashed her my winning smile. Part of me just wanted to reach out to her and continue to hold her, caress her smooth skin, taste her, worship her body, but the confused look in her eyes told me this would turn out to be something other than a wonderful morning spent in bed with a goddess. She might not have any memory of what happened last night. Inside, I was disappointed. For me, the night was glorious–for the most part–but for her, it was something her mind would rather forget.

I opted for an asshole response, as though it could save me from an ache in my chest. "You don't remember?"

Her reply was quick and angry. "Would I ask if I did?"

Her fingers tightened around the shirt–my shirt–shielding her naked body from me. It bunched up higher and showed off her delectable thighs. "Veronica, I'm assuming you're naked by how tightly you're grasping that, and I'm–" I lifted the sheet off my groin. "Well, I'm also very naked. What do you think happened?"

Confusion washed over her face. She sucked in her bottom lip between her teeth. Her eyes filled with worry.

She dropped her gaze to the floor and her long, thick hair hid her concerned eyes. "I...I don't remember," she said quietly. Just as I suspected. "But please...get dressed."

This was not heading to the direction where I'd like it to go. She would not respond to my advances. She would push away everything. She would push me away. I could not be that person. I would not be someone she'd regret.

I brushed the hair off my forehead. "Funny," I began to say, swinging my legs over the edge of the bed. I reached down for my trousers and pulled them on. "I don't seem to remember a lot either. It's a shame really." A shame that she couldn't remember what could have been a wonderful night.

Her doe eyes widened when I turned to face her. "Maybe," I began, walking slowly over to her. "Maybe you should remind me." She took a step back. I could feel her anxiety through the shirt that she held like it was some kind of armour.

"What?"

Such sweet temptation. With a quick tug on my shirt, she appeared before me, naked. She gasped and for a second I thought she was going to slap me. At this point, any form of touch from her would set me off. But her hands fumbled over her body, covering her chest and that sweet spot between her thighs. I couldn't help a chuckle out of me as I put my shirt on, keeping my gaze pinned on her. Veronica turned away and pulled open a dresser drawer, taking out a shirt from it.

Her behind was just as tempting as well, all of her. Before she could pull the hem of her shirt down over her upper half, I spun her to face me and covered her lips with mine. I filled that kiss with all of my pent-up desire and hunger. Instead of pushing me away, as I suspected she would do, she relaxed. Her body sagged against mine, her lips opened up and let me in. Her hands stroke my chest.

I got lost in that kiss, in her. Sweet, sweet Veronica. Her body moulded nicely against me. I traced the softness of her waist and hips under her cotton shirt, and then all the way to her behind. Then she pulled away, and gave me a light shove. Her eyes revealed so much in that short time. She didn't expect her own reaction to me, but it gave me so much more to hope for. I was afraid of what else she would do or say when her eyes hardened. So I laughed, hoping that it would ease the tension, then she swiped her arm over her lips.

"What happened?" she spat angrily, but her eyes spoke of other emotions.

All I could offer was deniability. I shrugged. "Lots of drinking. You were doing this incredibly sexy dance in the club," I said, remembering the alluring show she put on. "It was kinda cute too. Then you asked me to take you home, we kissed, got naked, then you know..." I let her fill in the missing parts in her mind. I winked and made noises with my puckered lips. Dread filled her and a blush reddened her cheeks.

Veronica hopped back into her bed, hiding underneath the sheets. Just as I thought, she was ashamed of being with me... or nearly being with me. It was a hard strike on my ego, but more than that, it was a shock to my heart. Would she ever see that we could be good together? Would she see me other than a Casanova who was incapable of being loyal to one woman? I could be loyal. I'd had previous monogamous relationships, but nothing stayed, none ever lasted. I thought at first that it was all my doing, that it was never part of me, until the moment I met Veronica.

I couldn't let her blame herself. I couldn't let this be an

embarrassment for her. Even if I wanted to shout it out, let the whole city hear it, I couldn't very well let them know that the woman I wanted had thought I was someone else. To soothe her, I sat on her side. "Veronica," I calmly said, "There's nothing to be ashamed of. You were such a good…"

She groaned and I couldn't continue when a single finger appeared above the white sheet. "Please don't say it. Will you just please go away? Just leave, okay?" Her voice was so low and quiet and caused my chest to tighten. Would she let me hold her and tell her that everything would be all right? Could I promise her that right now, knowing full well that she still had feelings for my best friend? Would she feel the same if she knew that I was willing to give up everything for her?

I inhaled, feeling the burn in my chest. Not knowing what else to say or how else to get on, I stood. i didn't want to leave her, not like this. But Veronica was a strong woman. She'd find a way to recover from this. She was also smart. Maybe not today, but later on, her mind would clear and she'd know exactly what had gone on last night., or more appropriately put, what hadn't gone on.

I looked around for the rest of my clothes and realized that the rest was probably outside her bedroom door. Before stepping away from the bed, I closed my eyes and inhaled, committing every single part of her bedroom in my memory–the floral quilt that laid on the foot of her bed, the white and pastel furnitures that were placed carefully along the walls, the smell of fresh flowers in the air, the tiny summer dress that hung on a hanger on the back of her bedroom door. Then, I thought of her, of Veronica. After having the chance to touch her, to feel her, how could I ever forget. It would forever be a part of me, even if she tried to push me away.

For now, I would let her go. It would fare better for me to let her find her way into my arms.

With one last look at the figure hiding underneath the blanket, I slowly made my way out the door, almost tripping at one of my shoes just outside. Then the other was a good foot away. I straightened the lamp that had been knocked over and checked to see for any damage. Everything else seemed okay. With hope hanging in the air, I looked back to the closed bedroom door. Would she come out after me? If she hadn't already, she probably wouldn't. So with a lump lodged in my throat, I mussed my hair up and left her apartment. One day soon I would return and I could show her how much she had changed me. And when that happened, she would never forget even a second of it.

ABOUT THE AUTHOR

USA Today Bestselling Author, Michelle, is addicted to romance. She believes in happily ever afters and loves writing about couples who get there.

When not writing, she props her feet up on her favorite lounger and binges on Netflix shows, or reads one or two books at the same time. She enjoys red wine, dark chocolate, cake, and can talk your ears off about delicious food. Travelling is high on her list, whether alone, with friends or family.

Michelle lives in Ontario, Canada with her husband, two amazing children and a cuddly maltese-yorkie dog named Scarlet.

DON'T MISS UPDATES ON UPCOMING WORKS, SALES OR GIVEAWAYS, SIGN UP FOR MICHELLE'S BI-WEEKLY NEWSLETTER: BIT.LY/MJQUINNNEWSLETTER

www.michellejoquinn.com
michelle@michellejoquinn.com

Available Now!
    Levi and Veronica's story continues in...
    Proposing Bliss

All he wants is a perfect proposal.
But all she wants is the truth...

The sexy and former playboy, Levi Laurent is ready to marry sweet, romantic wedding planner, Veronica Soto-Stewart. After a crazy and rocky start, Levi knows they can withstand anything--as long as he keeps his past buried deep... But when Levi and Veronica travel overseas to meet his ailing grandmother, Levi's past comes barreling forth, nearly suffocating both of them.

Now, it's time for Levi to open up to the one woman he can't bear to lose. But will Veronica agree to "for better or worse" once the Laurent secrets are revealed?

DOWNLOAD YOUR COPY
    www.michellejoquinn.com
    READ ON FOR BOOK 2 CHAPTER EXCERPT!

PROPOSING BLISS

EXCERPT

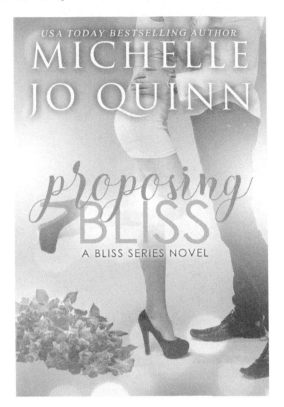

UNE AFFAIRE AU RETENIR

LEVI

TWO YEARS AGO...

*T*he night began like any other night—with me bored out of my head. I shook hands with the right people, talked business with others, and kissed a few too many women—who replied with subtle and some not-so-subtle gropes. In a black, tailored tuxedo, I stood beside my date for the gala, Louisa Marie Alfonso-Parker. Though her divorce wouldn't be final for another week, she thought she should make a new start, soon. And she had targeted me for trial-and-error purposes. By the way the night was going, I was leaning more toward error.

Throughout the night, I kept wondering what in the world had possessed me to accept her invitation. She was gorgeous, but her personality was drier than the Gobi desert. No amount of single malt could drown her mind-numbing political tirade.

My phone buzzed in my pocket, and I fished it out, hoping it was a means of escape. As I viewed the name on my screen, I was reminded that there were worse people out there than my date *du jour*.

"Olivier, must you work all the time? It's time to play, dahlin'," Louisa said through gritted teeth, and her nails skimmed the side of my neck.

I cringed, removing her claws before she drew blood. She hated not having anyone's full attention. "I won't be long," I told her, and ignored the plumes of dark smoke coming out of her ears.

The phone call I was about to take was rather...delicate, or indelicate depending on the other person. I didn't need an audience. Dodging the attendees in varied black-and-white attire, I made my way to one corner of the grand ballroom before answering the call.

"Ophelia?" I kept my voice flat. No need to excite her.

"Hello, lover," she drawled.

The wannabe actress/model had been a huge pain in my derrière ever since I'd made the mistake of taking her on a date. It had been a dare.

Huffing out a breath, I looked up to the gilded ceilings.

"I thought I asked you not to call me again." *Many times over.*

"Oh, but you weren't serious." I could practically hear her silicon-plumped lips pouting. "When are you coming home? I'm cold and lonely."

"I made it clear that I didn't want to see you anymore, remember? Remember when you keyed my new car?" Just the thought of what she had done to my Tesla made my blood pressure rise to dangerous levels. "I won't file charges, but you promised not to come near me again." Calm, I had to stay calm.

A sharp intake of breath came through the line before a maniacal laugh pierced my ear.

"You were just playing hard to get." She purred and moaned. "Check your phone. I sent you a selfie that will make you want me back." I didn't trust the confidence in her voice.

A ping sounded from my phone. I pulled it away from my ear to see what she had sent me. I shouldn't have, but I was glad I did. For there she was. All of her cosmetically-altered, naked self was spread-eagle on *my* cloud-grey sateen sheets. The ones on my bed, in my master bedroom, which Ophelia shouldn't have access to. As soon as I ended the call, I needed to reconsider acquiring a restraining order.

"How did you get into my penthouse?" I yelled at the phone, garnering stares and unwanted attention from people around me.

"I have my ways." Her voice took on a salacious tone. "So are you coming back soon?"

I *had* been patient for far too long. "All right, Ophelia, stay put. Do not move." I enunciated those last three words. Before she could say anything else, I disconnected and tapped in another number. "Jerrod, explain to me how someone was able to enter my apartment. The same woman who vandalized my car yesterday."

The head of security of my building stuttered an incoherent response. Not many had witnessed or experienced an angry Laurent. Jerrod went right into action, not making any excuses. He promised to handle my intruder personally and, if the authorities had to be contacted, that I would receive immediate reports. I then called my lawyer for the R.O. and had him get in touch with Blackwood Security for a more reliable and current system for my penthouse.

I had just ended that last call when, through the doors I stood next to, came a woman in a simple black dress, ass first. *Delightful.* Facing away from me, she leaned over a rolling tray, pulling it out from the kitchen. Staring right at that tempting behind, I didn't move fast enough. Her buttocks bumped me right where they should, but her right heel pierced my foot.

Alerted, electrified, and high on the buzz, I grabbed her hips just as she turned.

"Oh my goodness! I'm so sorry!" She pressed a hand on her chest.

She was a goddess.

Everything slowed down. All I could hear was the swift tattoo of my heart. The rest of the world disappeared into a puff of smoke. No one else was present except her and me.

The neckline of her 50's-style dress displayed a décolletage waiting to be explored. A string of pearls wrapped delicately around a neck that was aching to be kissed. The smooth skin of her jaw begged me for a nibble. And when my eyes met hers, cliché as it might sound, I felt that I had died and gone to heaven. My mind was a dense fog, but the sight of her was clear as day, as illuminating as the sun, as bright as the stars. *Be still, my beating heart.*

"You can let go of me now." Her voice somehow broke through. I gazed at her again, from her crown of caramel braids down to pink toes peeking out of her black, unadorned shoes. "Let go...please."

I followed the resonance of her voice—as though I could see it—from the edge of her neckline, up to her elegant throat and to heart-shaped, pursed lips. Then, one by one, she extracted my fingers from her hips, and daintily plucked the top of her dress and righted it.

"You can stop staring at my cleavage," the goddess admonished me. My eyes dropped to my hands, to the electrified parts of my skin she had touched.

When I looked up again, I stepped back from the disdain and clear disgust on her face. She might as well have called me 'pervert'. Possibly remembering where we were, her pursed lips and furrowed forehead melted into a slightly more serene countenance.

Any other time, I would have thought she had a screw loose, managing to go from one emotion to the next in one second flat. But I'd dealt with my fair share of crazies, and there wasn't any doubt in my mind that she wasn't one. She was pure and simple and beautiful.

And I had to know her.

But the first words that came out of my mouth weren't entirely what I had in mind. "There wasn't much to see." I was an idiot. What I'd meant to say was that I wasn't staring at her breasts.

Before I could rephrase my words, she "humphed!" her way around and back to the task at hand, angling the cart toward the main bar. As she stepped away, she muttered, "Should have stepped on your other foot too."

A quiet laugh escaped my mouth. It was something I hadn't done in a while, and it sounded strange. All I could do was watch the swing of her glorious hips as she moved forward, fast.

I muttered out loud this time, "Be still, my beating heart," and placed a hand over the erratic tattoo in my chest.

"Levi!"

I had trouble turning away from the goddess and toward the source of the voice which had called me. A man in his late sixties with an antalgic gait waved as he ambled up to me. His heaving paunch pushed the limits of the buttons on his shirt.

"Santiago, how are you doing?" Still reeling from the excitement of bumping against the sweet-looking woman, I shook his hand with gusto.

He returned my greeting with a big smile on his face. "Very well, son. Still surviving. How's your dear grandmother doing?"

"Martina was doing great last time I spoke to her."

Santiago leaned closer and jabbed my side with his plump arm. "It's okay, son, you can tell me that she's angry as the devil himself. How did her grapes survive the early frost?"

I shook my head and raised my hands in front of me. "You've known her far longer than I have, Santiago. You know how she gets." As tender and loving my grandmother was with me, she was a wrathful demoness when things didn't go her way. She had a love-hate relationship with Mother Nature, and oftentimes she would be found sleeping beside The Farmer's Almanac. "I've read reviews for your wine. Congratulations! Now that you've reached the top, isn't it about time to retire?"

The older man guffawed and coughed, clasping and adjusting his collar. "Never! I will be harvesting those grapes until my last breath. Now, tell me, son: Martina has taught you all her secrets. Isn't it time you branch out on your own? Run your own vineyard?"

I scratched the back of my neck. "Not in the stars, Santiago, not for me. It's best for people who have the heart to get shit done, who don't mind all the work and dirt on their hands."

"I wouldn't blame you." Santiago ducked his head and peered around us, waving a hand in the air. "Who in their right mind would give up waking whenever you want, with any woman you want, and only getting up to party all over again, eh?"

"Who indeed?" It was hard to explain, but there was a sudden emptiness inside as I said those words. I glanced to my left, and almost too easily, my eyes found *her* again, talking amicably with one of the bartenders.

What would be her views on this matter? On someone like me? I wondered, while I watched her from afar, the goddess with the sweet smile who had captured my heart.

֍

THROUGHOUT THE NIGHT, I tried in vain to find out who she was. No one seemed to know her, or even cared to figure it out. She was like a ghost haunting the ballroom, flying from one corner of the expansive hall to the next with little effort. After a while, I accepted that most, if not all, the event's attendees were rich, self-centered bores.

During dinner Louisa asked me to take a seat next to hers, and there I sat, but my mind roamed and my eyes darted from one area to the next. After desserts, I spotted her talking to Evelyn Witham, the chairwoman of the charity for which the fundraising gala was held.

There it was, another chance to figure out who the mystery woman was. Could I redeem myself? "Louisa, there's Evelyn." I nodded my head slightly in their direction. "Do you know who's talking to her?" I hoped that my voice did not betray me.

"Hmmm...I've never seen her before." Louisa pursed her lips, which reminded me of an anteater.

How could everyone else not notice her? "She's been here all night."

Louisa extended her neck and leered at me. "Maybe she's the help." She said the last word like it was a curse. "Viola would know. Viola," she called across the table, and Viola duBarry did not hesitate to appear interested. "Do you know who that girl is talking to Evelyn?"

"I think she's the event planner," the woman replied.

I bit the inside of my lip to stop myself from asking more questions, from appearing too eager.

"Planner? I thought Jayleen did this? Did they fire her? I just saw her at the club last week, and she'd been going on about this whole night," Louisa pressed.

Viola flattened a hand on her chest and leaned forward, but did not lower her voice. Meekness was lost to some of these women. "That's what I heard. Apparently, Evelyn found out Jayleen took some of the funds for personal purposes. Jayleen does have a new convertible."

Louisa quirked her eyebrow, while I remained, with bated breath, waiting for these two women to confirm whether my goddess was indeed the planner.

"Where did they find this one?" Louisa flicked a finger over her shoulder, like a fly had been annoying her. "I've never seen her in the circle before. She can't be new. Why would they get someone new to replace a veteran?"

"Maybe they wanted someone with fresh ideas," I put in, careful not to inflect my tone and betray my true emotions.

Louisa turned to me and scoffed. "Have you not seen what Jayleen can do? She planned my wedding!"

"And that's a great example? You're getting divorced after six months of marriage." I was preparing my own grave if I didn't stop mocking Louisa.

"Apparently, Evelyn worked with her in some art gallery opening, or something a couple months back," Viola added.

Louisa turned her head again, wrinkled her nose and said, "Look at her. She can't even afford a proper couture gown for tonight. You can practically smell the mothballs from here."

That was enough to tip me over. "I'm surprised you even knew what mothballs are, Louisa." I stood abruptly and straightened my suit jacket. "I thought the only balls you knew were your ex-husband's old, hairy ones." I strutted away from the table as I heard a collective gasp.

Once I was a few feet away from the goddess and Evelyn, my heart thumped like a high school drum line in my chest. I couldn't count each beat, and I tried—and failed—to steady my breathing, lest I sounded like I had run a marathon when I reached them. I knew she sensed me. Within a quarter of a beat, our eyes met, my line of vision blurred, I grinned like a fool, and my step faltered. She did not return my smile.

Whether she had heard of me, recognized me, or just understood the type of person I was in a matter of seconds, she didn't like me, and it showed. Her head nodded once, and a small smile played on her pink lips as she turned her attention back to Evelyn, before hastily leaving her side.

I was a mountain of patience, and I welcomed challenges.

"Evie," I called.

"Levi, you're looking rather dashing tonight." She

placed a hand to my cheek as she welcomed a swift kiss on hers.

"Just tonight?"

She laughed.

"Who was that you were just talking to?" I was tired of skirting around the issue.

Evelyn laughed again. "I can always depend on you to keep me entertained. She's none of your business, my dear boy." Evelyn Richland reminded me of my grandmother. Beautiful, even at her age, and like Martina, she had a pure heart.

I offered a charming grin. "C'mon, Evie, all I need is a name."

"Levi," she began, holding my hands in hers, and staring me straight in the eye, "She is the type of girl who believes in romance, in being swept away, not only by charm and dashing good looks—" She waved a hand at me. "—but by true love. She is a girl who believes in happily ever after, and Levi…Veronica deserves it."

Veronica. My throat constricted at the mention of her name. "I believe in all that too." Not until I said the words did I understand what they meant and that I, in fact, was honest saying them. There was a heaviness in my chest, like I had been punched in my solar plexus, which knocked the air out of my lungs until I could find a way to recover. I pulled at the bow tie around my collar, ensuring that it hadn't tightened.

"Dear Levi, you may think you do, but it hasn't seemed that way for years. I've watched you with other women. I've seen how you are, heard of what you've done to them. Best to stay away from Veronica. A girl like her deserves to be loved purely and honestly."

Evelyn was an intelligent woman, capable of growing her own empire with her head high and her integrity intact, much like Martina. I had had the privilege of acquiring her wisdom through the years, and it would be wise for me to listen to her now. But my heart was a stubborn machine, and I was a stubborn man.

"Levi, dahling, there you are!" Louisa's hand snaked over my arm and up my shoulder, digging her nails in. "Hello, Evelyn, another lovely event as usual."

"Louisa, I see you've moved on without thinking, once again."

The two women threw words at each other. Meanwhile, my heart began its fast tattoo once more, and it told me one thing: Veronica was nearby. I watched her cross the room weaving through a sea of people. I held my breath as she collided with a man. His drink spilled all over the front of her dress, and his hand stroked too aggressively over her chest. My hands fisted at my sides, and I was ready to grab his grubby hands away from Veronica.

One of the bartenders interfered and handed Veronica a cloth, while turning the man away. Two other staff approached and guided the man, who was clearly inebriated, out of the ballroom. She and the bartender surreptitiously exited the ballroom through one of the side doors, which led to the terrace.

"Excuse me, I have something..." I didn't finish what I wanted to say. I yanked my hand away from Louisa's grasp and ignored her calling my name.

I had to find her, to check and see that she was okay. The crowd had moved toward the middle of the room where the dance floor had been set up. Taking a different door on the side, I slipped out into the cool night. The threat of rain hung in the air.

"What an ass!" The deep timbre of a man's voice boomed. "Your dress is never going to be the same, Nica."

Nica? Was that a shortened version of Veronica? I

preferred her full name. I moved closer, hiding behind a topiary. The pulse in my neck thumped madly.

"I know. And it's my favorite, too. Are you sure I can't have it dry-cleaned?" I remembered the sweet tone of her voice from earlier. This time, there was a hint of sadness in it. I wanted to walk over there and kiss the frown away.

"No, hon, 'fraid not. You can try to hand wash it but be very, very careful. It's real vintage."

Her laughter suspended in the air like sleigh bells on a wintry night. I committed it to memory. One day, I would elicit those sweet giggles from her, among other sounds.

"Real vintage? Is there such a thing?" she asked.

"You know what I mean. Well, I'd better get in there before Pyotr gets wild with the vodka. You coming in?"

"I will in a few. I just need to breathe for a bit."

Through the spaces between the leaves, I saw the tall bartender wrap Veronica in his arms. "We're so proud of you. Last-minute, and you came up with this amazing event." He kissed the top of her head. How I ached to do that.

"Thanks, Gerard. Seriously, thanks for tonight. I couldn't have done it without you guys. I'll be back in, straight to the kitchen. I wanna raid those unserved desserts."

As I pressed against the plant, the leaves rustled. The bartender and Veronica looked up. I cursed at myself. And when the man, Gerard, said, "I think you should come in now. It's not safe here. There might be *perverts* in the bushes," I cursed myself again.

Veronica took his advice, tilting her head to the side to check on the intrusion. Me. They walked back into the ballroom, leaving me cold and angry at myself for losing that first chance of alone time with her.

And it was my last and only chance that night.

When I returned to the gala, a hand gripped my arm. Cynthia Benjamin greeted me with a wide smile on her face. She was as close to an aunt as I could ever have. "Cynthia!" I kissed both her cheeks.

"I didn't know you were going to be here. Who was the lucky lady?" Cynthia asked, flattening the lapels of my jacket.

"I was *unlucky* enough to say yes to Louisa Marie Alfonso-Parker." Cynthia hissed. "Yes, I know, I know. It was better than the alternative."

"Which was?"

I wasn't ready to admit that I'd accepted because I didn't want to be alone. Misery sure loved company. "I'm not entirely sure. You're a bit late to the party."

"Fashionably late, my dear. We had some issues with Isobel. I swear that girl will be the death of me." She rubbed her temples, trying to ease thoughts of her rebellious teen daughter.

"You just think that because your firstborn is near perfect. Speaking of whom, has he told you?"

"Yes—" She clapped her hands together. "—and we can't be happier. I'm glad the decision came from him. Although I have a feeling I have you to thank as well." She patted my chest.

"It was all Jake's idea." It had been. My best friend, after several years of being the fascinating, talented doctor he was in some other part of the world, had decided to return to California to be closer to his family. "Build roots," he had said, "fall in love. Start a family." Just two nights ago, while on the phone with him, I'd thought he'd lost his mind. I thought he'd contracted dengue fever and had been completely delusional. Jake and I had approached life like a game, always competing to see who would end on top, even when it came to women.

Two days ago, he'd confessed that he'd been exhausted and lonely, and searching for a real purpose, for true happiness. Despite his love for what he'd been doing, something was missing from his life. It was time for him to grow up, and he had advised me to do the same. I'd laughed at him but regretted not telling him that I had been feeling quite lost as well.

Until tonight.

"We're so proud of him." Cynthia's words brought me back from my recollections.

"As am I." And that hit me harder than a brick wall. I immediately zeroed in on Veronica, huddled behind the bar, sneaking a bite of something into her mouth.

Evelyn had advised me to stay clear of Veronica, because I wasn't the right man for her. I could be. I could turn myself into someone Veronica would be proud to call hers. It didn't matter that her vintage dress was old; she cherished it, which meant she wasn't enamored by glitz and glamour. I'd witnessed enough men—wealthy, good-looking, of different pedigrees—approach her throughout the night, and all she did was politely smile at them and walk away.

She wanted romance.

She wanted happily ever after.

She wanted true love.

I could be the man to sweep her off her feet. And I knew how to start.

After excusing myself from Cynthia, I searched for Santiago.

Before the event ended, I walked out of the grand ballroom without Louisa's arm wrapped around mine, with my own new venture, and my thoughts filled with a goddess in a black vintage dress, Veronica—the woman who would turn my life around.

***

Want to Read More? Proposing Bliss is available in ebook and paperback formats.

www.michellejoquinn.com

ALSO BY MICHELLE JO QUINN

www.michellejoquinn.com

THE BLISS SERIES

Planning Bliss

Proposing Bliss

Chasing Bliss

Santa Bébé (A Christmas Bliss Novelette)

Finding Bliss (Winter 2017)

WHEN HE FALLS (A New Adult Novel)

WHEN SHE SMILES (Coming 2018)

LOVE IN BLOOM (A Collection of Short Stories)

STANDALONE

THE MISTER CLAUSE (A Holiday Romance)

HARLEY (A Rockstar Romance)

WINTER'S KISS (part of IMAGINES ANTHOLOGY)

SUMMER OF BUTTERFLIES (Coming Soon)

Fancy a romance with a bit of suspense?
Check out:
Nothing but Trouble
By Elise Noble

When Ella Goodman's surrogate grandma died, her last wish was simple - she wanted Ella to get off the sofa and have an adventure.

Ella's not the impulsive type but she's left with little choice - if she doesn't complete Edith's wish list, she'll end up homeless.

As Ella drifts from one disaster to the next, she has one goal: Finish the challenge. She's not going to enjoy herself and she certainly isn't going to fall in love...is she?

http://www.elise-noble.com/nothing-but-trouble

Made in United States
North Haven, CT
29 December 2022

30309195R00168